# "So beautiful, Aislynn."

He reached to touch her hair, noting that the fine strands seemed to cling to his callused fingers. "So soft."

A barely audible sound escaped her, drawing his gaze back to her face. He watched her lips part and her breathing quicken. He found himself unable to tear his gaze away from those sweet pink lips.

Aislynn's voice was husky and questioning as she whispered, "Jarrod?"

Jarrod's head spun. Whether it was from the feel of this beautiful woman in his arms, or from the wine, he did not know. And at this moment, he did not truly care.

He could never in his life recall wanting to kiss anyone as badly as he did Aislynn in this moment. And if there were reasons for not doing so, he could think of none of them.

He bent and placed his mouth on hers....

# Praise for Catherine Archer's recent titles

### Summer's Bride
"A delightful read!"
—*Romance Reviews Today*

### Winter's Bride
"A compelling, innovative tale...
with lush details and unforgettable characters."
—*Rendezvous*

### Fire Song
"This finely crafted medieval romance...
(is) a tale to savor."
—*Romantic Times*

# Dragon's Knight

## CATHERINE ARCHER

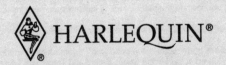
HARLEQUIN®

TORONTO • NEW YORK • LONDON
AMSTERDAM • PARIS • SYDNEY • HAMBURG
STOCKHOLM • ATHENS • TOKYO • MILAN • MADRID
PRAGUE • WARSAW • BUDAPEST • AUCKLAND

ISBN 0-373-29206-6

DRAGON'S KNIGHT

Please address questions and book requests to:
Harlequin Reader Service
U.S.: 3010 Walden Ave., P.O. Box 1325, Buffalo, NY 14269
Canadian: P.O. Box 609, Fort Erie, Ont. L2A 5X3

This book is dedicated to
Mt. Hood Hospice in Sandy, Oregon,
for all the wonderful work they do.

## Chapter One

Aislynn Greatham moved through the high-ceilinged, drafty rooms of Bransbury Castle, with only half her attention on whence she was going. The rest of her mind was centered on thoughts of where her brother Christian might be.

And if he would ever return.

Her father, the baron of Bransbury lands and keep, grew more morose with each day that passed. He asked the same questions each time they were together. Where could his son have gone and why? What could have possessed him to leave without telling his father? For the thirteen years Christian had been gone to the Holy Land. Had this not been long enough for him to be without his son and heir to his lands?

Aislynn could make no answer to any of these queries. She did regret not telling their father when Christian had confided in her that he was leaving. Christian had been so certain that he would return within a fortnight, had, in fact, given his solemn word on it. He had also assured her that he would be free to tell her every detail of his mysterious mission on his return.

Aislynn sighed, catching the first scents of the roasted fowl that she herself had seasoned that afternoon. She felt no pangs of hunger though she had eaten little that day. She greatly dreaded sitting at table with her father, having to bite back her own fears. For, more troubling than their father's worry, was Aislynn's thought that her brother had not returned because he could not.

Visions of him, ill…or worse, had begun to assault her day and night.

Those visions had driven her to do something that made it even more difficult to face her father. She had written to the friends Christian had spoken so much of. She had not bid her father's permission, fearing that in his pride he would not give it.

Although she had asked for no more than information concerning her brother's whereabouts, she secretly hoped and prayed that they would come to Bransbury. Christian had told her much of Jarrod Maxwell and Simon Warleigh, whom he had known since fostering with them even before the three of them had accompanied King Richard to the Holy Land. Not only his love, but his admiration for their strength and abilities was abundantly clear.

Surely in the event that Christian was not with them, such men could find her brother.

Her father, his leg having never healed properly after a fall from his horse, was in no condition to search further than the immediate surroundings for his son. Moreover, he had no notion of where to start his search.

''Dear God,'' she prayed, as she slowed her steps at the end of the corridor that led into the hall, ''even if Simon Warleigh or Jarrod Maxwell do not wish to help us, please let them send word soon.''

To hide her anxiety, she took a deep breath and schooled her features to appear calm. Stepping into the Great Hall, with its wide hearth and high, narrow windows, Aislynn gathered the strength to appear hopeful—not only for her father's sake, but all those at Bransbury keep. As she passed through the hall, she observed, with approval, the clean, scrubbed surfaces of the trestle tables that were set up for the evening meal. Many of the castle folk had already gathered in their accustomed places, chatting as they waited for the food to arrive from the kitchen. But there was a decided solemnity to their expressions.

She was sure they had noted their master's recent melancholy and were moved by it, not to mention their own uncertainty at the disappearance of the heir to the lands. Strong leadership could mean the difference between peace or war. Aside from being a strong leader, her father, though a reserved and quiet man, was a fair and just overlord. These qualities made him well loved by his folk.

Aislynn was taking her place at the high table when her father, Thomas Greatham, lord of Bransbury keep, entered with several of his men. She could see the weariness in his lean face as he removed his gloves. It was also apparent in his slow, measured step that did much to disguise his limp as he moved toward her. She was glad of the heat from the fire as the men's entrance brought with it a breath of chill air that made gooseflesh appear on her arms even beneath the heavy sapphire velvet of her gown.

As her father took his place, she noted a sheen of frost in his mustache. He looked to her with a hopeful expression in his periwinkle-blue eyes, eyes he had passed on to both of his children. "Any word of your brother?"

Regret made Aislynn look down at her folded hands. She took a deep breath then faced him with a fixed smile. "Nay, Father, not yet. But I am sure he, or word of him, will come soon." It was something she said each day and she no longer imagined that it offered any comfort.

The naked disappointment that came over her sire's face for a brief instant made her wish there was something, anything else she might do to help. There was nothing.

Not for the first time she considered telling him about the letter she had sent to Christian's friends. She dismissed the notion instantly. There had been no reply. Better that he not know in the event that no word came. Not only might he be angry with her for sending it, he would surely be even more disheartened.

She spoke with forced cheer. "And you, Father, what of your day?"

He frowned. "The blackguards will not give me rest of late. Llewellyn's constant efforts to plague me have been extended to his neighbors on the Welsh side of the border as well. Obviously there is some trouble brewing there, but I have been unable to glean any hint of what it might be."

Aislynn sighed. The problems of holding the lands

along the border did not abate simply because they had other worries. "Have you contacted Gwyn?"

"I have questioned your intended, but he seems to know naught, though he is deeply troubled by his neighbor's obvious quest to wreck havoc with us all."

Aislynn sighed again. Gwyn ap Cyrnain was the one of the few Welsh lords who had reached out in any kind of friendship to them. He had done so to the point of offering for Aislynn's hand in marriage. Her father approved of the match and Gwyn had been a friend to Aislynn in the long years when her brother had been away. The marriage would strengthen her father's position with Gwyn's countrymen. She had agreed. That Gwyn seemed in no great hurry to see the matter settled suited her most well.

Gwyn was a good man, a solid man, not only in size but in heart. With him she would create a stable base about which their children would gravitate. It would be a family such as she had always wished hers had been.

To the getting of those children she gave little thought. Although Gwyn had kissed her on the day their marriage contracts were signed over a year gone by, she had felt nothing but the same filial affection toward him that she always had. She did not bemoan this fact, for she had no notion of experiencing love such as was told in tales of romance. Family was what mattered to Aislynn.

Her father sighed now, bringing her attention back to him. He said, "As you know, under normal circumstances, I do my duty here gladly. It is only now, with Christian gone and with no explanation that I chafe under the responsibilities of keeping matters in check.''

She touched his hand gently. ''I understand.''

There was no more conversation between them as the trays arrived from the kitchen and the meal began.

Aislynn did not take her father's distraction as any insult to her person. In the years she had lived alone with him he had been a good father, if somewhat preoccupied with his duties. Only after Christian's return from the Holy Land had he been more garrulous at mealtimes. That was, until her brother's disappearance.

Aislynn was making every effort to eat the food, when the door to the hall flew open wide, bringing on a rush of cold air.

Like all those present, she glanced up, thinking the new arrival must simply be some latecomer for the meal, and stared. For the man coming toward them was not a resident of the keep or the surroundings lands.

Aislynn was quite sure that had she seen this man about the demesne she would certainly remember it. As he moved toward them with both casual grace and alertness, she noted the exotic quality of his appearance. His hair was black as a raven's wing, his skin darkly tanned, though most other men were paling as they all did at winter's approach. When he halted before the high table, she saw that his eyes were no less dark than his shoulder-length hair, their centers lost in that seemingly depthless darkness.

Even before the stranger began to speak, Aislynn realized who, in fact, this man was.

Jarrod Maxwell.

She had met him once, many years ago. It had been before Christian had left on crusade. She and her father had gone to bid her brother Godspeed where he was camped with King Richard's army. Her father had allowed her to go off with Christian, who had, of course, gone looking for his friends. They had seemed to forget her until someone had shouted out that the king had arrived. The throng had risen to watch the king pass by. It had been Jarrod Maxwell who had lifted her up on his shoulders so that she could see above the heads of the many soldiers. Everyone wanted to watch King Richard as he passed within a mere stone's throw of them.

Though she had been but six at the time, Aislynn had not forgotten that day. Her memory of it was sharper than that of her mother, who had died three years before.

Her brother had gone into fosterage only months after her mother's life had been taken in a tragic accident when the horse she rode stepped in a hole and tumbled upon her. Though Aislynn had been very young at the time, barely recalling her mother as more than a warm scent, Aislynn had learned her father had lost much of his joviality upon her mother's death.

This in no way surprised Aislynn. She knew her father blamed himself for his wife's death. The night before she'd left Bransbury for a visit to her sister's home, he had awakened from a vivid dream that foretold her death on the journey. Yet he had been unable to convince her that she must not go. He felt that he had not tried hard enough to convince her of the danger.

But Aislynn did not wish to think on this, for it

had all happened long before she could remember. She must concentrate on the man before them.

And truth to tell that did not prove difficult.

Christian had told her that his friend had been born of an Eastern woman while his father was on crusade and that he had brought the child home with him after she died. That exotic heritage was stamped on this man in not only his coloring but in the flowing ease of his stride, in the noble set of his wide shoulders, and the regal angle of his head. He was garbed as any other knight, in a burgundy velvet tunic and a flowing cape of fine wool with a dragon clasp that was fashioned in the same manner as the one her brother wore on his cape. Yet it was also easy to imagine him in the Eastern robes of the people in the many sketches Christian had drawn on his travels.

Christian had shared tales of the many women who had sought the exotic knight's favor wherever they had gone. And suddenly as those black eyes met hers for a brief moment, Aislynn knew a feeling of resentment for all those faceless dames.

Quickly she looked away, telling herself how very mad such a thought was even as the man began to speak. "My lord Greatham, my name is Jarrod Maxwell. I have come as quickly as I could in answer to the letter concerning Christian's disappearance."

Her father's tone was dull with confusion. "Letter?"

Aislynn watched from the corner of her eyes as Jarrod Maxwell nodded, a crease appearing in his brow at her father's obvious confusion. "Aye, it came to Avington by messenger some days gone by."

Her father said, "I sent no letter."

Aislynn, feeling her sire's assessing gaze upon her, looked into his blue eyes. "I sent it, Father. Christian had just returned from Avington when he set off on this mysterious quest of his, and I thought that those there might know where he had gone. Or that he might even have gone there as he has before." Her gaze flicked to the dark knight, and away. "I cannot deny that I did hope Christian's friends might even come to our aid. They are, after all the years they spent in the Holy Land together, as much family as we are to Christian. Besides, Christian himself once told me if there was ever any reason, I should not hesitate to call upon them as I would him."

Her father's voice was filled with disapproval. "Daughter, that all may be true, yet it does not explain why you would do this without consulting me?"

Jarrod Maxwell spoke up, drawing her gaze back to him. "If you will permit, my lord, I can not disagree that your daughter erred in not begging leave before writing to Avington. Yet Simon and I are indeed family to your son and come to your aid in finding him gladly." There was a coolly assessing expression in his dark eyes as they rested upon Aislynn for a brief moment. She felt a strange sense of unrest, though she was not sure why.

The fact that he glanced away again, clearly dismissing her, should not have brought such a prodding of displeasure. She told herself that it was because he had had the very nerve to express his own disapproval of her writing without her father's permission.

But his easy dismissal was especially irritating when she had been so immediately taken with the sight of him. Which was ridiculous of her, given that she was to be married. Yet for reasons she could not understand she found her gaze going to the knight once more as he bowed to her father, his lean-jawed countenance and strong nose in profile. Jarrod Maxwell was indeed as handsome a man as any maid might long for.

She pushed away this thought when her father spoke her name with irritation. "Aislynn!"

He watched her with a glowering expression and she realized she had not answered him. She addressed him hastily. "I deeply regret that I did not tell you, Father. I know how worried you have been, how frustrated in your efforts to find Christian. As I said, I thought that if naught else Warleigh or Maxwell might have some notion of whence Christian has gone. I…" She blushed again, looking down at her hands, feeling very self-conscious as she felt Jarrod's gaze upon them.

Her father raised her chin to look at her. He continued to scowl, yet she noted that most of his irritation with her had already passed. He said more gently, "In future I will thank you to recall that not only am I your father but the lord of these lands. You will not take such action without my consent."

She nodded, for there was no denying that she had acted rashly. Then in spite of her displeasure with Jarrod Maxwell, she faced him. She was glad that he had come to aid them. Surely he had come because he thought he could help find Christian. She asked hopefully, "Do you have any idea of where Christian might be?"

His expression showed clear regret as he shook his head, making his rejoinder to her father rather than to

Aislynn. "Nay. I am sorry, but I have not the least notion. When he left Avington he said only that he was going home, and, though he seemed a bit preoccupied, I thought little of it after all we had been through."

She tried to tell herself that her disappointment was brought on by his words, rather than by his continued disregard of her. Chagrined, she found herself studying her folded hands once again and wondering if she had gone quite mad in the intervening moments since this man had walked into the keep.

Even though Sir Jarrod Maxwell addressed his host rather than Christian's young sister, he could not help being aware of the disappointment that emanated from her. He flicked a glance over and saw the pain that tightened Aislynn Greatham's delicately beautiful profile and washed the color from that creamy skin. He fervently wished he had another answer to give, which surprised him.

He did not even know the girl.

She took that moment to look up across the table, laden with the evening meal, and Jarrod was held by a pair of startling cornflower-blue eyes. He found himself truly looking at Aislynn Greatham for the first time. There was a restive fragility about her, the type of restlessness as displayed by a butterfly. Her skin was like porcelain in contrast to the dark blue velvet of the head covering that framed her face. Her honey-colored lashes were thick, her lips, pink and pleasingly formed, her cheeks sweetly curved above the slender line of her jaw. He felt a stirring inside him, a desire to touch, though he knew that he could not

do so, for to touch a butterfly was to destroy its ability
to fly.

He was shocked at this fanciful thought, for it was
so unlike him.

It was not the first time he had thought of this girl.
Many years ago when he was a boy of fifteen, he had
met her when she, so small she could barely be more
than a babe, had come to bid her brother, Christian,
Godspeed before his journey to the Holy Land. She
had been such a little child, straining to see King
Richard as he rode by the troops, who had gathered
for the journey. He had felt an unfamiliar twinge of
affection and protectiveness, reaching down to lift her
up. She had weighed next to nothing as he had raised
her up to see above the crowd of soldiers.

Now there was a difference in his reaction to Christian's young sister that he could not quite put his finger on. And, strangely, he felt an intense reluctance
to attempt to name it.

Jarrod had no personal interest here other than to
find Christian.

Even as she watched him, her gaze darkened with
some deep emotion that he could only read as sadness. He felt that tug in his belly once more and deliberately focused his attention on her father again. ''I
take it, my lord, that you still have no idea of your
son's whereabouts either.''

Lord Thomas Greatham shook his gray head.
''Nay, I do not.'' He bowed with studied politeness.
''But really, sir, you need not concern yourself with
our difficulty. It was wrong of Aislynn to bring you
all this way.''

Jarrod frowned. ''Not at all, my lord. As I said,

Christian is as my brother. I am happy to be informed that there is a problem, as was Simon who would have come as well if it were not for his duty to his lands, not to mention his new bride.'' Simon was indeed well and happily occupied, having found more bliss with the daughter of his enemy Kelsey than Jarrod would have thought possible. But he did not wish to think on that now, nor the fact that any thought of Kelsey reminded him of the untimely and unjust death of The Dragon, the very man who had brought himself and his two friends together as fosterlings.

The loss of his foster father still brought a wave of pain. The Dragon had taken an angry lad of thirteen and taught him that he was the master of his own fate, had not only made him knight but a man. Jarrod chafed under the knowledge that he and his friends had been denied retribution against Kelsey by a king who loved those who were of like nature as himself.

Knowing these thoughts gained him nothing, Jarrod looked to Lord Greatham. ''Neither Simon nor myself would have you do aught but contact us about this matter.''

Jarrod recalled Aislynn's obvious understanding of their brotherhood, and felt an unwanted rush of kinship toward her. He knew again a strong pull of awareness that centered in his lower belly. Instantly Jarrod called himself firmly to task.

He forced himself to look at her again, to see her clearly as the child she was. It was almost with relief that, as he swept her form, which was enveloped in a gown of heavy sapphire velvet, his eyes told him that she was indeed a tiny waif of a girl with fragile bones. And her blue eyes were, as they had been the first time he saw her, too large for her heart-shaped face.

He also recalled a blond braid of so pale a shade that it was not readily forgotten. His gaze slid over the hood that completely concealed her hair. The honey of her brows and lashes made him wonder if it had darkened as many children's did as they approached adulthood.

At the moment, his eyes met those blue ones again and he saw that they bore an expression of uncertainty as well as sadness over her brother's disappearance. He found himself thinking that he would do whatever he must to see that sadness gone from her eyes. To see her smile.

His gaze went to those lips, which were not smiling now. Her tongue flicked out to dampen the lower lip, which seemed more full than before. He felt a stab of awareness and found himself once more looking into the blue eyes that were watching him with an expression he could not begin to name.

The baron's voice intruded on Jarrod's thoughts like a cold draft as he said, "I appreciate your enthusiasm, sir, but I am certain you must have your own matters to attend."

Jarrod blinked and turned back to the other man. "Forgive me, my lord, but I have nothing of more import to attend. At the same time, I do not mean to press myself where I am not wanted." He squared his shoulders, frustrated with the need to convince the other man to accept his help. He sensed the depth of their concern as well as his own. Tact was not one of his virtues, but he ventured, "I understand that I am as determined to find your son as you yourself are, my lord. I am but another pair of hands, another horse, to aid the efforts that are already being made. I would do whatever I can to locate him and see him returned home without delay.''

Lord Greatham sighed heavily, rubbing long slender fingers across a tired brow. ''I know not what you could accomplish, sir knight. Thus far none of my efforts or those of my men have gained so much as one hint of where my son has gone.'' The baron took a long, deep breath. ''It appears as though my son rode out from this keep and disappeared into the mists.''

Jarrod bowed. ''I assure you, I have naught else to demand my attention than finding Christian.''

He could see the continued strain on the older man's face, even as indecision creased his brow.

At that moment the woman reached out to put a comforting hand on her father's arm. And Lord Greatham, proud man that he was, put his hand over hers as if it was she who needed comfort.

She whispered, ''Pray heed his offer, Father. Sir Jarrod is as worried as we and mayhap he can help us. I...Christian was gone from us for such a very long time and now...''

Her anxiety moved Jarrod to a feeling of protectiveness that amazed him. He also felt moved by Lord Greatham's pain as he sighed. Jarrod listened with relief as he said, ''I will accept your aid in the spirit it is offered.''

Jarrod bowed again, knowing that he could not afford the weakness of becoming too attached to Christian's sister, or his father, for that matter. The only relationships he'd ever experienced with anything approaching satisfaction were those with Christian and Simon. And they needed nothing from him, accepting his loyalty and love, not requiring it.

Jarrod had never been needed by anyone, nor had he himself needed anyone, not his father, nor his half brother, nor his moth— He stopped himself before the last thought could fully form. Jarrod was greatly aware of his own good fortune. As the bastard son of an Eastern woman and his father, he had been brought back to England and lived in his father's noble household until he'd overheard his younger, legitimate, brother Eustace begging their father to send him away. Having never felt that he truly belonged in the household of his father's legitimate wife and son, he had requested that he be sent away into training as a knight.

His father had agreed with his accustomed lack of emotion and Jarrod had fostered with The Dragon at thirteen, those two years being the best of his life. And even after his foster father had been betrayed and murdered by The Dragon's own half brother, Jarrod had simply gone on to a new fosterage, leaving England with his new lord and not returning until early in this year. As Simon and Christian had also made the journey, staying on in the employ of the Knights Templar, when most others had returned to England, he had been more than content for the thirteen years he had remained in those hot desert climes. He had only ventured to return when they had, feeling no more tied to the East than he was to England.

He would remain, as he has always been, free to come and go, by his own will. He would keep his mind on what he had come here to do. ''I thank you, sir, and will begin at whatever task you would have me do with all haste.''

Lord Greatham inclined his own head, seeming almost relieved now that the matter had been decided. ''You may do what you think best in this. Truth to tell, I find I have a scarcity of inspiration.''

''I thank you, my lord, for your faith in me.''

The older man shrugged. ''Give more credit to my son's high opinion of you.'' He eyed Jarrod with a respect that did nothing to disguise the pain he was feeling. ''Your quest will wait till morn. For tonight you will accept not only our thanks but our hospitality.'' He gestured to one of the servants who stood nearby. ''Bring our guest a seat as well as a cup and plate.'' He then turned to Jarrod again. ''Please, take a place at our table.''

''Thank you, my lord. I would be grateful as well as honored to sup with you.''

Jarrod seated himself on the bench that was brought forward. In spite of his hunger, he found himself picking at the food presented to him. Resolved to remain unmoved by these two, he cast not so much as a glance in Aislynn Greatham's direction.

Yet he was uncomfortably aware of Aislynn throughout the remainder of the meal. With the baron it was easier. They talked of hunting and other such pursuits, seeming to stay away from more personal issues. He felt the baron was not eager to reveal more of his inner feelings than had already been given away.

Even when Aislynn rose before the meal's end, begging fatigue, he kept from looking directly at her, though he was aware of a certain stiffness that emanated from her small person. Only then did he finally look into her delicate face to see that she was watching him with a look of hurt confusion in her blue eyes.

Jarrod kept his surprise severely in check. As soon as she noted his attention, she looked away, making a hasty departure.

Once she was gone, though, Jarrod realized that he was indeed behaving quite madly. He was decidedly wrong to think he could prevent being moved by Christian's sister to some extent. She was frightened for him and Jarrod loved Christian as his brother. It was only natural that he would feel a strong connection to the sister Christian loved and who obviously loved Christian. He could not ignore her in his short time here, nor did he wish to.

She was feeling badly enough without his being rude. One did not have to become attached to show kindness as he had toward many in his life.

## Chapter Two

Aislynn paused before the door that led to the private chambers and peered back toward the high table. Aye, Jarrod Maxwell was indeed still there. He was not some figment of her imaginings, that strange and fascinating man who had come walking into their lives with that cool breath of wind. And yet he had managed to sit the whole of the meal without one word to her, talking with her father as if she did not even exist.

She would certainly wish him at the far ends of the earth were it not for her certainty that he would find Christian. Even as she thought this, she could not forget the way he had looked at her mouth. She had felt a rush of something warm and womanly inside. It was something she had never felt when Gwyn looked at her. Not even when he had kissed her that once.

Whatever was the matter with her?

Though Jarrod Maxwell was quite undeniably the most interesting and handsome man she had ever seen in all of her life, she must stop this. She certainly had no reason to think the knight was interested in her. She must not allow herself to imagine some connection between them. Instead, she needed to be about the task of readying his accommodations.

As her father had said, the knight should be shown the utmost honor and hospitality they could bestow upon him. Christian's chamber was vacant at the moment and quite spacious. It should serve their guest quite well.

Without further ado Aislynn went to the kitchens and charged her women with readying a bath. She then made her way to her brother's chamber to prepare it for Jarrod Maxwell herself, determined to behave as the daughter of her father's noble house. Yet, as she was spreading the clean linens on the bed, the bed Jarrod Maxwell would soon lie upon, she noted with alarm that her hands were trembling. Quickly, she told herself her trembling was only due to her excitement and hope that the knight might actually be able to help them find her brother.

When she moved to place the soft white pillow upon the bed, she could not deny an unexplainable thrill at the vivid image of his dark head upon it. She took a deep breath and held the snowy pillow tightly to her breast.

It was with a start of surprise that, at that very moment, she heard her father's voice behind her in the open doorway. Along with it came the unmistakable deep tones of the man who was so much in her thoughts.

She swung around to face them with a guilty start, dropping the pillow onto the floor.

Her father motioned Jarrod Maxwell into the

chamber as he addressed her. "Aislynn, my dear, Margaret informs me that Sir Jarrod is to have Christian's room during his stay."

Aislynn nodded, not meeting her father's gaze as, with a pounding heart, she bent to pick up the pillow and toss it upon the bed. Telling herself that the men could not have known her thoughts even if they had seen her hugging it, she replied quickly, "There is no point in his having less comfortable accommodation when it is vacant. Sir Jarrod will have some measure of privacy here." As she motioned toward the large wooden tub, she realized that the knight's name felt strange and at the same time welcome on her lips, which only disturbed her further.

Hurriedly she went on evenly, determined to behave as if she welcomed this man no more than she would any other guest. "The women are heating water for a bath as we speak."

Jarrod Maxwell held up a hand, shaking his black head. "There is no need—"

Her father interrupted him. "Nay, do not demure, sir knight. Allow us to thank you for your help by way of our hospitality."

The other man subsided, bowing, his stance tense, as if he were uncomfortable at being the object of their consideration.

Aislynn found herself studying Jarrod Maxwell as he stood there with her father. This new awkwardness was a sharp contrast to the grace and power that seemed his accustomed demeanor. What a strange mixture of reticence and confidence he was. No wonder Christian held him in such high esteem.

Again Aislynn felt an unmistakable stirring inside

her. He raised a strong hand and raked it through the raven darkness of his hair while he listened to her father. At that very moment those black eyes found hers and she felt herself flush. He held her gaze for just one moment. "Lady Aislynn."

Quickly she looked away, moving to make sure the towel she had draped over the bench was not too close to the fire, though she already knew that it was not. Far from being pleased that he had acknowledged her, she was unaccountably flustered, her heart thumping in her breast.

Deliberately Aislynn occupied herself with wandering about the room, putting away the few items her brother had left out. The two men's conversation became no more than a soft murmur in the background, though the deep timbre of the knight's voice kept her senses in a heightened state.

So successful was she in distracting herself that she ceased to even attend their conversation until her father's voice rose as he said, "What do you mean, the side of one of the pots has cracked?" Aislynn looked up to see that her father was addressing Margaret, the head woman at Bransbury, who stood at the entrance to the chamber with a perplexed frown creasing her brow.

The slender, dark-haired Margaret looked from him to Aislynn. "I did not mean to trouble you with this matter, my lord. I intended to inform Lady Aislynn. The iron hook that held the pot of bathing water over the fire came loose, causing it to fall."

Her brow creasing, for a crack in one of the enormous pots was a calamity indeed, Aislynn started forward. "I will see to it, Father." She would be glad of an excuse to leave them.

But her father halted her with a raised hand. "Nay, Aislynn, you have had much to occupy you. See to our guest. I will attend this matter myself. I wish to see how badly the pot is damaged."

"But…"

It was too late. He was gone and with him, Margaret.

She heaved a silent sigh. Clearly she had been too effective at appearing busy.

And now she was yet more determined to appear so. She did not wish to attempt to make polite conversation. But Aislynn could feel the knight watching her. She could not bring herself to look at him, not now without her father's presence to buffer her feelings.

Desperately she looked about the chamber. The fire burned clean, the tub was ready for filling, the linens were laid out, the bed was turned down. There was nothing left to do and his attention upon her was near tangible, though Aislynn pretended not to notice.

She felt a flush staining her cheeks. Surely she had blushed more in the past hours since Jarrod Maxwell's arrival than ever before in her life.

It was with a start that she heard him speak her name. "Lady Aislynn?"

She looked across the length of the thick carpet that marked the center of the room and into those black, depthless eyes. There was no expression in them that she could read. "My lord?"

He motioned about the chamber. "Would you

mind if I have a look about? I might be able to find something that would help us in our search for Christian.''

Instantly she shook her head, blushing anew as she realized what her thoughts should truly be occupied with—her brother and finding him. "Nay, please do so, but I do not know what you might find. My father and I have been through everything. There seems to be nothing here beyond my brother's clothing and his drawings.''

"He left his drawings? When we were in the Holy Land he never went far without them.'' His dark brows arched. "Perhaps I will begin there.''

Aislynn started toward the chest at the end of the bed and was aware that he was moving toward it, too. When she halted before it, she reached out to the latch. A strange but unmistakable jolt flashed through her as her hand came into contact with warm flesh and she pulled her hand back. In that brief contact, she was aware that the skin she had inadvertently touched was smooth and hard. The skin of a man's hand.

Jarrod Maxwell's hand.

Her gaze lifted and she saw that he was now standing close enough that she could see the fine lines at the corners of his mysterious black eyes. He took a step backward, murmuring, "Forgive me. I but thought to do something for myself rather than have you wait upon me.''

Her heart pounding, Aislynn saw that his mobile mouth had turned down in a frown. Rubbing her still trembling hand against the back of her skirt, she wondered if he was aware of her own reaction to that inadvertent touch.

She answered hastily, attempting to cover her confusion. ''There is nothing to forgive. You simply startled me.'' She was decidedly unhappy with the breathlessness in her voice.

Surely it was surprise that made her tingle from the top of her head to the tips of her toes—startlement.

He bowed, not meeting her gaze now, and Aislynn turned back to open the chest. She found herself speaking too quickly. ''As I told you, we have searched everything. Though there are hundreds of renderings, none of them gives any hint of where Christian might have gone.''

With the lid thrown back, the few sheets of parchment, which lay on top of Christian's best garments, were revealed. ''These are most recent of those we found. All the others are over there.'' She pointed across the room toward another larger chest against the gray stone wall. ''They were obviously made before his return to England.''

She could feel the heat of Jarrod Maxwell's body as he bent over her. He seemed to have forgotten that awkwardness of a moment ago as he looked more closely at the drawings.

Aislynn swallowed hard, a shiver racing through her. Taking a deep breath, she moved back carefully so as not to actually touch him while giving him a better view. Sir Jarrod, thankfully, did not appear to note her reactions, which was a relief of great proportions. For they only seemed to grow more inexplicably extreme by the moment.

She watched as the dark knight reached out to take the top drawing, holding it close as he studied it, frowning with obvious concentration. Curiosity overcame her reluctance to be near him, and she leaned in to look at the drawing. She was forced to rise up on toe tip to see it clearly.

Noting her action, Jarrod Maxwell looked down at her. "You are very small," he commented as he held the drawing lower, seeming unaccountably pleased at his observation.

Finding no explanation for why this would be so, Aislynn determined to ignore it. She had never been particularly troubled by her size. It had in no way prevented her from doing anything she wished to do. She turned her attention to the rendering.

She had seen it before, of course. It was done in charcoal, as were all of Christian's renderings. In it a man lay upon a bed, his face creased with pain and sadness. In the corner of the parchment was drawn the form of the dragon brooch. Out of the corner of her eye, she looked to where Sir Jarrod had thrown his cloak upon the end of the bed, recalling that he had worn it his when he'd entered the hall.

Aislynn knew from Christian that it was Sir Jarrod who had had the brooches made and that their friend Simon Warleigh had one as well. Although it had seemed odd that her brother would draw the brooch on the corner of the page, neither she nor her father had been able to assign any particular significance to it.

Jarrod's gaze continued to hold obvious concentration as he looked from the drawing of the sick man to the brooch and back again.

Aislynn could not stop herself from asking, "What is it? Do you find something of significance there?"

The knight turned to her with an expression of intense concentration. "I am not sure, but the man in the drawing is a soldier who came with Isabelle and Simon when they left Dragonwick some weeks ago. He was injured in his efforts to help Isabelle and Simon escape from Kelsey."

Aislynn heard the barely suppressed rage in his voice as he said the name Kelsey. Through her brother, she knew what ill Kelsey, who had murdered The Dragon, had wrought, and also of the anger that seethed inside the three men who had fostered together. But she noted a depth of venom in this man that went even deeper than that which Christian had displayed.

She listened as Jarrod went on, his voice now softened by regret. "Though we thought the wound was not serious, Jack became ill and died. Christian, although he knew him little, spent much time at his side. Seeing Jack so ill, and knowing he had meant only good in helping Isabelle and Simon to leave Dragonwick, made me want to vent my wrath on Kelsey all the more." His jaw clenched tightly. "And that I can not do, for Simon and Isabelle's sake. We are too closely watched by King John, who was not pleased to have been coerced into setting Simon free."

Aislynn knew that it had been Christian who had convinced two very powerful nobles to speak on Simon's behalf, virtually blackmailing the king into setting him free. She wondered if Sir Jarrod had any

notion of how much he revealed of himself with this
tale. Clearly he had a great capacity for ire and a
love of vengeance, yet he tempered them for the sake
of those he loved.

Again, Aislynn was moved by the bond between
the three men, though she was not surprised to learn
that her brother had sat with the dying man. She had
been quite young when Christian had left Bransbury,
but his kindness to injured animals about the demesne was well remembered. She had missed his
gentleness, his warmth, when her father was so
locked in his grief over his wife's death. Though she
had understood as she grew older that a young man
must foster and become a knight, she had never
stopped hoping that he would return to Bransbury—
that they would be as a family.

Christian's return had made her dreams a reality,
for a time. But now they were once more in a state
of loss. She would leave no avenue unexplored in
her desire to have Christian home.

Yet she could not see what this drawing might
have to do with her brother's disappearance. Puzzled, she watched as Sir Jarrod quickly leafed
through the other drawings, setting them into the
chest before going back to the first one, the one de-
picting the man who had died.

Again she asked, "What is it that you see?"

He shook that dark head. "I am not certain. There
is just something. Somehow it seems that Christian
may be saying that the brooch, The Dragon, is connected to Jack."

"But even if that is true, I do not see what it can
have to do with Christian's being gone. Perhaps the

man simply made him remember past times at Dragonwick.''

The knight raked a hand through his thick hair, taking a deep breath and setting the drawing aside. ''Perhaps you are right, Lady Aislynn.''

The sound of her name on his lips brought her back to an instantaneous awareness of all the feelings she had been attempting to deny. Her gaze came to rest on the lean line of his jaw, the curve of his heavy black lashes, the suppleness of his mouth.

A strange heat moved in Aislynn's belly. At that moment Sir Jarrod turned his black fathomless eyes to her, his gaze as deep as the darkest night and just as unreadable. Aislynn could not move, could not even breathe properly, for her chest felt...

Suddenly realizing that she was staring at him, Aislynn feared that all that was going on inside her would be revealed in her eyes. Deliberately she focused on the fire, the stone floor, the open door. Anywhere but on the dark knight.

Good heavens, had she gone mad?

Her brother was missing. That was the knight's only reason for being at Bransbury. Even if he were interested in her, it would not be appropriate now. Even if she were not engaged, which she was. Even if her marriage was not significant to the peace on her father's lands, which it was.

The sound of slow footsteps approaching in the hallway outside made her cast her gaze to the doorway. Her father appeared there. He came forward into the room, taking in the fact that Jarrod was holding her brother's drawing in his hands.

He looked to Aislynn and she said, ''Sir Jarrod

wanted to know if he might look through Christian's things and I said yes.''

Her father nodded. ''That is well, for I have said he might have free rein to do whatever he thinks might aid him.'' He moved to examine the drawing. ''I too thought there might be some hint here yet I can see nothing. What is your opinion?''

Jarrod shrugged. ''I see what you see, my lord.''

Her father sighed and made a slicing motion. ''Enough for this night. You have journeyed far and must rest.'' He turned to Aislynn. ''The pot did fall and must be replaced, Aislynn, but we have made use of another. The water will be ready shortly.''

Aislynn felt her cheeks heating again. She had completely forgotten the broken pot, which was certainly unusual for her. She took great joy and pride in the overseeing of the keep.

Her father went on, unaware of her discomfort. ''You will be abed before you know it, Sir Jarrod.''

To her surprise, the knight turned to her with a frown of apology. ''Pray forgive me, Lady Aislynn. I had not thought until this moment how late the hour has grown. You should have sought your own bed some time gone. I'm sure you will soon be eager for me to leave Bransbury if my presence keeps you up past the hour when your father prefers for you to be abed.''

She frowned, blinking. He was speaking to her as one might a child.

Her father nodded. ''Aye, Aislynn, as Sir Jarrod has indicated, the hour grows late for you as well.''

Aislynn did not remind her father of the fact that she was often at her duties until far past this hour.

"Perhaps it *is* past time for me to retire. Good night, Father."

She bowed in Sir Jarrod's general direction and slipped toward the doorway as her father halted her, kissing her on the cheek and saying, "Good night, little one." It was something he had said countless times, but this night, before this man, it gave her a decided feeling of discomfort.

She was infinitely aware when Sir Jarrod's dark eyes fixed on her and it was all Aislynn could do to meet them as he said, "You have my thanks, Lady Aislynn. I will not allow myself to impose upon your usual routine again. I know how the young need their rest."

She felt the chagrin that flashed from her own eyes to his. Then quickly she forced her gaze to fall, bowing and making a hasty exit.

Was the man mad? And what was wrong with her father, to have treated her like a child before the other man? Needing her rest, indeed. She was a woman, some nineteen years of age.

Her reactions to Jarrod Maxwell had not been those of a child. But this thought brought only deeper discomfort, for she would never have him know that.

Not sure whom she was angrier with—herself, her father, or the knight—she stalked in the direction of her chamber. And as she went, she could not help wondering that one of them had not offered to carry her poor exhausted little person to bed.

The momentary image of herself in Jarrod Maxwell's arms caused her body to heat in a new and far more disturbing way that made her groan her anger aloud.

Jarrod rose early and went down to the meal.

Although his attention was mixed and had been since arriving at Bransbury, he did his utmost to concentrate on what must be done to find his friend. Jarrod could not help feeling that there was something about that drawing of Jack, something that kept prodding at the back of his mind. Yet he could not quite determine what it might be.

He remained distracted by thoughts of Aislynn Greatham. Although he had realized that he was drawn to her because she was Christian's sister, that realization had not lessened the surprising strength of his reaction to her.

In that one instant last night when he had touched her hand, and then again later, for the briefest moment, when she had seemed to be looking at him as if…

He shook his head to clear it. He did not want to think about the way she had been looking at him, nor his unfathomable response, that strange tugging inside him. She was Christian's sister.

It was far better for his peace of mind to think on the obvious anger in her gaze as she had left his chamber the night before. Clearly she was an unpredictable young wench to show such resentment in the face of his and her father's consideration of the late hour.

Jarrod paused at the entrance to the hall and realized that only a few of the servants were stirring. He felt a sense of relief that he need not linger to break his fast with the family. It was surely due to his uneasiness over not only Aislynn's but also her father's making such an effort to see him made comfortable.

Jarrod was not accustomed to being the brunt of such coddling. He was a soldier, not visiting royalty. Even at Avington, with Simon and Isabelle, he had gone about, as he was accustomed to, without so much fuss.

Last night had been his first bath in a tub in some time. His baths were taken in whatever body of water he might come across. And that was the way Jarrod preferred it. He required no luxuries and wanted none. He neither wanted to become soft, nor to become beholden to anyone.

Yet he could not deny that the warm tub of water would have been relaxing had it not been for the fact that he kept getting images of a pair of periwinkle-blue eyes each time he closed his own.

With a silent groan of frustration, Jarrod approached a slender, dark-haired woman in a clean woolen gown and said, "Might I trouble you for a slice of bread and meat?"

As she passed an assessing brown gaze over him, putting hard, muscled arms on her narrow hips, he realized it was the woman, Margaret, who had come to Christian's chamber the previous night. "You may, my lord, but would it not be better to eat a proper meal?"

He shrugged. "Perhaps. Yet I would get an early start."

She nodded. "As you will, my lord." She paused then before going. "It is good of you to come, my

lord, to help to find our lord Christian.'' He could
see the sudden misting in those brown eyes. ''We
are sore grateful to you.''

Feeling uncomfortable with her emotion and gratitude, Jarrod nonetheless reached out to put a hand
on her shoulder. ''He is my friend.'' He was not
acting out of some selfless wish to help, but out of
his own desire to find Christian. Jarrod wished they
would all see that.

Her gaze registered understanding and she bowed
deeply in return, then went on her way.

His discomfort with her thanks, with all of their
thanks, had not lessened as he received the food with
a self-conscious nod and strode from the hall. As
quickly as his horse could be fetched, he left the
keep, turning his mount to the open countryside at a
gallop.

Although Jarrod knew that Lord Greatham had
questioned everyone in the immediate vicinity of
Bransbury, he began at the beginning. He needed to
set some order in his mind to his own search.

The village lay nestled to one side of the castle,
but Jarrod moved directly off to the left of it. He
meant to leave the village for later as he moved
around the demesne in a circular motion.

Each man, woman and child must be thoroughly
questioned. Without even realizing, someone might
have seen Christian as he left. If he could find such
a soul, Jarrod would then know which road and direction he had taken.

Yet thorough as he was, helpful as all he spoke to
were, Jarrod learned nothing new that day, even
though he spent all the hours between leaving the

keep and long after dark on his effort. Neither did he the next day.

Though he did see and discuss what he had been about with her father, Jarrod did not see Aislynn Greatham during either of those two days, returning to the keep after she had retired. He told himself that he had no care for this either way.

His last thought each night was of her, but this was because she was Christian's sister and he was sympathetic to her pain.

# Chapter Three

Aislynn woke quite early, after a restless night—as each night had been since Jarrod Maxwell had arrived at Bransbury. She kept telling herself that his speaking to her as if she was a child did not plague her in the least.

Yet her agitation worsened when she remembered how she had felt as his black eyes looked directly into hers. It was as if he were looking into her soul, making her feel far from the child he believed her to be.

She tried to wish Jarrod Maxwell had never come to Bransbury, but the very notion was shockingly painful. Surely it was due to her belief that he would be able to help them find Christian.

Even though there had been no real developments in the days the knight had been at Bransbury, she was not willing to relinquish hope. She was, in spite of all that had happened in her life, including the early death of her mother and her brother's long absence, an optimist at heart. And it was this sense of optimism that she drew on to assure herself that she would conquer this strange fascination with Jarrod Maxwell.

She parted the heavy rose velvet curtains at the side of her large oaken bed and stepped out onto the carpet that covered the cold stone floor beside the bed. There was no sense in building a fire when the day's duties would keep her from returning to the comfortably furnished chamber for more than minutes at a time. Shivering, Aislynn dressed warmly, as she always did on chill mornings, in a shift, a heavy underdress of dark green linen, and an enveloping over gown with wide sleeves that showed the tightly fitted sleeves of the gown beneath. She then donned her veil, barbette and a warm cap with pearl trim that matched the butter-yellow brocade of her gown.

Leaving her chamber, she went to the kitchen, which lay at the end of a long corridor off the hall, as she did each morning before going in to break her own fast. One of the duties she most enjoyed was flavoring the large pots of stews and boiled meats that were served at the midday meal. The herbs that she grew in her own garden served as a constant inspiration for new and interesting combinations of flavor. And many about the keep said that the teas she brewed from her herbs were quite effective at alleviating minor ailments of the head and stomach.

This day she paused at the entrance to the long narrow chamber with its well-scrubbed counters, great ovens and wide hearth. With one of the two enormous pots that hung from iron hooks on either side of the hearth broken, only one rested over the low-burning fire. Although this made keeping up with work in the kitchens difficult, the women had managed to do well thus far, roasting more of the meat than was their usual custom.

And strangely Aislynn had not even thought on the matter of how much thyme might be added in to a particular recipe in relationship to the amount of rosemary, or any other such combination since the first night Jarrod had come to Bransbury.

Jarrod, whose mysterious black eyes made her heart pound each time he looked at her.

With irritation she realized that she had allowed her thoughts to go back to that man once more. Sharply Aislynn returned her attention to her responsibilities.

It should have soothed her that all was in order, as it was every morning with Margaret awaiting her instructions on which of the containers of herbs and spices would be used this day. It did not.

Margaret had mothered Aislynn since her earliest memory and Aislynn loved her. As a small child she had often been held close to the woman who was lean and wiry from constant activity. Even at rest, the head woman seemed always about to jump up and see to some task.

Yet the fact that she had inadvertently seen Jarrod Maxwell comforting Margaret in the hall on his first morning here had left Aislynn uncomfortable in Margaret's company. She had been so moved by the brief gesture that she had not shown her presence, but had stayed out of sight until he was gone. And each time she saw Margaret she was reminded of his kindness.

As Aislynn approached, Margaret swung around from where she stood stirring the pot and smiled at Aislynn. "Good morrow."

Aislynn nodded. "Good morrow."

''What think you this morn?'' She nodded her head toward the row of small containers in which the flavorings were held, the main stores being kept in a cool dry cellar.

Aislynn looked at them and frowned, her mind devoid of any inspiration. Finally she admitted, ''I have little hunger and naught seems appealing to me. What think you?''

Margaret looked at her closely. ''Are you well, Aislynn?''

She avoided looking into those brightly observant brown eyes, fearful that all she was trying not to think on would be revealed to the woman who knew her so well. She spoke the truth without telling all of the truth. ''Aye, I am concerned for Christian.''

Margaret clearly failed to note any undue disquiet in her mistress, asking, ''Have you seen Sir Jarrod this morn?''

''Nay, why do you ask?''

''I wish to catch that lad before he sets off without anything to eat. We must have a care for his well-being for he seems to have little enough, if any.''

Aislynn bit her lower lip, guilt stabbing her sharply. In spite of his shortcomings, Jarrod Maxwell was a guest at Bransbury. It was her duty, as the lady of the keep, to have a care for his comfort.

She held up a hand. ''I will see to it. You have enough to attend without adding that to your other duties.''

Quickly, before she could give herself time to think, Aislynn went back down the corridor that connected the kitchens to the main part of the keep. On entering the Hall she cast a glance around the chamber.

She did not see him. Hurriedly she asked one of the serfs who were assembling the trestle tables. "Royce, have you seen Sir Jarrod?"

The serving man nodded. "Aye, he went from the keep some minutes ago."

Clearly the knight meant to leave without eating, as Margaret feared. Aislynn hurried out into the cold morning after him, knowing he would first fetch his horse.

The stable came into her sight just in time for her to see a mounted Jarrod Maxwell emerge from the wide double door. He started across the greensward toward the gate and she called out quickly, "Sir Jarrod."

He swung around immediately, his dark gaze searching her out with obvious surprise and what looked to be reluctance. But it was quickly masked by cool civility as he turned the white stallion and came toward her.

Not caring for that expression of reluctance, however brief, Aislynn raised her chin as she waited for him.

Sir Jarrod halted the restless stallion at her side. "May I be of assistance, Lady Aislynn?"

In spite of her irritation with him, she answered, "I thought to see that you had something to eat before you left the castle." A desire to hide any real interest in him made her add, "Actually it was the head woman, Margaret, who thought of you. I simply realized it was my own duty and not hers to see you were looked after."

His lips curved into a smile that did not reach his eyes. "You have done your *duty* by me. You may rest easy."

She grimaced, wrapping her arms around herself as she realized that it was not her intention to be surly no matter what his opinion of her might be. "I did not mean to imply... Aside from your being here to help us find Christian, you are a guest at Bransbury. We do not receive many guests and it is not only my father's but my intent that you be treated with the utmost hospitality and honor."

Those dark eyes changed, narrowed, studying her with an expression she did not understand, and Aislynn could no longer hold them. She looked at the ground as a shiver took her and she wrapped her arms about herself.

He said softly, "You've come out without your cloak."

His changed tone made her raise her head.

Before she could even think, Jarrod Maxwell was on the ground beside her, slipping his own cloak about her shoulders, the cloak that was still warm from the heat of his body. There was a new tingling along her flesh that had naught to do with cold.

Immediately she made to remove the cloak, whispering, "Please, there is no need for you to..."

He reached out to hold it together in front of her and Aislynn looked up at him, her eyes caught once again by his as he said, "Do not be silly. You are cold." His gaze softened as did his voice, the huskiness of his tone making her shiver in a different way, a pleasurable way. "I do thank you for your concern for my well-being and it has already been brought home to me that you and your father are kind and generous folk. But you should not have come out here without a cloak.''

''I simply thought to catch you before you could leave the keep without some sustenance.''

A soft laugh escaped him. ''Let me assure you. I am quite unaccustomed to being fussed over and am more than able to look after my own needs.''

She was surprised at the huskiness of her own voice as she replied, ''So you have said, but mayhap you should allow yourself to be looked after. At least a little.''

He looked away from her, his gaze distant. ''Nay, there is nothing to be gained in becoming soft.''

She frowned at this. ''It is not softness to allow others to show kindness. The receiving of kindnesses takes as much strength as the giving of them. You seem willing enough to care for others but unwilling to receive care.''

His lips twisted wryly, his expression suddenly patronizing. ''What would one of your tender years know of such things?''

Her frown deepened as a wave of renewed ire swept through her and she groaned in frustration. ''Why do you persist in saying such things to me?''

His black brows arched high in obvious amazement at her animosity. ''What things?''

She put her hands on her hips. ''You address me as if I am a child.''

''But you are a child.''

She raised her head high, made bold by the anger running through her veins. ''I may be small of stature, my lord, but I am no child and you should know this.

Many women are several years wed by my age. I myself will be married ere many months have passed.''

A strange ripple of something dark and unreadable passed over his exotically handsome face, leaving as quickly as it had appeared before he said, ''But how could this be. You were an infant when last I saw you.''

She sighed. ''I was six and more than thirteen years have passed. I am nineteen years of age.''

He took a deep breath, a flicker of uncertainty passing through his eyes now, as he seemed to be speaking more to himself than to her. ''But I thought...'' He drew himself up. ''Nonetheless, you are my friend...my brother's sister.''

Impatience tinged her voice. ''Pray what can you mean by that, Sir Jarrod? I have not said that I am not Christian's sister. And what has that to do with my age?''

He looked into her eyes, his own searching and confused as, far from answering her questions, he asked one of his own. ''How could I have been so very mistaken?''

Aislynn scowled again, drawing on anger to mask her own disquiet. ''That, my lord, only you can answer. Haps you have your own reasons for wanting it to be true.''

As soon as the words were said, Aislynn wished them back with all that was in her. Whatever could have possessed her to speak thusly? She certainly did not mean to imply that he had any interest in...

It was more than obvious that he did not. Any more than she was interested in him. She was to be married.

Aislynn was distantly aware of that displeased expression returning to his depthless black eyes once more. His voice was barely audible. ''Just what are you accusing me of?''

She tried to hold her ground, yet the madness of her words could not be defended. She faltered, sputtering, ''I...oh...I meant nothing...I...''

And suddenly Aislynn could think of nothing save getting away from that measuring black gaze. She parted the cloak and dropped it to the ground before he could move to halt her. She then swung around and ran from Jarrod Maxwell as quickly as her feet would take her.

In some ways the morning after Jarrod's encounter with Aislynn passed in the same fashion as previous ones since his arrival at Bransbury. He questioned, in an orderly fashion, each man, woman and child in his path.

Yet his attention was divided as he went from farm, to woodsman's croft, to mill, spiraling out from the immediate area around the demesne to the next village and learning nothing. He could not forget the conversation that had passed between himself and Aislynn. He could, in fact barely credit that it had even taken place. Recalling the flash of womanly fire in her eyes, the noble dignity of her stance, in spite of her anger when she had told him her age, made him wonder afresh how he could have been so very wrong.

Again he recalled her seething outrage when she had informed him that she was to be married. Jarrod could not halt a renewed rush of disbelief as well as an unmistakable and unexplainable sense of regret, both of which he quickly dismissed.

He had only felt protective of her—brotherly. It was those brotherly feelings that made him hesitate at the thought of her being wed. Any brother would wonder if his sister was ready for marriage, even one who was, by her own declaration, well into her womanhood.

If he had only been thinking clearly he would have told her this.

He could not do so now. For any attempt at explanation might be misinterpreted as…well, he was not certain how it might be misinterpreted. He only knew it might be.

God's teeth, he swore as he realized that he had turned the stallion off the path without even realizing it. Had he not told himself that he would not become involved with those here at Bransbury?

There would be no explanations made to the noble lady Aislynn. He would finish his tasks here as quickly as possible and be on his way. In the meantime he would not allow Aislynn Greatham to get beneath his skin.

It was his own lack of concentration, as much as hunger, that drove him back to the keep earlier in the evening than on previous days. These things, and the realization that he would need to remain away the whole of the night if he was to go on to the next village.

The sun was still fairly high over the curtain wall when Jarrod rode through the gate into the bailey. He realized that his passage was marked by many, as it had been since his arrival. Jarrod knew that the castle folk hoped he would be able to find the young lord, as he was called here at Bransbury.

Jarrod took his horse to the stables and gave him a good rubdown, before supplying him with a portion of feed. The stallion was not only a mount but also a companion to him. The well-proportioned horse, with its flowing white mane and tail had been bred in the Holy Land. It was smaller than most destriers, but its stamina and strength were equal to its beauty.

When he left the stable, Jarrod started toward the great gray form of the keep. His path led him near to the low stone structure of the kitchens. As he drew closer, he became aware of a group of people gathered around a wagon from which hung numerous goods.

A tinker. Jarrod was suddenly brought to alertness.

Here would be someone he had not questioned concerning Christian. And perhaps Lord Greatham had not done so either, for the peddlers did not linger often in one place but quickly moved on to the next likely sale. He knew his host was not in the keep this day, but had gone to make another attempt to negotiate a peace between the feuding Welsh.

Jarrod approached the group around the wagon with a determined step. It was not until he was directly upon the eight or ten women who ringed the wagon, and the short, dark man who stood beside it, that he realized that at the forefront of the group stood none other than Aislynn Greatham.

A wave of not only reluctance, but more shockingly, intense awareness washed through him and Jarrod's feet came to a standstill. Shocked after all he had resolved within himself this very day, Jarrod found himself stepping backward into the shadow of the wall.

He told himself that he was not avoiding the woman, he would simply rather question the tinker alone.

None of those gathered around the wagon seemed to have taken any note of his presence, though Aislynn did glance in his direction briefly and he held very still. He felt an uncommon relief when she turned back to the tinker, who began to extol, in eloquent terms, the virtues of the huge iron pot that rested upon the ground before him. When he was finished he cast a beaming smile upon the lady of the keep.

Jarrod watched as Aislynn shrugged, saying, "I might be able to put it to some use."

The peddler's dark eyes continued to smile with good nature as he nodded. "Aye. This pot will be invaluable to the lady who purchases it. It will hold more laundry, more stew, more of whatever a lady might choose than either of those in yon kitchen."

Aislynn shrugged and Jarrod realized that she wisely neglected to mention that one of those now had a crack in it. To do so would very likely influence the value of this one. She said with perfect unconcern, "How much?"

The man named a price.

Aislynn laughed softly. "I could not find my way to paying more than half that amount."

The man held up his hands. "I am a man of business, my lady. I must recoup the cost to myself in order to feed my five children." He named a sum that was halfway between his own first figure and hers.

Again Aislynn shrugged. "I am sure that some other lady will be happy to pay that amount." She turned away.

With a heavy sigh, the man threw up his hands. "For you, Lady Aislynn, only for you would I make such a sacrifice. The pot is yours."

She swung around, reaching for the purse that hung from a cord at her tiny waist, even as she motioned to the women. Two of them moved to take up the pot by its handle and carry it into the kitchen.

The peddler made a great show of continuing to emit heavy sighs as Aislynn dropped the coins into the palm of his hand. But there was no mistaking that his eyes had lost none of their humor. Neither did they disguise the trace of self-satisfaction in the curve of his lips.

With the transaction completed, the fellow grinned once more. "Now I wonder if I might interest either you, or any of your women, Lady Aislynn, in a bit of anything more frivolous."

Without waiting for a reply, he swung around and flipped up a shutter along the side of the wagon to reveal a tray full of fripperies. Among them were inexpensively made bobbles, threads and ribbons.

As if of a single mind, the women stepped closer, Aislynn included.

Jarrod watched as Aislynn reached out to finger the end of a periwinkle-blue ribbon, then a much deeper sapphire one, which lay beside it. One of the women said, "The darker one would match your new gown, my lady. Of course, it would not be seen lest you leave your head uncovered."

Aislynn nodded and picked up the dark ribbon.

"You are right, Therese. I need not always wear a covering on my head, even in winter." She placed another coin into the tinker's outstretched hand.

Not being one to ever have had a great interest in hair ribbons, Jarrod was surprised to find himself not only noting her purchase with some interest but with a decided disappointment at her choice. Not that he disliked the dark blue. It was certainly a color he would be more likely to prefer for himself. It was simply that the lighter shade matched her eyes.

Appalled at his own fanciful thought, Jarrod gave his head a vigorous shake.

Unconsciously he slid even further back into the shadow of the wall. He remained there until Aislynn and her women had concluded their other numerous interactions with the tinker. Gladly he watched as Aislynn stepped back, gave a final nod of her head and led her women into the kitchen.

Only when he was certain they were not coming back did Jarrod approach the tinker. The small energetic fellow had already begun to hang various items on their accustomed hooks.

The peddler looked up with a smile of welcome as Jarrod came to a halt beside him. "How may I serve you, my lord?"

Jarrod shrugged. "I was wondering if you might have happened upon the young lord Christian on the road some weeks past."

The fellow shook his head. "Nay, my lord, I did not, though I do recall seeing him here at keep the last time I was at Bransbury. The lady Aislynn was so happy to have him home that she had to tell the tale of his return from the Holy Land to even me, a lowly tinker.''

Jarrod could not help feeling a sense of disappointment, though he'd had no real reason to believe he would learn anything from the man.

The tinker went on. '''Twas a sad thing to hear that Lord Christian was missing as I arrived this day. He was not long at home and I only really spoke with him twice.''

''Twice.'' Jarrod's brow furrowed with sudden concentration.

''Aye, the lady showed him to me when I came that day, all excited she was to have him home. As I said, he was a good sort, spoke to me man to man, not condescending as some nobles are wont to do. And he was no different when he came to me that night when I camped on the hillside outside the keep, as I do each time I pass through these climes.''

Jarrod was listening very carefully now. ''He came to your camp?''

''Aye, he came down to my camp and talked with me while we shared a bottle of wine. Asked me about the places I had been and seen, which are considerable in my work.'' He rolled his eyes, laughing. ''The stories I told him and all the others I could have told if we'd had more than those few hours under the stars. Not that Lord Christian didn't have his own stories to tell about him and his two friends.''

Jarrod restrained a sigh as he realized that this information, however entertaining it might be in other circumstances, only served to frustrate him now.

Finally the man said something that made the fine hair on the back of his neck prickle in alert. ''Young lord Greatham, he seemed fair disappointed that I knew very little of a wee village called Ashcroft. I was sorry not to be able to tell him something of it other than that I've heard another of my trade mention the place. There seemed nothing of interest to say of it for he said it's such a small village, and very isolated, that there's little gain to be had there. No great family lives there, such as the Greathams here at Bransbury.''

Jarrod took a deep breath, trying to think calmly, to understand what this might mean. ''You say Lord Christian was very disappointed that you could not tell him how to find this Ashcroft?''

''Aye, I'd say so. It was not anything he said, mind you. But I've something of a good eye for reading people after making my living at selling goods. A man has to know when to give a good-natured nudge when a customer is uncertain, or to leave go. If he pushes too hard he won't be welcome in a place next time and if he has no enthusiasm for his craft…well…his children do not eat.''

Jarrod could not doubt the man. Had he not watched the exchange between him and Aislynn? Not that she had gotten the worst of the bargain. She had acquitted herself quite well in Jarrod's opinion, though he was fairly certain she had ended in paying the price the tinker wished to receive for the pot.

Even if he wished to doubt the significance of the exchange between the tinker and Christian, he could not do so. For now, at long last, he had some bit of information to begin his search for his friend.

Thus if the tinker said Christian had been disturbed when they'd discussed this Ashcroft, Jarrod was determined to figure out why. He frowned. "But you say you do not know the location of this village?"

The other man shook his head then sighed. "Nay. I am sorry that I can offer you no more information than I have. As I said, it is remote, and perhaps if I think on the matter, the one who told me of it had just recently come from the north, toward Scotland."

North toward Scotland. This brought an immediate thought of Kewstoke, his father's lands, which were not far from the Scottish border. But Jarrod did not wish to think on this, nor of his feelings of grief when he had heard of his father's death from a nobleman who had recently come from England some years ago in the Holy Land.

He must concentrate on what the peddler had told him. Though it was, in fact, precious little to go on, it was something. Jarrod bowed to the man. "You may have, in fact, been of some help to me. I am in your debt."

The tinker bowed. "Then I am very glad to have been of service." He gestured to his laden cart. "As for being in my debt, have no care for that other than to recall that I am a salesman. Should you have need of anything of a material nature, I would be happy to provide it."

Jarrod knew there was unlikely to be any opportunity for him to make any purchases from the man.

The tinker laughed, shrugged and began gathering his goods together once more. As Jarrod watched, he reached out to close the shutter that would once more hide the tray with the ribbons Aislynn had examined earlier.

The periwinkle-blue ribbon caught his eye as be-

fore, bringing an unexpected idea. Seeing Aislynn
with the tinker, watching her as she fulfilled her duties
with wisdom and adroitness made him realize anew
that he had been mad to ignore her. What harm could
there be in offering a small token of peace?

Jarrod reached into his belt and removed a coin. "I
will have the pale blue ribbon."

The tinker quirked a brow and glanced toward the
door where Aislynn had disappeared some minutes
gone. "A very good choice, my lord."

Jarrod made no reply to this obvious innuendo as
the tinker reached to his own purse, for the sovereign
Jarrod had placed in his hand was far too dear a price
for a bit of ribbon. Jarrod stopped him. "Nay, pray
keep it. As I said, you have done me a service."

The tinker bowed and said, "And now I am in your
debt, my lord."

Jarrod nodded absently as the man's assumptions
brought a surge of discomfort. With the bit of ribbon
in his hand he now felt somewhat uneasy, especially
as the image of Aislynn's delicate face and those wide
and beguiling blue eyes came strongly in his mind.

He suddenly realized he could not give it to her. It
might only further confuse things between them. She
might very well misinterpret his action, as the peddler
had.

An honorable man did not give such gifts to a
woman who was to be married. The Dragon, who had
been the man to teach Jarrod so much of honor, had
never mentioned this specifically. But Jarrod knew, in
spite of the fact that he had little experience with gentlewomen. His sense of right told him as much.

Nay, he could not give it to her, but neither did he wish to keep it. Only the fact that he would cause the peddler to speculate further kept him from dropping the bit of silk to the ground where he stood.

# *Chapter Four*

Aislynn listened with amazement to her father. "The peddler has told Sir Jarrod that your brother had sought information about a village called Ashcroft. Sir Jarrod believes, as I do, that he may, in fact, have gone to this place."

"Ashcroft." The name was utterly unfamiliar, but Aislynn's joy overwhelmed any accompanying surprise. In her excitement Aislynn leaned closer to her father. Sir Jarrod had accomplished what they had not.

She had not seen Jarrod Maxwell since that horrible confrontation this very morning. Her face heated at the very memory of it, though she was buoyed by a sense of righteous indignation.

Unaware, her father answered, "Sir Jarrod told me just minutes ago when I met him as he was leaving the keep."

She looked down at her folded hands. "He is not coming in to the meal?"

"Nay. He is determined to seek further information concerning this village."

This brought her upright. "What do you mean—seek further information? Can Sir Jarrod not simply go there?"

"The peddler knew no more about the location than that it may be in Scotland. Scotland is a big country."

She sighed. "Then my happiness is premature."

"Nay, daughter." He reached out to put his large warm hand over her cold one. "Sir Jarrod has said that even if he learns nothing more this day he intends to simply head toward Scotland and see what can be learned on the way. He will leave on the morrow."

Jarrod was leaving on the morrow! Aislynn felt a rush of emotion that left her limbs weak, her chest tight.

As her father went on, she forced herself to attend him. "Sir Jarrod is determined. I believe that if any can locate this village, he can. And if he does locate it, he may indeed find your brother there or at the very least further word of him."

Aislynn forced herself to nod. She wanted her brother found and she did not care in the least that Jarrod Maxwell would be leaving them in order to find him.

She *was* glad the irritating man would be gone from Bransbury. Life would go on much more smoothly and peacefully without him.

A sudden rush of memory of the times when their eyes had met and the strange sensation that had come over her made her feel weak and uncertain. When Jarrod Maxwell looked at her, Aislynn felt, well, alive in a way she had not been before he came.

"Aislynn?"

The sound of her father saying her name intruded upon these thoughts. Her voice was breathless as she answered, ''Yes, Father.''

The frown that creased his brow left her with the impression that he had been trying to gain her attention for some time. His words confirmed it. ''Aislynn, attend me, please. Are you well?''

She nodded quickly. ''I am simply so very happy to know that Sir Jarrod will set out immediately.'' She could hear the lack of conviction in her words.

He nodded. ''You will, of course, see that Sir Jarrod has all he needs to begin his journey—food, warm furs, perhaps even a tent, and whatever else he might require.''

Now Aislynn frowned in consternation. She did not wish to have any more contact with Jarrod Maxwell.

She could not tell her father this. Yet neither could she bear the thought of facing the knight. She smiled tightly. ''Father, I am sure that Sir Jarrod will not require anything beyond some food. He brought no such luxuries as you suggest when he arrived at Bransbury.''

He scowled at her. ''I am surprised at you, Aislynn, for this attitude is quite unlike you. We could do nothing about the circumstances by which Sir Jarrod traveled to us. We can do something about the circumstances under which he leaves us. Especially so when it is for our benefit that he has undertaken this journey.''

She flushed, looking down at her hands, which she had clasped tightly in the lap of her apricot velvet skirt. It was badly done of her to respond as she had.

And even more importantly she felt a reluctance for her father to wonder at her odd behavior.

Aislynn spoke very softly. "Your point is well taken, Father. I will see that Sir Jarrod has all he will accept by way of making his journey as comfortable as possible."

He nodded. He seemed suddenly distracted now, seeing her, yet not seeing. His distant voice told her why. "I have received word that, far from being quelled by my visit to him, Llewellyn has continued to harry his neighbors, though none claim to know the reason why. They are saying that he is calling in every man upon his lands for questioning. If I can not leave this chaos in order to find my son, making the one who will search for him comfortable is the least we can do."

Aislynn bowed her head. "I will see to it this very moment, Father."

As she moved off to the kitchens, Aislynn resolved that, even though she meant to carry out her father's wishes with no more complaint or hesitation, she need not have direct interaction with the man she had been avoiding, until all was done. Sir Jarrod would very likely be glad to have little contact with her as well.

It was not until some hours later, long after most of the keep had sought their beds that Aislynn was finished making arrangements for their guest's journey. She wiped her hair back from her brow with a weary hand, feeling a sense of accomplishment in spite of her fatigue. Leather bags had been packed with foods that would keep well for several days. The freshly aired furs, as well as a small but sound tent, were ready to be secured to the donkey she had designated to carry the provisions.

She knew she had delayed telling Jarrod Maxwell of her preparations for him long enough.

She had no fear of waking the man who so occupied her thoughts. Margaret had informed her that he had returned to the keep a short time gone. Margaret had further insisted a jug of warmed wine, as well as bread and meat, be sent to Christian's chamber.

Where he might have been until so very late at night, Aislynn did not know. Nor, she told herself, did she care. Her business with him was purely out of necessity.

Yet she could not help wondering if he was avoiding her as she was him. For some reason the thought prickled, which made no sense whatsoever.

She raised her head high as she made her way down the passage that led to her brother's chamber.

Yet as she came to halt outside the narrow oak door, she hesitated, biting her lower lip. She could hear no sound from inside. Perhaps she was wrong in thinking the knight would still be awake and Jarrod Maxwell had already gone to sleep. She certainly did not wish to waken him, not when he was starting a long journey in the morning. Perhaps one of the servants could inform him of the preparations she had made on his behalf in the morning.

Even as she continued to hesitate, a soft scraping from inside the chamber made her frown with chagrin.

The knight was awake. And she had promised her father.

Taking a deep breath, Aislynn raised her hand and

knocked softly upon the heavy portal, so softly that even she was hard-pressed to hear it. Immediately realizing Jarrod could not possibly have heard, she raised her knuckles and rapped again. This time the noise was much more forceful. It sounded, in fact, quite demanding. She stepped back instantly, startled at her own temerity.

Jarrod had been drinking deeply of the dark red wine since the serving woman had brought it. He had returned to the keep tired in both mind and body. Yet he knew that if he climbed into the bed, he would not sleep. He would lie awake thinking of the compelling young woman who had managed to so disturb his peace without even trying. A young woman whom he was unlikely to ever see again. Even when he found Christian, there would be no reason for him to return here.

He would be free to go on as he had before with no ghosts to haunt him but those of his past. Yet he drank more wine than was his custom in an effort to dispel the reluctance he felt at leaving Bransbury. Surely it was because he was so tired. The journey from Avington had been long and he'd had precious little sleep since arriving. And he was to set out again in the morning with nothing more than the name of a remote village as guide.

His unrest had nothing to do with the blue eyes of the female who had so forthrightly declared herself a woman and then insisted that he had some reason for not seeing this.

The very thought made Jarrod reach out for the cup again. He raised it to his mouth just as an imperious pounding sounded at the door. He sprang up, knocking over his stool as a jolt of adrenaline raced through him. Quickly he strode to pull the door open, his mind whirling not only from the wine but concern as he wondered what could be amiss to warrant such a pounding.

Jarrod stopped short. For on the other side stood a wide-eyed and diminutive Aislynn Greatham. Diminutive, he reminded himself, but very much a woman.

He spoke quickly. "What is amiss?"

She shook her head quickly. "Nothing. I simply wish to speak with you for a moment before you retire."

His heartbeat eased only slightly as he scowled down at her. "When I heard that drumming, I thought something had occurred, that something was wrong."

"Nay, there is nothing wrong." His frown deepened and she finally noted his displeasure as she sputtered, "Forgive me, Sir Jarrod, I..."

Nothing, she had pounded upon his door like that for nothing. His head was spinning from the wine as well as irritation, and without stopping to think, he took her arm and pulled her inside the chamber.

Her eyes widened in shock. "What are you...?"

He let go of Aislynn, closing the door with a decided firmness, before rounding to face her. "I have no wish to discuss the matter in the hallway. What do you mean summoning me thusly in the dead of night?"

Now it was her brow that creased in not only displeasure but defiance as she glared up at him. "I attempted to beg your pardon for that. But you would drag me in without listening."

"I am listening."

She took a deep breath, clearly trying to calm her own anger, though he could still see traces of it in the high color along her cheekbones. "My father asked me to ready a few items for your journey. I simply wished to tell you that I had done so." She looked down. "You are leaving in the morning, are you not?"

Jarrod was amazed at the amount of regret that stirred inside him as he looked down at her bent head. "Aye, I am leaving in the morning." With no small effort he called himself to task and added, "There was no need to ready any supplies for my journey. I shall not be taking them. I prefer to travel light, making my way as I go."

She shrugged those slight shoulders. "Nonetheless, my father asked me to make the things ready for you." She looked at him then, her gaze direct, her nose tilted at a proud angle. "I was simply doing as he requested of me. He is a kind and thoughtful man."

He nodded, not willing to try to fathom the strange expression in her gaze. "Aye, that I will uphold. Your father is a kind man." He paused, honesty making him add, "And you are also kind, Aislynn."

"You do much for us."

He knew she meant his search for her brother and again felt a strange sense of regret. He pushed it aside. "I have told you that I have my own stake in finding Christian."

Aislynn watched him closely. "So you have said. Have you no one of your own?"

A shaft of pain pierced his chest, a pain that

shocked him, for he had thought himself long over this ancient hurt. The hurt of not having a home, a family of his own.

He felt her continuing to watch him as he moved to the table and picked up his cup. He downed the remainder of the contents and filled it again. And without knowing why, or even that he had been going to do so, Jarrod told her the truth. "Nay, my father is dead. And my half brother, who is now baron of his lands..." He shrugged. "Let it suffice to say he would not exactly welcome me with open arms."

He did not look at Aislynn, but he felt the difference that came over her, a compelling softness that seemed to call to him, to urge him to rest in her womanly warmth. Again Jarrod emptied his cup.

The wine warmed him as it flowed out into his blood, warmed and numbed him, but did not ease that inner wanting. Slowly he sank onto the chair beside the table.

When she began to speak, his gaze found her face, the loveliness of her in the candlelight, which played over each delicate feature. So caught was he in just looking at her, in seeing the beauty he had not wanted to see, it was a moment before her words really registered in his mind. "I can not imagine what it would be like to be so very alone. Although there has been sorrow in my life, there has always been the promise of my dreams coming true, of my brother coming home, our family being whole again. My family, my father, my brother, marrying and having my own home and children someday, these things mean the most to me."

Married, that was right. Aislynn was to be married.

Jarrod felt a renewed sense of unrest. He listened carefully as she went on, "My mother died when I was quite young. My father...he was not himself for a time afterward and it was during this time that Christian left us." He looked at her, saw the sadness in her gaze, the glisten of tears she refused to shed. "You have no notion of how good it was to have him returned to us. He brought new life to Bransbury—to my father. He must be found. I can know no true happiness until it is so."

Jarrod took the unused cup from the tray on the table and poured some of the wine into it. Without saying a word, he held it out to Aislynn.

Taking a deep breath, she moved forward and Jarrod rose. As she took the cup, he motioned her onto the chair. She took a drink of the wine, her gaze fixing on the flickering glow of the fire in the hearth.

Jarrod drank from his own cup. Even in his wine-clouded state, Jarrod wished he had some words of comfort. He did not, but her distress weighed heavily upon him. He told himself that it was her own sympathy for him, misplaced as it might be, that made him wish for some words of comfort.

Aislynn drew him back from these thoughts, whispering, "Have you discovered anything more of this Ashcroft? Have you any notion of how to get there?"

Jarrod shook his head. "Nay, but with the name in my possession all I need do is ask directions along the way."

She sighed. "I am so glad that you have learned this much and am grateful for your efforts, but my worry has been little eased. It still makes no sense that Christian would remain away from Bransbury lest something had happened. I can not credit that he would break a promise to me lest something was dreadfully awry.''

He could not argue with that. Christian did keep his promises. ''It is true, he does. Yet that does not mean something has happened to him. There could be any number of reasons for his being delayed.''

She turned to him, her gaze direct. ''You do not really believe that naught is wrong or you would not have come all this way to find him.''

Jarrod could not meet those wide blue eyes, which seemed to see too much. ''You must not allow yourself to become fanciful in this. I am certain that all is well.'' As he said the words, Jarrod told himself that it had to be true.

Suddenly, he felt the chafe of waiting till morn to set out to find this village. He had always preferred action to conversation. Words were too easily distorted. As had been the loving and loyal words of The Dragon's brother only days before he had betrayed him.

Aye, Jarrod would be glad to begin his new course of action. He did not wish to examine the accompanying thought that his restlessness was stronger than ever in Aislynn Greatham's presence.

Jarrod took another long drink of his wine.

Aislynn raised her own glass. She too took a long drink before setting it back down, staring at her slender fingers as she twisted them around the base.

Jarrod found himself studying her averted profile, the dusky fringe of her lashes, the sweet curve of her cheek, which was pale cream in contrast to the apricot velvet of her cap. There was a definite trembling in the mouth that had pursed so many times with anger in his presence. He was drawn to her vulnerability, beckoned by it. She was so very delicate, so small, and seemed as if she would be so very easily broken. At the same time he realized what strength lay inside her. He had seen it time and again over the past days in the way she looked after her father—and in the confrontations with himself.

She lifted one hand and wiped it across her cheek. It was a furtive gesture and, if he had not been studying her so closely, Jarrod might have missed it.

Yet he was watching her. And he realized instantly that she was crying.

An intense jolt of protectiveness tightened his chest.

Before he could stop himself, Jarrod moved around the table to her side. Acting purely on instinct alone, he reached out and put a hand on her shoulder. The bones felt fragile under his hard, callused hand. He swallowed as she looked up at him, her periwinkle eyes damp and unguarded in the light of the candle.

Jarrod spoke roughly, awkwardly. "Pray do not cry, Aislynn. I will find him."

Rather than stopping the tears as he had hoped, this made them spill over onto her pale cheeks in a flood of sorrow. God's blood. He had not meant to make things worse.

Now what was he to do?

Jarrod's experience with women had not involved much in the way of comforting. He refused to remember the one woman for which he would have done anything. She who had wanted none of him. That pain was too great to bear…

Aislynn was here—now, and she seemed to welcome his care. He raised his other hand to the soft curve of her cheek. ''Aislynn, I...please do not weep so. I promise you that I will bring Christian home to you.''

She peered up at him, her face pale, her gaze now searching, afraid to hope. ''How can you make such a promise?''

He took a deep breath. ''Because I am that certain I will do so.''

She sniffed. ''Truly?''

He forced himself to hold her eyes without wavering, although his felt hot from not only the wine, but the loveliness of her. ''Aye, truly.''

Before he knew what she meant to do, she had leaped up from her chair to throw her arms about his neck. ''Thank you, thank you so very much. I simply could not bear it if he were not to return to us, nor could Father. Father is really not as strong as he appears, you know. His leg, it pains him so at times. That is the true reason that he has not gone after Christian.''

Jarrod stood very still. Aislynn was soft and yielding against him, so delicate, while at the same time decidedly woman. Feeling a distinct and decidedly unwanted stirring deep in his lower belly, he recognized it for what it was instantly. Desire. Jarrod tried to breathe evenly.

He told himself that he must think clearly here, must not allow himself to feel this way. He would concentrate on the fact that he must now do whatever he had to in order to bring Christian back, no matter how difficult it proved, or how long it took.

Yet as he stood there, he continued to be aware of

other feelings and thoughts, the gentle, warm, woman scent of her, the press of her breasts against that area between his chest and belly, the heat that flickered gently but distinctively in his own blood. These sensations reminded him of the fact that he was a man and Aislynn was a woman.

She sighed, her breath stirring the fabric of his tunic over his heart. And finally he could deny his senses no more, giving in to them as he recognized that Aislynn indeed was small. But far from feeling like a child in his arms, there was a definite womanly roundness to her diminutive form. Her breasts were round and firm against him and as he slowly slid his hands further down her back, her narrow waist curved into hips that were perfectly proportionate to the rest of her.

Though he willed it not to, his heart thumped in his chest. He was aware of the increased tugging in his belly, the heady hints of desire that thickened the blood in his veins.

Aislynn became very still in his arms and, though he knew that he should not do so, Jarrod looked down. Straight down into those glorious damp periwinkle eyes, with their spiky wet lashes. Again he put his hand to her cheek, his fingers brushing the edge of her cap, and suddenly Jarrod was beset by a desire to see her without it. With trembling fingers, he reached up and pushed it back from her forehead, never breaking the contact with her gaze until the heavy mass of moonlight slipped free. Only then did he allow his gaze to take in the shimmering length, which fell to her hips. "So beautiful, Aislynn." He reached to touch it, noting that the fine strains seemed to cling to his callused fingers. "So soft."

A barely audible sound escaped her, drawing his gaze back to her face. He watched her lips part and her breathing quicken. He found himself unable to tear his gaze away from those sweet pink lips.

Aislynn's voice was husky and questioning as she whispered, "Jarrod?"

Jarrod's head spun. Whether it was from the feel of this beautiful and surprisingly shapely woman in his arms, or from the wine, he did not know. And at this moment he did not truly care.

His gaze went back to her mouth—so delicately full—so inviting.

He could never in his life recall wanting to kiss anyone as badly as he did Aislynn in this moment. And if there were reasons for not doing so, he could think of none of them.

He bent and placed his mouth on hers.

For a brief instant, Aislynn became very still, her heart thudding in her chest, which felt too tight to breathe. And then she pressed her mouth to Jarrod's, unable to do anything else, though she had no understanding of what had happened here. Perhaps it was sympathy, or his own sadness that made him take her in his arms. She did not know. She knew only that it had somehow become something far different, and she wanted this difference with every fiber of her being. She felt the strength and suppleness of those lips on her with a sense of disbelief, but also a heady rush of some strange unidentifiable longing. It made her heart race and her blood quicken in her veins.

Aislynn could think of nothing save the thrill of

these sensations. She wanted to be closer to Jarrod and she pressed herself as closely to him as clothing, skin and bone would allow.

His lips parted and she felt her own follow suit, felt the hot inner dampness of his mouth. Aislynn's belly spasmed and her fingers tightened on his tunic with near desperation as she raised up as high as she could go on the tips of her toes, wanting to increase the pressure of their lips.

As if he sensed her need, or perhaps because he was as eager as she to deepen their contact, Jarrod lifted her up against him. Aislynn sighed with pleasure and relief as she finally put her arms around his neck, holding him to her as he did her to him.

And he went on kissing her, nibbling, tasting, exploring her lips and mouth until her head was whirling. But, far from confusing her, this only served to make Aislynn certain that she wanted more, that the ache growing inside her could only be assuaged by closer and closer contact with this man.

Jarrod's head was spinning with the wine he had consumed and his own powerful reactions to Aislynn. He was overwhelmed by her open and sensual responses to him, driven to have more of her, of her passion.

He wanted—needed—more.

When Jarrod suddenly took his hot mouth from hers and held her slightly away from him, Aislynn feared that he might put her down. But he instead settled on the bench she had just vacated in one swift and sure motion, then pulled her squarely across his lap.

Immediately his lips came back to hers. But only

for a moment before they left her mouth to trace a trail of heat across her jaw and down the tender flesh to the base of her throat.

Aislynn's head fell back and she was grateful for Jarrod's strong hand on the back of her head, for she felt so weak she could not hold the weight of it. When his hot mouth came to the edge of her gown, her heart began to beat so loudly that she was certain he must hear it.

Jarrod, thwarted in his efforts to press his mouth lower along her silken flesh by the heavy velvet, reached up to cup her breast in his free hand. His eyes closed as he felt the nipple harden against his palm through the denseness of the fabric.

The quickness of her breathing, the heaviness of her lids drove him on. He turned Aislynn more fully against him, running his hands down her sides to her bottom. Again the velvet and whatever else she might be wearing beneath it frustrated him, for though he could feel the shape of her it was just not intimate enough.

His voice was husky with desire as he moved to kiss her again, whispering with an impatient groan, "Pray, why do you wear such heavy gowns, Aislynn? There is no need to cover yourself so fully."

Aislynn did not move her mouth from his, trying to think of some answer for this strange question when all she wanted to do was feel. Finally she murmured distantly, "For warmth. Have you not noted the chill in this keep?"

When he groaned again, his arms encircled her more closely and she reveled in the feel of her own body as it awakened wherever he touched her. She was aware of her own softness, the curves of her breasts, hips, her thighs, in contrast to the hardness and strength of his body.

When his large hands splayed across her waist, slipping down to hold her hips, hold her more tightly to him, she felt a new surge of heated warmth in her stomach. As her breathing quickened, her mouth seemed to open of its own accord, searching blindly for his.

And found it. Jarrod's tongue slid inside and Aislynn's breathing ceased entirely. A soft moan of longing escaped her and her fingers slipped into the dark hair at his nape, holding him more fully to her mouth as his hands continued to glide over her, molding each curve.

She realized that she felt her own desire to touch him, to explore his hard masculine form. Aislynn's questing fingers slid down, across his chest. The muscles tightened distractingly as they passed beneath her fingers, and she thrilled at the sheer powerful maleness of him.

Jarrod rose again, this time keeping her in his arms, and moved across the floor. Aislynn knew where they were going. Knew and could summon no thought or emotion save relief that the ache inside her would surely soon be eased.

Jarrod laid her back on the bed and kissed her once, deeply, before easing away. Aislynn saw him reach for the hem of his tunic, and a sudden breathless disbelief that this could all really be happening made her close her eyes.

When a muffled groan that was far different from the previous ones that issued from his lips sounded, her lids flew open. Jarrod stood beside the bed, his tanned chest bared, one hand reaching up to rake his hair back from his brow as he stared at the object in his hand.

She whispered. "Jarrod?"

He did not look at her but continued to stare at whatever he held in his hand. "Dear God, what have I done?"

It was a moment before Aislynn's surprised and passion-dazed eyes could make out what he was holding. And even after she could fix upon the scrap of blue ribbon, she could find nothing about it to cause him to pull away from her.

He wiped a trembling hand over his face, again saying, "Dear God!"

She rose on boneless legs and took a step toward him, reaching out with a hand that she saw was quaking even more than his. "What is it, Jarrod?"

Still he did not look at her. "I...what we... This is wrong. I do not want this."

Her voice was dull with the pain that stabbed through her, but she held her head high. "You are right. We should not have drunk the wine when both of us were feeling so badly. You had told me of your having no family and then you comforted me about Christian. We...I let our mutual sympathy for each other..."

She got no further as he ground out, "Do not waste your pity on me, Aislynn. I have my freedom and that is the way I want things to be. It is you, Aislynn, who welcomes ties, you who are to be wed."

She froze. "Yes, I..."

He turned to stare into the fire, speaking in a hoarse whisper. "Just go. I beg you."

Not knowing what else to do, Aislynn spun about and, somehow, not only found, but managed to open the door. She moved down the corridor to her chamber feeling as if she were crawling through a dense fog.

All the while she could hardly fathom what had occurred between them. Even more confounding was the way it had ended.

Telling her that he did not want it!

It had been Jarrod who had kissed her, not the other way around.

But for whatever reason he had done so, there was no misunderstanding his true position. He had made it all too clear that freedom was the one thing he desired, the freedom to come and go as he would. He wished for no ties to Aislynn, had reminded her that it was she who was to marry.

Yet how was she to forget that Jarrod Maxwell had kissed her, caressed her. And what kisses, what caresses. Aislynn had never imagined that a man's lips upon her could feel thusly, his hands upon her body. She had been enraptured—enchanted from the moment Jarrod had kissed her. It was as if he had somehow, by placing his lips on hers, worked an invisible magic upon her that had set her entire body alight.

And to him it had meant nothing.

As she moved to her bed, she still felt as if she were seeking her way through that fog of confusion.

She ran her hands over her face. If only she had not drunk the wine, perhaps she would now be able to think more clearly.

Even if he was determined to be free, how could Jarrod simply end it as abruptly as he had? And what had the ribbon he had been holding to do with it? Was it possible that there was a woman involved, a woman who understood that he would not be bound?

The thought brought on such a wave of anguish that Aislynn was unable to stand. She sank down on the edge of her bed.

Thinking about the way his arms had held her, the way his hands had touched her, she could not help wondering how this could possibly be. Surely no man could behave that way if he loved another.

Aislynn could not understand Jarrod Maxwell at all. She only knew that she wanted him still. She put her hands to her head, wishing she could block it all out. Would that Jarrod Maxwell had never come to Bransbury, had never awakened her.

She crawled beneath the cover fully clothed. It was mad to spend so much of her energy on worrying over why he had drawn away from her. He had never pretended that he was here for any reason other than Christian's well-being.

There was no need for her to worry about what would happen between them now. Jarrod Maxwell would be gone in the morn. Unfortunately, Aislynn felt less comfort in this thought than she would have wished.

# Chapter Five

A loud and insistent pounding on her chamber door woke Aislynn. It came only a short time after she was finally able to go to sleep. Waking from her dream was not any easier than accepting the contents of that dream.

Her and Jarrod, kissing, touching…

Aislynn reared up in the bed, her face flushing as she felt the heat of those images. They were as shocking as the events that had taken place the previous night in his chamber.

In that dream, far from rebuffing him, she had responded with a passion that left her breathless and shaken. With a groan of frustration she leaped from the bed, running across the cold stone floor in bare feet. As the pounding came again, she pulled the door open.

In the light of the single candle he held stood her father's squire, Phillip.

"Whatever is the matter, Phillip?"

He bowed. "Pray forgive me, Lady Aislynn. Your father bids you come to his chamber in all haste."

"Has something happened to my father?" Anxiety caused her voice to be harsher than she would have intended.

There was no mistaking the unease in his young face as he replied, "I know not. I was told nothing but to come for you."

Aislynn swung around and took her robe from the end of the bed, sliding her feet into leather slippers. As she began to shrug into the robe, she realized that she was still wearing her clothing from the previous day.

She flushed anew and tossed the robe to the floor, feeling Phillip's gaze upon her as she did so. Without meeting those eyes, she motioned him toward the door, hurrying after him when he rushed to obey. She arrived at the door of her father's chamber to find that it was standing open, the light from many candles spilling out into the darkness of the hallway.

Going inside the comfortably appointed chamber, Aislynn searched for her father. She found him behind the heavy ruby velvet curtains of the enormous carved bed, which had been opened wide. His back was propped against a mountain of cushions, the bedcover pulled high on his chest. The wideness of his blue eyes and the deep flush that stained his lean cheeks told of his distress.

Aislynn rushed to his side and took his shockingly cold hand in hers. "What has happened, Father?"

He pulled her down on the bed beside him as his troubled blue eyes met hers. "Aislynn, I have had a dream."

"A dream, Father?" She could hear the perplexed quality in her voice.

He gripped her hand tightly, almost painfully. "Aye, a dream. I dreamed of your brother, of his being ill."

A spasm of fear passed through Aislynn. She was well aware of the fact that her father had dreamed of her mother's demise. And that dream had come true. Her voice was barely audible as she whispered, "Ill, dear heaven. Was he…?"

Quickly he soothed her. "Nay, in my dream I was told that he would be well."

"Thank God."

"Aye, thank God, but I was also told that it would be a woman, fair of face and form who made him so."

"A fair woman?"

He gripped her fingers too tightly. She felt his gaze moving over her, over her pale hair. "Aye, Aislynn, and there is none more fair than you. I was also shown a dark vision of this woman as she made an infusion from boiled water and herbs. Though I could not see her face, it can only be you who is meant to save your brother."

"But how am I to do that?"

"Sir Jarrod will take you to him."

Her whole body tightened with disbelief and rebellion. "Nay, I…" Quickly she stopped herself from saying the words that sprang to mind. "He would never agree to do so."

Her father frowned. "And why would he not, daughter. He has professed his desire to do whatever he must to see your brother brought safe home. You will accompany him on this journey to Ashcroft."

Aislynn clamped her lips tightly. Never would she

tell her father what had happened the previous night. Neither could she imagine going anywhere with that damnable man. She was even less inclined to go when none of them had a clue as to how far they might be going, or how long it might take to arrive at their destination.

"What is it, Aislynn?"

"It seems a drastic measure. We do not know that Christian has been anywhere near this village even if we would be able to locate it."

Though she was not looking at him, she knew her father was shaking his head. "We do not, but I feel that you must go with Sir Jarrod, that he will find Christian even if he must go further afield than we imagine at this moment." She met his compelling blue gaze, so like her brother's as he went on, "You must see that there is no other explanation for why I would have this dream. Clearly you are the one to save your brother, and Sir Jarrod is our only hope of getting you to him. After…after what happened to your mother… If I had only heeded the dream I had the night before your mother died, I might have her with me still." His eyes and tone were raw with pain and regret. "We can not take the risk of ignoring this warning, daughter."

There was nothing Aislynn could say to this. She knew how her father felt about his wife's death. She also knew that she could not ignore his dream any more than he could.

There was nothing for Aislynn to do but nod her acquiescence. "I will make ready, though we cannot rely on his agreeing." She said carefully, "We have neither of us spoken with Sir Jarrod. He may, indeed, refuse to take me with him.''

Her father took a deep breath. ''Then I shall throw all to the winds and take you myself.''

Looking at her father and the determination that lay beneath the pain on his dear face, Aislynn felt a rush of sympathy and love that left her weak. In spite of his own physical limitations and his duty to his lands, her father would do this for love of his son. ''I am certain Sir Jarrod may be reasoned with.''

He closed his eyes, sighing with obvious relief, then looked at her again as he said, ''Of course, you can not go with this man alone, friend to Christian that he be. With Llewellyn in an uproar, I can hardly spare a man right now, but I will send Sir Ulrick with you.''

Aislynn shook her head now. ''He is one of your most experienced knights. You will need him here at Bransbury.'' The knight was getting on in age, but he was still a powerful man and a skilled fighter.

Her father's brows rose. ''He and he alone will I trust with your safety.''

Aislynn made no reply, realizing that she was speaking with her father as if this was really going to happen. As if she was indeed going off on a journey with Jarrod Maxwell.

With a great act of will, she called upon the inner strength that had sustained her through the loss of her mother, her father's prolonged grief afterward and her fear now for Christian. She could very well end in having to help convince the man to take her with him. But how could she do so without making him think…?

She called herself to task again. She would do what she must.

Jarrod woke with a pounding head.

But it did not pound so loudly that it blocked out the memory of the things he had said and done the night before. As he raised his hands to his burning temples, he was not sure that the remembering was not more agonizing than the headache.

If only he had not consumed so much wine. If only Aislynn Greatham had not come along with her big sad eyes and compelling femininity. He'd been helpless in the face of the longing she awakened in him.

It had only been seeing the pale blue ribbon as it had fallen from his tunic that had stopped him from...

It had been that ribbon, which he had realized he could not give to an engaged Aislynn, that had brought him to his senses. Thank the Lord in his heaven for that blue ribbon.

Though the light outside the shutters was not fully dawned, he threw back the cover with a grunt of frustration and leaped from the bed. He would be away, now, before he could even inadvertently run into the diminutive temptress.

Ignoring the pain in his head, telling himself that he deserved it and worse, Jarrod shrugged into his garments. He then moved to the door and jerked it open.

As he stepped into the hallway, his less than keen gaze came to rest upon the young fellow whose head banged backward against the hard stone wall. While moving to massage the spot, the boy sprang to his feet. "Sir Jarrod."

Jarrod scowled. He recalled having seen the boy, who he believed was called Phillip, serving the baron on several occasions. He replied as evenly as he could, considering the state he was in, "Yes."

The young man confirmed his thought. "I am Phillip, squire to his lordship. I have been sent to fetch you to Lord Greatham."

"How long have you been waiting here?"

Ruefully Phillip shrugged. "I know not, my lord. I fell asleep."

Exasperation colored Jarrod's tone. "Why did you not waken me and have it done?"

The boy's expression was quite earnest as he replied. "I was told not to, my lord. You were only to be brought to the baron after you had awakened."

Jarrod could feel himself scowling more deeply. It made him uncomfortable the way the baron and Aislynn—

His thoughts halted with a painful jolt. He would not think on her or anything about her.

He nodded in the direction they must take to get to the lord's chamber, again ignoring the slice of agony the motion brought. "Let us be at it then. I would be away as quickly as possible."

The odd look the squire cast in his direction did not sit well. But Jarrod told himself he was simply imagining things. Phillip seemed an odd enough sort of lad at best, and Jarrod would be ill served to make overmuch of his expressions.

All the same it was a relief to step into the room and see his host sitting beside the fire waiting for him. Though he felt that sense of relief, he was instantly aware of an even more powerful and indefinable tension. Without conscious thought he scanned the room. With unfailing instinct, he found Aislynn where she stood beside an open chest at the head of the bed.

He didn't want to look at her. He did not want to meet her vulnerable blue gaze, but he could not prevent himself from doing just that. An instantaneous wave of awareness moved through him, tightened the muscles at the joining of his thighs.

With an ultimate act of will, he focused his attention on her father. "You sent for me, my lord."

The baron rose. "I did, Sir Jarrod. There is something of import that I must tell you. Ask you."

Jarrod raised his hands in supplication. "Pray then ask. I would be happy to do what I can."

The baron nodded. "I am very glad to hear you say that." He took a deep breath and let it out slowly. "I would ask that you would take my daughter, Aislynn, with you when you leave Bransbury this day."

Jarrod knew that his own eyes had widened with horror and shock, yet he could do nothing to disguise it. "You can not be serious. It would not be proper for me to travel alone with a young gentlewoman."

The baron frowned then, taking a deep breath before he went on. "Forgive me. I see that I have begun badly. I will explain myself more fully."

Jarrod could think of no explanation that would make such a thing credible, or make him agree to it. Yet he stood silent, waiting.

Thomas Greatham spoke earnestly. "Last night I

dreamed that my son lay in a bed, his face wet with
fever, his body racked with heat. In the dream he
was gravely ill, indeed. And then there came a voice,
a voice of peace and reassurance. It told me that he
had been sent aid, aid in the guise of a woman, a
woman fair of face and form.''

The baron looked to Aislynn, as did Jarrod. He
said, ''Are there any more fair than my own daughter?''

Jarrod could not deny this. With her pale hair falling in a tangle down her back, her blue eyes wide
with some indefinable emotion as she watched her
sire, she was indeed fair on all counts. He knew a
rush of desire, of wanting, so intense that it weakened him.

Again, with great effort, he turned away to address
her father. Filled with confusion about his reaction
to this woman, Jarrod tried desperately to counter his
host's words. ''It was a dream, my lord. I do understand how one can be disturbed by dreams, yet they
are just that—dreams. Even in so grave a matter, one
does not act on what can only be a nightmare.''

The lord of Bransbury shook his head, his eyes
burning into Jarrod's. ''Unless one has had such
dreams prove true in the past.''

Jarrod frowned as the baron continued. ''I had a
dream of disaster before my wife was killed. I told
her of it but made no further effort to prevent her
from departing on the journey she had undertaken.
She did not return to me.'' His voice broke and Jarrod could hear the pain that was still raw after these
many years. ''You must take Aislynn with you. I
will send a man, a knight of great strength and honor

not only to act as chaperon, but to help protect her from any harm you might meet along the way.''

Jarrod felt the tug of her where she stood there beside the bed. It told him that he could not do this. Acting purely out of self-preservation, he ground out, ''Nay. You ask the impossible.''

What the baron might make of that, Jarrod did not care as he turned and strode from the chamber and down the hall. He must be away from this place, from the emotions that ran out of control inside him.

''Wait, please,'' Aislynn called out behind him. Jarrod swung around to face her as she halted no more than two steps away from him.

Aislynn looked up at him, her eyes direct. ''I pray you hear me in this, sir knight. My father loves me greatly, as well as being a man of pride. He would never ask this of me or you lest he felt it must be done. He believes that my brother may very well die if I do not go to him.''

He took a quick breath, not able to break the contact of their gazes as this reminded him of his own concern for his friend. ''And you? Do you believe that Christian will die if you do not go to him?''

She squared her shoulders. ''I...can not but think there is a possibility of that.''

Jarrod shook his head. Although he did feel for them, he could not bring himself to agree to the mad, impossible notion of traveling with Aislynn Greatham after what had passed between them the previous night. Especially since his feelings for her rested just below the surface even now, like a strange tingling current.

''I...'' she began then halted, her gaze uncertain

as she glanced away. Her eyes met his once more and she squared her shoulders. "There is something which must be addressed, I think, so that we may go forward here. What happened last night was a mistake that I do not hold you responsible for. I do not imagine that you have developed some attachment to me. You have made your true nature, that of one who prefers freedom and adventure well-known to me." She took a deep breath. "We had both of us drunk too much of the wine and I was feeling so badly. I know that you were only trying to comfort me. There is no reason to imagine it would ever happen again."

Jarrod watched her closely. Her explanation of the events may have eased his mind if he had not reacted to her so very strongly on seeing her again just now. Something about this woman interfered with his ability to guard himself and his emotions.

She took a step closer to him. "Please, I beg you, sir, to remember your assurances that you would do whatever you must to return my brother safe home. Even if you have doubts in your own mind, heed the fact that my father and I do believe that I must accompany you, that Christian might well die if I do not…" Her voice broke. Those suddenly limpid blue eyes held his no matter that he tried to look away from the pleading he saw there, the desperation.

As that now familiar sense of protectiveness rose up inside him, Jarrod realized that he was lost. He could not deny her. In spite of all the reasons against his agreeing, he could not refute his pledge to do what he could to help his friend.

He would simply have to put aside this mad attraction.

With the decision made, Jarrod was finally able to break the contact of their gazes. Taking a deep breath, he said, "Come." He then moved back into the baron's bedchamber, remaining infinitely aware of Aislynn's presence behind him.

The baron, now standing before the fire, was speaking to his squire. "I will take as few men as…"

He halted, looking up as Jarrod entered the room.

Jarrod moved to stand before him. He could feel the three of them watching him.

Now Jarrod would not meet Aislynn's gaze, nor her father's. "I will take her."

The baron drew himself up. "I do not wish for you to act out of coercion."

Jarrod shook his head. "I have not been coerced, my lord. I have simply had time to think. I will be pleased to have your daughter accompany me. My intent, as is yours, is to do what must be done to see Christian home safe and well. I pray you allow me to undertake this quest as I have pledged."

Jarrod could feel Aislynn holding her breath as her father stood silent. At last he said, "I will accept your offer." Her relief was palpable.

Jarrod addressed Aislynn without looking at her, his tone harsher than he intended. "You must be in the courtyard ready to travel within the hour."

He felt her stiffen, but she said only, "I will be ready, sir."

Jarrod spun away and left the room. He was awash

with doubt over what he had just agreed to do, yet
there was nothing for it now. He had given his word.

Surely though, it would not be so very great a trial.
He need not even speak to the woman lest it was
necessary. It would be a journey of haste and difficulty, not some day out undertaken for pleasure.

All would be well. Christian would be found and
Jarrod would immediately deliver his sister into the
tender and capable care of her own brother.

The notion almost eased his unrest. Almost.


Jarrod was ready and waiting when Aislynn and
her father came down the steps of the keep at exactly
the appointed time. Her promptness should have
pleased him. It did not.

As he watched them from atop his own horse, he
saw the knight, which her father had introduced to
him as their traveling companion, step away from
his own stallion to greet them. Sir Ulrick seemed a
good enough fellow in the few moments Jarrod had
spoken to him when he arrived from the knight's
quarters with his belongings.

Lord Greatham nodded to both Jarrod and the
other knight. "My lords."

Jarrod bowed as did Sir Ulrick.

Sir Ulrick then moved to wait beside the chestnut
mare that Aislynn would ride. After a polite nod toward Ulrick but not even a glance for Jarrod, Aislynn
turned back to her father. "I...goodbye, Father."

Jarrod told himself not to be offended by this as
the older man looked down at her with obvious love
and sadness. He wanted no familiarity between them.

Yet Jarrod felt a tug of something gentle inside

him as he watched the baron touch her cheek. "You are a good and loving daughter. As well as a sister."

She took a deep breath. "We will find him." In spite of his desire to remain distant, Jarrod once again found himself moved by their care for one another and Christian. And though he wished to deny it, he felt a yearning for that kind of care.

He forced himself to attend as Aislynn's father spoke again. "Would that I were going with you."

She sighed. "I will be well." She motioned vaguely toward Jarrod, then smiled at Sir Ulrick. "I will be in more than capable hands."

Her father enfolded her in his arms. And then she was turned toward her horse.

It was at this precise moment that a commotion at the castle gate drew not only Jarrod's attention, but that of all of those present. He watched as a mounted man came thundering through the gate, which had already been opened in preparation of their leaving.

It was obvious that the man who came riding toward them was a giant even at first glance, his legs hanging long in his stirrups, his great bulk seeming to dwarf the pony he rode. He slowed, taking in the tableau in the courtyard with obvious surprise. Yet he seemed to recover quickly, for he rode to where Aislynn was standing with her father and leaped from his horse before it was fully drawn to a standstill.

Somehow Jarrod knew immediately that this was the intended bridegroom, the "good and dependable" husband-to-be, who would give Aislynn the life she had always longed for. Aislynn moved toward him with wide eyes, appearing more childlike than ever in comparison to his towering height and enormous shoulders. "Gwyn!"

Jarrod assured himself that the tightness in his chest was due to the fact that it seemed incredible that anyone would agree to wed the delicate Aislynn to such a hulking beast. Yet whatever she or her father had been thinking, 'twas none of his affair.

The giant frowned down at her. "Are you going away?"

She nodded. "I am." She pointed to her father. "Father has had a dream of Christian and he believes that I must go to him."

The large man took a deep breath. "Then of course you must do so." As soon as this was settled, the giant seemed to lose interest in the subject. His expression was clearly troubled as he said, "It is most fortunate that I have managed to come here before your departure, for I have something of great import to tell you myself."

She put her hand on his arm and Jarrod felt a trace of discomfort wriggle in his belly. He tried to ignore it when she said gently, "Pray tell me what it is."

The big man took a deep breath, letting it out quickly as he glanced about, pausing for a brief moment on her father's attentive face. He then turned back to her before addressing her father, watching her closely as he said, "I beg your leave to speak to Aislynn in privacy for a moment."

The baron nodded. "You may certainly do so, my son. As her intended, there is no need for you to even bid permission for a private moment. It is your right."

For some reason, his saying this only caused the

tightness in Jarrod's chest to move lower, to grip his belly in an unrelenting hold. And it only seemed to increase as he watched the man lead Aislynn away.

Aislynn followed Gwyn around the side of one of the smaller outbuildings without demure, though she could feel the attention of the others upon herself and her intended. She was especially aware of the intense scrutiny of Jarrod Maxwell. Was he thinking the very worst of her, that she could have allowed herself to fall such a willing victim to his embrace when she was bound to the man before her?

It was certainly no worse than she was thinking of herself.

Deliberately she focused her attention on Gwyn. He was a decent man, her friend, and had been since they were children. She owed him her fidelity, did she not, even though neither of them had ever professed any romantic notions toward the other?

Not only her duty, but her honor and the peace of her father's lands lay in their eventual marriage. Not in the arms of a man whom she barely even knew and who declared his kisses a mistake.

Yet she could feel the compelling power of that other man's presence just out of earshot in the courtyard. She told herself it was because he would be impatient with her. He had made his desire for haste well-known to them all.

Yet she would attend to whatever Gwyn wanted to tell her. And she would do so with her full attention.

She heard the resignation in her own voice as she

looked into Gwyn's familiar and obviously anxious gray eyes. "Tell me what is amiss."

"Aislynn, I..." He halted and started again. "You know of my cousin Leri?"

She nodded, taken off guard by this question, uncertain of where this might be going. "You have spoken of her to me." Aislynn had never met the other girl, as she was the daughter of Llewellyn, the man who plagued her father with his unruly ways.

He held her gaze. "Leri has run away. She is with child."

Aislynn tried not to display the shock she felt. For she knew that in spite of his differences with Llewellyn, Gwyn was fond of Leri. "I...you must be quite concerned on her behalf."

He nodded. "I am. I must go to her."

Aislynn shrugged. "Of course. I would not expect you to do otherwise."

A wide smile curved his lips as they met her own with a loud smack. The next thing she knew, she was being drawn up into his strong arms. "I knew you would understand."

She could not help smiling back at him as he then held her away from him. Was this what had caused him to seem so disturbed? Why ever would she mind if he went to offer support and guidance to his cousin? She spoke gently. "You must go with God, my friend. I am moved that you would inform me of your going, for I myself was set to leave in search of Christian without even telling you."

Gwyn shrugged. "I could hardly find fault with you in that now, could I?"

Distractedly Aislynn shook her head, leaning

around the edge of the structure, her gaze brushing the others where they waited near the front gate. She could not help noting the fact that Jarrod Maxwell was staring in their direction and his expression was far from pleased. Inwardly she winced, knowing she was delaying them most grievously, and after she had so boldly and definitively informed the ill-humored knight that she would be of no trouble to him.

"Aislynn, I..."

She turned back to Gwyn, interrupting him, albeit with a smile. "I would gladly hear all on my return, but I pray you understand now, that I must away. The others await me."

He drew a deep breath, seeming almost relieved. "I too should be on my way, for I delayed in going to Leri only long enough to speak with you."

She touched his arm. "Then make haste."

He bowed. "We will sort it all out later."

Aislynn nodded, her relief at being on her way great. She started around the side of the outbuilding and he followed, casting a quick glance over the party, his gaze lingering for longer on one of them. Aislynn did not need his inquiry to tell her who it was. "Who is the strange knight? The one on the white stallion?"

Aislynn looked down, trying to hide the sudden rush of guilt she felt, knowing it would serve neither of them for Gwyn to suspect she had any attraction to the man. For it was certainly dead now, killed by his disregard for her. She spoke more evenly than she would have thought possible. "He is my brother's friend, Jarrod Maxwell. He has come to help find Christian.''

''Then he is most well met,'' Gwyn said. He then added, ''Though he does seem a dour sort if he is to be judged by his expression.''

Aislynn could not keep her gaze from going to that set profile, which was now averted as they approached. Nor could she help seeing that, in spite of his anger, the clean line of his jaw, the noble angle of his nose and wide brow beneath that crown of raven-black hair were more pleasingly assembled than any countenance she had ever viewed.

Because of her irritation with herself, she answered with more heat than she intended, ''I care not for his mood. I simply do as my father bids me.''

Gwyn stopped her with a hand on her arm, looking closely at her. ''The lout has not treated you ill? He has not…?''

Aislynn felt herself flushing, knowing she had given her betrothed the wrong impression. ''Nay, have no worry for that. Sir Jarrod has not forced himself upon me.''

And indeed this was true. She had been all too willing in what had passed between them.

Again she found her gaze going to Jarrod as she finished. The rigidness of his body told her that she need have no worry as to it ever occurring again.

She did not look at Gwyn directly as she moved forward again, fighting her own unexplainable regret. ''You will forgive me, but I really must be on my way now. They have been waiting for some time.''

Gwyn fell in beside her. "I only wanted to be assured that all was well."

She cast him what she hoped would pass for a smile, and said, "All is well," although all was far from being well. Thankfully he seemed to accept her words.

Aislynn moved forward, hugging her father quickly now, feeling her heart ache just slightly at the knowledge that she was leaving him for the first time in her life. She soothed herself with the thought that it would surely not be for long as she went to her mount.

It was Gwyn who helped her onto the mare, not bothering with the stirrup at all but lifting her up in his huge arms and depositing her in the saddle. He put a hand over her own on the reins and spoke softly, gently, his eyes holding hers. "Go with God, Aislynn. We each must follow our own path this day."

It seemed an odd way of saying goodbye, but Aislynn said nothing of it. She replied simply, "I will see you ere long."

Before anything more could be said, Sir Jarrod called out in a rough voice, "Let us away then." He urged his mount through the open gate. His perturbation was clear in the stiff line of his back and set face.

Sir Ulrick, who led the donkey that carried their supplies, looked to Aislynn. She nodded to him. With a last glance at first Gwyn, then at her father's dear and uncertain face, Aislynn forced a smile in spite of the anxiety that tightened her throat.

She would not bring her father more guilt than he

was already feeling over not undertaking this journey himself. Surreptitiously she took a deep breath and prodded her mount to follow the knight, aware of the fact that the sound of his horse's hoofbeats were already fading as he gained distance from them. It was little comfort to feel Sir Ulrick fall in behind her, no matter how desperately she wished it to be.

She somehow doubted that even the knight's presence could prove enough buffer between herself and the cold disapproval of Jarrod Maxwell.

# Chapter Six

Aislynn stared into the flames of the fire. She did not want to think about Jarrod Maxwell, who had departed the camp before Ulrick, who had gone to get more wood. She hoped the dark and distant knight would remain out hunting until she was long in her tent.

If only she had something to occupy her time. But she had already rummaged through their provisions for the last of the fresh bread Margaret had sent. She was cold and tired, and felt utterly useless without her accustomed duties to perform. What could have possessed her to undertake this journey of misery?

She thought back to the last time she had been truly warm. That had been the morning at Bransbury, two days gone by, when she and her father had convinced Jarrod Maxwell he must take her with him. Even now she could hardly credit that she'd had the courage to leave the keep with him.

In the ensuing days, Jarrod Maxwell, damnable knave that he was, had spoken not one word to her. Every word came by way of Sir Ulrick. And then it was only what she needed to know, such as that they were stopping, or that it was time to rise.

Repeatedly she had reminded herself that she did not care what Jarrod Maxwell thought. His behavior toward her was of no concern as long as he took her to her brother. She was doing this to find Christian and that was all that mattered to her. If he was ill as her father's dream had foretold—she couldn't allow herself to think of anything worse—she would be able to nurse him back to health. That her father trusted her, and her alone, to carry out this task made her even more determined to do so.

A rustling off to her left made Aislynn look up. She expected to see Ulrick coming back with his wood. He rarely left her alone for more than moments.

A frown creased her brow as she saw it was not Ulrick but Jarrod Maxwell who stepped out into the tiny clearing. He cast a quick glance about and frowned when he failed to locate the other knight.

A wave of devilment made Aislynn's brows raise high. How, she wondered, would he manage this situation? Might he, at last, be forced to actually speak to her?

Chagrin followed quickly on the heels of her amusement as he moved toward the fire, not so much as glancing toward her again. He carried several hares, which had already been dressed and skinned. Quickly he hung these over the makeshift spit that Ulrick had fashioned before leaving. Jarrod then strode to where the packs lay on the ground nearby and occupied himself with rummaging through them.

Aislynn bristled. Rising abruptly, she said with icy

sarcasm, "I am fair done in by your consideration and civility, sir."

He swung around to face her, his gaze both shocked and guarded at the same time. He frowned. "Your pardon?"

"You, sir knight, are without doubt the rudest man I have ever had the misfortune to be in close contact with."

His scowl darkened, those black brows straightening over equally black eyes. "I am sorry that you feel thusly, Aislynn. I have intended no insult."

The words did not soothe, but only served to inflame her outrage as she strode to stand over him. "You intended no insult. Pray what is it that you do intend by making such a great show of pretending I do not exist. I know you did not wish for me to come with you, yet I had no notion that I would be so illtreated."

He glared up at her. "Ill-treated. I have not treated you ill. I have…I have…"

Aislynn put her hands on her hips. "You have…?"

He grimaced. "I have been much occupied with my plans to discover more information about this Ashcroft."

"Too occupied for common civility."

Jarrod rose, his own expression stubborn. "I had no idea that you expected me to make idle conversation. I had thought that we would do well to avoid undue contact. I had thought that you were concerned with nothing more, as I have been, than finding Christian."

There was no mistaking what he meant by undue contact and she felt herself flush to the roots of her hair. At the same time, she could not control that deep inside there was a part of her that wished for undue contact. Utter frustration with herself and him made her grind her teeth as she replied, "Make no mistake, sir knight, I have no desire for *undue contact*. I am speaking of nothing more than politeness. Possibly a 'good morrow, Aislynn.' Or a 'chill weather, isn't it.' Heaven forbid the thought that you might even discuss your plans concerning where we are going, or what we will do when we get there? You have shared that much with Sir Ulrick."

He scowled. "Perhaps I am simply not adept with the ways of chivalry and therefore find it difficult to make such conversation with one of your sex."

She felt the blood fair race through her veins with anger at this characterization of himself as a bumbling oaf. "That is preposterous, Jarrod Maxwell. I know well enough that you have a way with words when it suits you. Not to mention a way with one of my sex."

Jarrod's dark gaze narrowed as it fixed on her mouth. Then abruptly he stepped back, his eyes unreadable as he replied, "Mayhap my lack of expertise in such matters caused the very incident you take as proof of my prowess."

Aislynn's anger burst into dazzling sparks of fury and she cried, "Lack of experience? Pray discontinue this attempt to toy with me. Christian has told me of your women." For Christian had informed her that Jarrod had no deficit of female companions, that they flocked to him like bees to an exotic flower. The very thought of it made her ache inside and she sputtered, "And do not try to make me believe that the blue ribbon you keep is not a reminder of one of your conquests. Perhaps it is even a reminder of an ongoing liaison...'' She broke off, too disturbed by this notion to continue.

The moment Aislynn saw the unfeigned amazement and indignation on his darkly handsome face, she could have bitten her own tongue off.

He growled, ''Only one woman has ever meant more than a moment's companionship to me and she...nay I will not speak of that with you. You will not worm your way into places you do not belong.'' There was no mistaking the bitterness in his eyes. ''And what in the name of all that's holy was Christian thinking to tell you such things?''

She stiffened, immediately defensive of her brother, even as she felt hurt by his accusations. ''He meant you no harm. He was telling me of your adventures together and...''

Jarrod grabbed her roughly by the arms. ''The women he spoke of were not, I assure you, gentlewomen. They were quite clear as to what they were about.'' His black gaze bored into hers. ''You, on the other hand, Aislynn, do not know what you are playing at. And pray what gives you the right to question my life, when you are to give yourself to that... that...hulking Welshman?''

She sputtered, ''Are you speaking of Gwyn? What has he done that you would think to denigrate or criticize him?''

His lips thinned. ''Have you not looked at him? He is four times your size. What could your father be thinking to agree to such a match?''

She put her hands on her hips. ''Now it is you who

go too far. As if his size had anything to do with anything.''

Those black eyes narrowed. ''Oh, I assure you that his size will be of great import to you at some point.''

Aislynn felt realization wash over her. Although she had never once considered her wedding night in such detail, and could hardly credit that Jarrod would have the temerity to speak on such a matter, she suddenly understood that they did make an incongruous pair. But she would not allow Jarrod Maxwell to know this. She drew a deep breath, not knowing why she would explain anything to this lout except that she felt the need to defend her friend. ''Gwyn is a kind and gentle man now, as he has been since I met him. I was ten and small for my age—'' she grimaced ''—as I have always been. Though he was no more than fourteen, he did not speak to me as if I were an infant, as many were apt to do upon first meeting me.'' She raked Jarrod with a cool glance. ''Gwyn sees me for who I am. He will have every care for me—unlike others might.''

''Are you perhaps referring to me?'' There was cold steel in his voice though she saw a trace of chagrin in his eyes. But she could not give credence to that softer emotion and thus told herself she was mistaken.

She glared at him defiantly. And then, before she could even think to deny him, Jarrod's angry mouth had closed on hers. For a brief moment—just how brief would be mortifying afterward—Aislynn resisted.

Then, as a streak of something warm and compelling flashed between them, she returned that pressure with all the yearning that had been waiting just below the surface since the night he'd first kissed her. Her lips softened, opening, inviting entry.

Thus it was with some confusion that she felt herself being set away. Slowly she opened dazed eyes, which she didn't recall closing, to look up at him. His eyes were dark, so dark the pupils were lost as he whispered harshly, "I am what I am, nothing less, nothing more."

Aislynn, not knowing what to say, what to do, nor how things had gone so dreadfully awry, simply put her fingers up to cover her bruised mouth. She murmured, "I...oh...I did not intend to goad. Please, forgive me."

Regret now colored those black orbs. "Oh, pray God forgive *me,* Aislynn. This is naught but madness. I have no right to question your father's choice for you, or to...I want nothing more than..."

She stopped him. "You do not have to say that you desire nothing so much as your freedom, I would not have it from you. And let me remind you, sir knight, when you tell yourself I have overstepped the boundaries between us that it was you who kissed me." He opened his mouth but she halted him again. "Oh, and have no fear that I shall think it anything but my punishment for trying to goad you."

His eyes darkened further, his lips tightening, but Aislynn had no care for his anger. She had endured enough, not only of him, but of her own unprecedented and seemingly irrepressible desire for him.

The crack of underbrush nearby drew his gaze from her. Aislynn swung around as Ulrick stepped into the clearing, his arms laden with dry wood. Both Aislynn and Jarrod stepped away from each other at the same moment.

Clearly oblivious to their awkwardness, Ulrick dropped the wood into a pile beside the fire and said, "The rains have made finding dry wood a chore, that is certain."

Jarrod nodded. His voice was husky with what she knew was suppressed rage. "We will arrive in Clumney on the morrow. There we will find more comfortable accommodations. At least for one night."

Aislynn did not look at him though this news surprised her. She hurriedly told herself it should not. Having known nothing of the knight's plans, anything was possible.

She ran trembling hands over her skirts as she made a great show of resettling herself on the log. Desperately wishing to avoid a chance meeting with either man's gaze, Aislynn told herself it would be very good to get in out of the cold. To perhaps even take a bath. Yet her agitation with herself and Jarrod was strong enough to dampen any pleasure the notion might have brought.

Why had she baited Jarrod so? Why did she care what he did, or thought of Gwyn, or how he treated her?

She wished that she were indifferent to him. But her reaction to his kiss had proved that she was not, for the very thought of it brought her to an aching desire for more kisses.

There would be no more kisses. And she certainly would not pry where she was not wanted, despite the fact that his violent reaction to her question about the ribbon had only fueled her curiosity about the knight.

Aislynn was aware of the men's quiet conversation but, in her misery, heard none of it. She roused somewhat when Ulrick moved to the fire to turn the rabbits upon the spit.

Without her permission, her gaze moved to follow Jarrod Maxwell as he came forward to use a stick to push the hottest of the coals closer beneath the now sputtering rabbits. It did not waver when he moved to put more wood on the fire. As the fresh wood began to flicker, the light flared up, warm and rosy, casting the lines of his face into sharp relief. His face was far too handsome for her peace of mind. As were those shoulders too strong, and the hands that placed the pieces of wood across the flames too deft.

At that moment he looked up and his black eyes, made infinitely more mysterious and deep by the flickering light of the fire, met hers. And for a brief instant Aislynn was sure that he could see all that was going on inside her, that he knew her every thought, her every yearning wish.

She felt herself flush from the top of her head to the tips of her toes. Hurriedly, not caring what he or Ulrick might think, she rose and went to the small tent, crawling inside. She lay there, unmoving, in the darkness.

Ulrick's voice came from just outside. "Are you well, my lady?"

She took a deep breath, her tone surprisingly even. "Aye."

His voice had not lost that edge of concern. "You have not eaten."

"I am tired." As if to emphasize her words, she

pulled the bedcover over her though he could not see this.

He answered with obvious sympathy. "We have traveled far this day."

Then she heard the softness of his footfalls on the damp earth as he moved away. Aislynn could not suppress a sigh of relief.

In what seemed like a very long time, she heard the sounds the two men made as they readied their own bedrolls. Her mind supplied her with all too vivid images of one of them, his strong frame outlined against the rosy flames.

Only then was she able to close her eyes in spite of her exhaustion. Unfortunately, even closed, her burning eyes were not free of images of herself and the exotic knight, images that kept her awake long into the night.

Jarrod led the small party forward with surprisingly little attention on where they were going, which dismayed him somewhat. This area of England, not far from the Scottish border, was not unfamiliar to him. His father's lands at Kewstoke were within a few hours' ride of the market town. Yet, though he was more restless than he had ever been in his life, it seemed to have very little to do with any lingering pains of childhood.

He could not help feeling badly about what had happened between him and Aislynn, about what he had said and done. Even the fact that she had almost gotten him to talk about…things he did not wish to discuss with anyone, let alone a wide-eyed woman who had far too much influence on him than he cared to admit, did not give him any excuse to completely forget himself.

Lord help him for telling her that Gwyn was a poor match for her, and why. Jarrod had thought of little else since seeing them together, but he'd had no right to say such a thing. And then to kiss her.

It had all started because she felt he had treated her ill. With a lack of civility, as she termed it. That had certainly not been his intent.

Damn her condemning eyes.

He had thought that he had found a solution to his difficulty in allowing Sir Ulrick to act as an intermediary. It had not prevented him from thinking of her, from casting covert glances toward her as she rode or sat beside the fire or talked with her father's knight.

It had not occurred to him that Aislynn would think him rude or become angry. She had made her feelings about his having kissed her, about her reluctance to travel with him, very clear, indeed.

Kissed her! His mind rebelled at calling what had happened between them that night at Bransbury a kiss. Yet Jarrod must find some way to distance himself from that night, from the powerful feelings that had driven him beyond rational thought and control.

She was to be wed to another man. A man who was kind and gentle—quite the opposite of her opinion of himself. And how could he fault her for that opinion when he had kissed her so brutally?

Jarrod had lain wakeful most of the night, angry with himself and her, wondering what new disaster the new day would bring between them. But he need not have concerned himself. This morn it had been more than obvious Aislynn was avoiding him. She had managed to ready herself for the day's ride without so much as one word to him, even through Sir Ulrick.

Jarrod should be glad of this, for he did not trust himself to hide the truth of his unrest from the other knight. At the same time, he was perturbed by her continued outrage. He had no intention of pouncing upon her as she seemed to imagine he was wont to do with women.

She had gotten the wrong notion of his expertise with women from Christian. Jarrod was eager to have a chat with his friend once he found him. Though there had been a number of women in his life, none of them had wanted more than the passion of the moment. It was the way he preferred to live. One could not count on anything but the moment. He had lost too much in his life—his father, his home, The Dragon—to believe any differently.

He reminded himself of this each time he was tempted to go to Aislynn to try to make peace. He would not wish for more than there was between them, even if she was not promised to another.

It was with some relief that he, at last, saw the town of Clumney, which he had deliberately chosen because of its busy market and the fact that he had a connection there, come into sight ahead of them. He had known that they were getting closer throughout the day as more fellow travelers appeared along the road. Here he hoped to gain more detailed information on finding Ashcroft.

Jarrod rode toward the center of the town, knowing that he would find the hostelry he sought there. This night he would not sleep with nothing more than the darkness and the aging knight between himself and the undeniable temptation of Aislynn Greatham.

Nothing could have induced Aislynn to ask Jarrod Maxwell anything, though she wondered whence they were going. Even if her very life depended upon doing so.

Yet, in spite of her anger and resentment of the man, she could not completely ignore her own excitement at being in Clumney. Never had she seen so many folk in one place. Never had she dreamed there was such a gathering of young and old, rich and poor, large and small alike.

Her gaze lingered on the fine fabrics of the ladies' garments, as they passed with their retinues of knights. She saw the awed faces of those as new to such sights as herself, the eager expressions of those with carts of goods to sell. And she deliberately breathed in the smells of the town, which consisted of the acrid scent of burning wood, both sodden and dry hay, the muck in the streets and the musky excitement of so many bodies all in one place. It was pleasant and unpleasant at one and the same time.

Jarrod guided them, seeming to have some notion of where he was going as he moved through the throng on his stallion. Sir Ulrick remained close behind with the donkey.

Aislynn was not concerned for her safety. She hardly imagined anyone would mark her a target in her travel-stained gown of amber velvet. In this disheveled state, she felt less than noteworthy and doubted she would be paid the slightest heed were she to wander the streets alone.

She drew up short as she realized that Jarrod had come to a halt before her. Looking ahead, Aislynn saw that they had stopped before a two-story structure with walls of whitewashed wattle and daub.

A neatly painted sign proclaimed it the Pheasant Inn. Jarrod Maxwell dismounted and handed his reins to a lad dressed in filthy gray clothing. The boy bowed and held out his hand for the coin Jarrod put into it. Aislynn could not help seeing the eagerness with which the lad poked the generous coin into his waist as he bowed with even greater deference.

Not wishing to acknowledge the warmth she felt at Jarrod's benevolence, Aislynn deliberately took the hand that Ulrick held out for her and slipped to the ground beside him. Jarrod had already turned to go inside. Her head held high, Aislynn stepped into the dim interior behind him.

Aislynn was in no way prepared for what she saw when she entered. There before her was Jarrod Maxwell locked in the embrace of a comely and voluptuous woman with a fall of lovely dark hair. She fair squealed with pleasure as she said, "By my eyes, Jarrod Maxwell!"

Aislynn felt her stomach churn with some unfamiliar emotion when Jarrod drew back and turned to her. "Sadona, this is the lady Aislynn Greatham. She is Christian Greatham's sister." The strain in his voice was audible to Aislynn's ears.

The woman bowed her head. "My lady."

Jarrod swung around to face the voluptuous beauty

once more. "We would like to break our journey here. If you have accommodation for us?"

The woman raised her brows and ran an assessing gaze over Aislynn. It was obvious that she was curious about what he was doing with Aislynn, but she restrained it, saying only, "If you are willing to share, we have room. We are quite busy just now with the harvest finished for some time on the surrounding farms."

Jarrod shook his head. "That would do well enough for me and Sir Ulrick." He indicated the other knight where he stood behind Aislynn. "The lady must have her own chamber."

"I do not see how I can…"

Jarrod put a gentle finger to her lips, and his tone was softly teasing. "Our journey has been difficult and the lady has not had a bath since we left her father's keep. And more pity that I do not know when the chance to sleep in a bed will come again. I would hold myself the most grateful of men if you could find a private space for her."

Aislynn felt a strange stirring that had nothing to do with the anger she had felt toward him over the past days. Here was a side of Jarrod that she had never seen, a disarming flirtatiousness that would melt the coldest of hearts like magic. What made it even worse to witness was that she would never find herself the recipient of it.

Her chest tight, Aislynn watched as the woman flipped a silky strand of dark hair back over her shoulder before putting her hands on those womanly hips. She cast Jarrod a wry grin. "For you, my lovely, I will find something." Even as he smiled down at her, she hurried to add, "But mind you it will be small."

Jarrod bowed. "You have my thanks." He smiled most winningly, his teeth white against his dark complexion, bringing about a fluttering sensation in Aislynn's own chest. "And could you arrange a bath for the lady as well?"

The woman leaned forward and to Aislynn's utter amazement kissed him full on the lips. "Anything, when you smile at me that way. But it will cost you extra."

Jarrod shrugged. "Of course."

Aislynn could barely believe that she had witnessed this intimate exchange, even if she was to be the beneficiary of its outcome. Jarrod had never once smiled at her that way. And what was he thinking to allow that woman to kiss him like that?

And she certainly did not wish to stay in this place, with this woman.

*Even if it meant having a bath.*

The woman now swung around and bowed to Aislynn. "If you will come this way, my lady?"

There was not a word Aislynn could say that would not give away all the tangled feelings inside her. Holding her head high, she moved to follow their hostess up a narrow flight of stairs to the upper floor. She was fully conscious of Jarrod and Ulrick behind her.

At the top was not so much a corridor as a long narrow landing, off which opened several doors. Sadona led them to one at the very front of the building.

Sadona opened the narrow door and stepped into a room that was illuminated by one tiny window. It was very small, barely long enough for a tall man and of an equal width. Aislynn watched as Sadona moved forward and took up one of two thin pallets that lay upon the wood plank floor, then dragged it out into the hall where they stood.

She waved Aislynn in. "Your private chamber, my lady." She then moved to the next door and opened it.

Aislynn, not knowing what to do, followed as Jarrod and Sir Ulrick were led into the next chamber. Peering in from the hallway, Aislynn saw that though the room was somewhat larger, the accommodations were no less rustic.

Here their hostess deposited the pallet she had taken from the other chamber with the four others that already lay upon the floor. She then swung around and said, "If you've no need of anything else, I've other work to attend."

He nodded. "There is one other matter." As she listened attentively he went on, "Do you know of a village called Ashcroft? I believe it is in Scotland."

Her brow creased in a thoughtful frown, then she shook her head. "Nay, I am sorry but I do not."

Jarrod bowed. "Again you have my thanks."

And again she leaned forward and kissed him. Sadona then patted him on one lean cheek before making her way toward the door.

Aware of her own wide eyes, Aislynn tried not to stare as the buxom woman bowed in passing and said, "I shall have your bath readied whenever you request it."

Not knowing what else to do, Aislynn replied with a quick nod of assent.

Sadona then headed back the way they had come. Aislynn tried even harder not to look at Jarrod as the echo of her footsteps on the wooden stair faded away. But she could not help herself, for the tormented churning of her stomach would not ease. He seemed occupied with his own thoughts as he moved to the door.

Sir Ulrick spoke into the silence. "These accommodations will not do for the lady Aislynn."

Jarrod swung around with a shrug. "I admit that they are less grand than I expected, but at least it will be warm and your lady will have a bath. It will only be for this one night as I fully expect to have a better idea of whence we go by morn."

In spite of her lack of enthusiasm for this place and for what had occurred between Jarrod and that woman, Aislynn spoke up before Ulrick could. "Pray have no concern for me. I am contented enough with the room." She did not wish to give Jarrod any reason to think she was causing difficulty.

He did not acknowledge her acquiescence other than with a brief bow. He addressed Sir Ulrick. "I will trust you to attend your lady until my return."

Aislynn stepped into his path without even pausing to think. "You are not going to leave me—us—here?"

He frowned. "I am simply going to roam about the market. There I intend to ask directions to Ashcroft."

She did not want to plead with him, but neither did she wish to remain here with that woman for hours—in that dark little room. "The day is still young and I will not trouble you. I…only wish to be out for a few hours, to see the town." Jarrod frowned, looking to Ulrick.

The older knight said, "I will see my lady is kept safe whilst we are about. You need not worry on that score."

The frown deepened as his gaze came to rest on hers. Aislynn met him with silent entreaty. Jarrod gave one sharp nod. "Very well then. You may come. But you will mind yourself and stay by Ulrick's side."

Aislynn's relief was mixed with resentment. Resentment that was due to his obvious reluctance. Not to mention his speaking to her as if she were a child. He had certainly not treated her like a child when he'd...

Aislynn stopped herself right there. She did not wish to think on what had happened, not even for a moment.

Jarrod sighed. "We'd do well to get on with it then."

Ulrick looked to Aislynn and she nodded. They followed as Jarrod moved again to leave.

Their hostess was not to be seen in the public room below. Of that Aislynn was not sorry.

In spite of all that had occurred, Aislynn felt a trace of excitement return as she followed Jarrod back out into the street. She was also buoyed by the protective bulk of Ulrick's supportive presence just behind her.

Other than to use his wide shoulders as a mark to guide her, Aislynn ignored the man in front of her. The sights, the sounds, the smells of the busy market kept her head swiveling from one side to the other as they passed through the busy throng. First her attention was taken by a young family, father, mother, children, all dressed in their finest as they strolled about the market. Then it was captured by a group of young men, talking and laughing loudly as they drank openly from large wooden tankards. Then her gaze fixed on the open windows of a smiling merchant's booth, more wares displayed for sale than she had ever dreamed of.

The scents of breads and roasting meat that rose from some of the booths left her mouth watering, for it had been days since she had smelled anything so inviting. She watched intently as two young boys ate roasted fowl from their fingers. It was not until Jarrod swung around to scowl at her from some distance ahead that she realized her steps had slowed too greatly.

Hurriedly she rushed to catch up to him. "Forgive me, Sir Jarrod. I was but looking at something."

Before he could say anything in reply, Sir Ulrick spoke up. "I believe my lady is hungry. As I am, my lord. It has been many hours since we stopped to eat this day."

Jarrod's scowl deepened and he looked down at her. Quickly Aislynn said, "Pray have no concern for me. I told you I would be no bother and I will not. I will eat when you are ready."

At that moment a hint of breeze wafted the smell of spiced meats over her again. Traitorously, her stomach gave a growl. Not a loud one, but loud enough for Jarrod Maxwell to take note.

He took a deep breath and let it out slowly, obviously searching for patience. "We will eat."

Aislynn bristled, raising her nose to a sharp angle. "I am not hungry. Let us go on."

With a noise of impatience, Jarrod Maxwell took her by the arm and turned her back toward the booth from whence those heavenly scents had arisen. Though Aislynn desperately wanted to resist him, there was no hope for such rebellion. The knight was far too strong and too arrogant to heed her wishes.

Ulrick said not a word, but his step was eager.

In no time at all, Aislynn was holding a steaming piece of chicken. Though, unlike the two lads she had seen only moments before, hers was wrapped in a clean scrap of fabric the merchant had found at Jarrod's insistence.

She soon held a piece of fritter in the other hand, the scent of cinnamon making her stomach growl anew. As they moved on in the crowd to eat their feast, Aislynn was aware that Jarrod also seemed quite intent on devouring his food. As was she for some minutes.

But when her hunger began to ease, Aislynn realized that Jarrod had finished his own meal and had begun to stop and chat with some of the folk they passed along the way.

She simply followed, now nibbling delicately at the sweet bread, making it last, as she had the ones Margaret had made when she was a child. As Jarrod stopped to talk to a man at one of the booths, Aislynn became aware of an odd prickling along the back of her neck. Frowning, she turned and saw a man. He stood on the far side of the booth at which they were now waiting for Jarrod.

Aislynn looked at him more closely. His dress and

bearing marked him a knight. He was a compelling figure, to be sure, in his enveloping cloak the gray of deep shadows, and dark coloring, which was most striking because of his intense gray gaze. But it was the fact that he was watching Jarrod Maxwell with animosity that held her attention. His narrowed eyes seemed to move between Jarrod's face and the area of his shoulder with equal heat.

She looked to Jarrod. She could see naught that might be of note but the dragon brooch, which held his cloak in place. She frowned thoughtfully.

For his part, Jarrod had clearly taken no heed of the man. He was conversing most intently with the merchant.

## *Chapter Seven*

**J**arrod had not wished to take Aislynn with him to the market. It was impossible to deny the longing in those lovely blue eyes. He suspected Aislynn did not wish to be left at the inn with Sadona. His face still burned as he recalled the way Sadona had kissed him and the condemnation in Aislynn's gaze.

He had found himself wanting to tell her that it was all perfectly innocent. Sadona was wed to one of the soldiers who had been with them in the Holy Land for many years, a man Jarrod called friend. But he realized that to explain the situation would be to imply that it was Aislynn's concern who kissed him.

It was not. He was to see to her well-being, and nothing more. He was free to kiss whom he would.

As long as that was not Aislynn.

Yet as they had made their way through the crowded streets, he could not help being moved by Aislynn's fascination and delight in everything around them. He noted the yearning glances she cast at the food.

Jarrod was filled with chagrin. They had traveled

the whole of the morning, not stopping as he had pressed on to arrive in the market town early in the day. The scents of roasting meat had made his stomach grumble to be filled.

As they'd eaten he'd risked a glance at her and seen the relish with which she licked the warm bits of apple from the tips of her slender fingers. He'd experienced an immediate tightening in his loins. She had done naught to attract him in any overt way. She was simply being herself, seemingly oblivious to him as she gazed about them, her blue eyes wide with interest, her cheeks flushed with excitement. The problem lay in the fact that her ingenuousness was one of the very things that seemed to draw him to her.

Desperate to distract himself, Jarrod paused at a booth they were passing. The man inside came forward eagerly, his gaze taking in their fine garments in spite of their layer of grime. Jarrod nodded. ''I wonder if you might spare a moment. I am seeking a village called Ashcroft. I was wondering if you might have heard of it.''

The fellow shook his head as he rubbed at his short gray beard. ''Nay, it does not have a familiar sound.''

Jarrod shrugged. ''Would you know of anyone who might? I was told that it may lie in Scotland.''

The fellow looked up, his brown eyes brightening. ''I can tell you who might know of this place. The potter, Wibert, has traveled in the north. He may be able to tell you how to get to this Ashcroft.''

It was not much, but Jarrod felt a rise of hope. ''Can you tell me where I might find him?''

The merchant nodded, pointing off to the left. ''He is in the next to the last stall.''

Jarrod bowed. "You have my thanks, sir."

The man shrugged. "Your thanks are well met."

With that Jarrod turned back to Ulrick and Aislynn. He noted that Aislynn seemed as if her thoughts had drifted far away. He tried not to take advantage of her distraction by letting his gaze linger on her face. But he could not help noting that the juices from the cooked apples had left a sheen on her lips. Lips that tasted like...

Roughly he called himself to order.

He said abruptly, "We go on now." He swung around and started forward....

Straight into the path of another man, their bodies connecting with unexpected force. The contact was jarring, but Jarrod stepped back immediately and met the other's gray eyes. "Your pardon, sir."

The other man, who was clearly a knight by his dress and manner, stared back at Jarrod with cold anger. "And pray why should I accept your pardon?"

Surprise made Jarrod's brows raise. He had not expected such a reply to his apology and chafed at the delay in getting on with his quest. At the same time he was not completely shocked at this reaction. There were those, who, as fighting men, had grown accustomed to conflict and searched it out at all times.

Even more than was usual for him, the frustration of the past days had left Jarrod with an itch to give vent to some action. Yet he was responsible for Aislynn's well-being and that was of far greater import than any impulse to give this fellow a taste of his blade.

He tried to diffuse the situation, reminding himself that there was no need to prove his own manhood by taking offence from such a one. "Then do not accept my apology, though it be given wholeheartedly. I will take myself from your proximity so as not to cause you further insult."

He started forward and the man moved to block his path. "Methinks not, my lord. For the insult you have already inflicted is cause enough."

Now Jarrod really looked at the man. He felt a rise of anger that was more compelling than his aggravation, but dampened it by reminding himself that he could not jeopardize Aislynn's safety in any way. And fighting in the streets with a hot head was surely doing just that.

From behind them came the sound of a voice. "Someone call for the sheriff!"

Jarrod turned to see it was the man he had just been speaking with. Again the merchant cried out, "Call for the sheriff, I say."

Two knights brawling in the streets would definitely be bad for business and they had begun to attract the attention of others, who were giving them a wide berth. Jarrod swung back around to tell his antagonist that he could ill afford the time spent on becoming involved in a legal difficulty.

The man was gone. Disappeared without a word or sign of his direction. Jarrod was as surprised by the fellow's behavior as before. But he was also grateful. He spun to face Aislynn, taking her by the arm. "Come."

She did come and without hesitation. The speed of her steps easily matched his own ground-eating strides.

It was not until they were out of earshot of the

scene, that he drew Aislynn to an abrupt halt. Immediately she swung around to face him, glancing about with obvious agitation. ''Why are we stopping here?''

Jarrod found himself speaking more harshly than he intended, addressing the knight rather than Aislynn. ''Ulrick, I would have you take your lady back to our lodging now. I will join you shortly.''

Jarrod looked at Aislynn as she issued a short hiss of exasperation. Her fair brow puckered as she looked up at him. ''But you can not…''

He heaved a heavy sigh, holding up a forestalling hand. ''I cannot risk another such interchange as that with you in my keeping. And I would try to get something accomplished ere dark.''

''But Jarrod, there is something you must know…''

He looked at her pleadingly, trying to make her understand that he needed her to cooperate in this. ''Aside from not having to worry about your safety I will be more able to move about quickly on my own. And you must realize that your father would be horrified if he knew what had just occurred, what could have happened.''

Ulrick spoke up. ''He is right, my lady. Anyone wishing you harm must first pass through me, but it is wrong to risk such a thing.''

Jarrod had no doubt that the powerful knight would indeed be formidable in protecting his mistress. Yet Ulrick saw there was no gain in seeking out such difficulty.

Aislynn shook her head, scowling at both of them. ''I will not be moved from this spot lest the two of you listen to me for one moment.''

Jarrod would humor her in this. But only for a moment. He did wish to get on with his purpose. He nodded sharply. "Speak on then."

Aislynn took a step toward him, her gaze now pleading. "That man, the one who attempted to engage you in a fight, he had been watching you in the crowd some time before and must have placed himself in your path deliberately."

Jarrod frowned. "Why would he be watching me, Aislynn?"

She shook her head, her gaze puzzled as well as troubled. "I know not. I can only tell you that he was and he seemed very intent on the dragon brooch you wear."

"Intent on the dragon?" Jarrod raised a hand to run it over the piece.

She glared at him. "Aye. I do not believe this can be such a shock to you after what just happened."

Jarrod sighed. "The man could have no particular interest in me, or my brooch. There can only be two others like it in all the kingdom. And Christian and Simon wear them. I have never laid eyes upon the fellow and find it impossible to believe that either of them would have." He looked at her. "Did you recognize the man, or even find him vaguely familiar?"

She scowled, shaking her head, though it was with obvious reluctance.

Jarrod continued, "The three of us have only been back in England for less than a year. Simon has been at Avington when he was not being held at Dragonwick. Christian has been with you at Bransbury when he was not with me. Few people in England would know us as adults. That the man would have recognized me makes no sense.''

She closed her eyes and took a deep breath, clearly searching for patience. ''Yet he did do so.''

Jarrod shrugged, wanting nothing more than to get on with what he had to do. ''I can fathom no reason for that, Aislynn.'' His tone became soothing. ''Beyond that, it behooves us to put this incident behind us. He is gone now and can do no harm, for we do not mean to remain in this vicinity.''

Aislynn looked to Ulrick. ''Can you not make him see reason?''

Ulrick shrugged his wide shoulders, though his gray eyes were understanding. ''Sir Jarrod must certainly have a care for himself, my lady. But he speaks true. What could be done now if the man did mean him ill? He is gone and we wish to continue our journey in the morning.''

Aislynn continued to stare at Ulrick, who looked down at the ground. She then glared directly into Jarrod's eyes. ''Then neither of you will heed me in this.''

He shrugged again. ''It is not a question of that. We simply see no reason to believe there is undue cause for concern.''

Without another word to either of them, she turned and stalked back the way they had come. Ulrick did not hesitate, but went after her.

Jarrod sighed again.

He didn't want to think that he might have hurt Aislynn, or that he had reacted too harshly. Aislynn had only been showing concern for him. Her concern was, in a way that was unfamiliar to him, strangely moving. Surely he could have...

Roughly Jarrod shook his head. He had important matters to attend. He simply had to put her and her opinion of him from his mind.

Yet as he strode through the crowded street his sense of regret, as well as an unexplainable ache of loneliness, would not be denied.

Aislynn wanted to stamp her feet in frustration. Jarrod Maxwell was, without doubt, the most onerous man in the kingdom.

'Twould surely serve him right if the strange and malevolent knight did mean him ill.

But the very thought left her feeling weak and physically ill. She suddenly knew that Jarrod's safety was all that mattered in this, in spite of the fact that he had so little care for it.

As soon as they reached the safety of her chamber at their place of lodging, she swung around and commanded, "Sir Ulrick, I wish for you to return to the market and learn what you can of that man. Though there is a great crowd there this day, a nobleman's presence is always of note to the common folk. Someone will know his name or something about him."

"I can not leave you alone, my lady."

No more than Aislynn was reluctant to bide her time in this small chamber alone. Even the thought that she might see the shameless Sadona could not deter her from her purpose. "You can. And you will."

She moved to the door and motioned for Ulrich to follow her as she pointed. "You see. There is a strong bolt upon the door. I will use it. And I swear upon my mother's memory that I will not leave or allow anyone but you or that dratted Sir Jarrod to enter.''

She paused for a moment, then added, ''Except for 'that woman' or one of her servants. For I mean for you to inform them that I am ready for my bath.'' Aislynn was not truly concerned with bathing now, but it would give her something to pass the time whilst she waited for word from her father's knight.

Ulrick, who had frowned at her disparagement of Sir Jarrod, looked far from pleased. ''Sir Jarrod is like to be angry with both of us.''

Aislynn raised her nose to a forty-five-degree angle. ''Pray let him be thusly. I care not what he thinks.'' Yet in spite of her hauteur, even she could hear the fear in her voice as she went on, ''I do care that he is not harmed. Not in attempting to do us a kindness. And mark me, Ulrick, that man does mean him harm. Mayhap learning who he is will help me to convince Jarrod that there is some danger.''

Ulrick took a deep breath. ''Very well then, my lady, but you must not leave this chamber. And you will not open the door even for your bath, lest it be brought by the landlady herself.''

Aislynn wanted to sigh at these extreme measures, yet she held his gaze without wavering. ''On my oath.''

After another long, tense moment, Ulrick bowed, but his expression continued to be disturbed as he left, closing the door firmly behind him. She was aware of him waiting in the hall and she moved forward shooting the bolt home loudly. Only then did the clump of Sir Ulrick's footsteps sound as he moved off down the hall.

It was Sadona herself who spoke from outside the door sometime later. "My lady."

Already chafing in the confines of the tiny chamber, Aislynn nonetheless moved to open the portal with reluctance. She did not wish to be in the same room with a woman who was very likely Jarrod's paramour.

When she did open it she saw that the landlady stood next to a wooden tub that was barely bigger than the cooking pots at Bransbury. The woman seemed completely unaware of her disappointment. "I've brought the tub. My girl usually carries the water, but I've promised your knight that I will do so myself."

Aislynn stepped back as Sadona shoved the tub into the room with her leather-shod foot.

Aislynn said with deliberate civility, "There is no need for you to go to such trouble."

The woman put her hand on her hip, wiping a strand of hair from her bright green eyes. "Aye, I've given my word and that is reason enough for me." With that she turned and strode from the chamber, presumably to fetch the water.

Being mindful of her own promise in the face of the other's integrity, Aislynn shot the bolt home once more. But she stayed by the door and opened it again the instant she heard her hostess's footsteps in the hallway.

The landlady stood there, as well as a comely maid of mid-teen years. Each of them carried two steaming buckets. But the younger set hers down and scurried

back down the stairs without speaking. As Sadona
brought her two into the room, Aislynn fetched the
other two.

Sadona seemed somewhat surprised but nodded her
thanks as Aislynn poured the water into the tub along
with her. She then moved to the door with the buckets. "Is there aught else that you require, my lady?"

Aislynn shook her head, but as Sadona turned to
go, she found herself speaking up, "Your pardon."

The older woman swung around. "Aye."

Aislynn felt herself flushing. "You are a friend of
Sir Jarrod?"

The woman's arched brows rose knowingly. "Aye,
a friend."

Aislynn could not fathom what that tone and expression might mean. She shrugged, feeling her heart
sink further although she knew she had no right to
ask. Jarrod had made it clear that he would not welcome her prying in his life.

The other woman smiled at her suddenly. "Saints
above, I must put you out of your misery. I am indeed
friend to Sir Jarrod, but pray have no concern, for that
is all I have ever been. He is also friend to my good
husband, Lewis."

Aislynn felt her spirits lift at this news while she
tried to deny her own feelings as she said, "What Sir
Jarrod might have done, or what he might do in future
are naught to me."

The other woman chuckled softly. "Forgive me,
for speaking thusly to my betters, my lady, but if that
be true I've three arms."

Aislynn felt herself flush from the top of her head
to the tips of her toes, as the woman went on, "And

there's far less worthy a man that a young girl could set her heart on in spite of his parentage. 'Twas he who lent the money to me and my Lewis to purchase this place.'' Her face glowed with pride. ''Though he's been repaid his investment in these two short years.'' She focused on Aislynn once more, ''Aye, there's far worse a girl could do than Sir Jarrod.''

Aislynn's eyes widened with horror, though she tried to hide this as she said, ''I fear you have the wrong impression.''

''Do I then?''

She felt the stiffness in herself. ''Aye, Sir Jarrod is not...we are not...you should not speak thusly.''

There was a sympathy in Sadona's warm gaze that made Aislynn's heart ache, even as the woman bowed again. ''Forgive me for presuming, my lady.''

Shocked, Aislynn held out a hand, ''Nay, I did not mean to reprimand you...you have not...I simply wish for you to understand the situation properly.''

The woman subsided.

Aislynn went on. ''I thank you for your kindness to me, madam. And believe it is sincerely meant.''

Sadona shrugged. ''I have seen the way you and Sir Jarrod look at each other. The way you looked at me when he kissed me. It does my heart good to see his feelings awakened again after so very long.''

Aislynn ignored her discomfort at this assessment of her and Jarrod's relationship. She was less interested in refuting it than she was in finding out what the woman was speaking of. ''What do you mean, awakened again?''

The other woman bit her lip, now seeming uncertain. ''I would not speak out of hand, my lady. Sir

Jarrod has been more than kind to me and my Lewis.'' She glanced down and she went on, ''You see I was no more than a camp follower when first I saw Sir Jarrod some eight years ago. If I had not been in that profession I would never have known of his attachment to Fatima.''

''Fatima?'' Aislynn whispered the name.

''Aye, lovely she was but quite a lot older than the knight. She was an outcast amongst her own people, who did not accept her profession. Sir Jarrod came to the camp several times to see her, but only talked until one night when he paid to go into her tent.''

Aislynn grimaced and Sadona shook her head as she said, ''Nay, have no worry. This is no tale of passion, at least on her part, for there was immediately a loud exchange, with her demanding that he leave and not return.'' Sadona sighed. ''You should have seen Sir Jarrod's face as he left, so dark with pain that one could hardly bear to look upon it.'' She took a deep breath. ''And I never saw him there again until she died some month's later, having been ill for long before any of us knew. It was then he came back, paid for the expenses of her burial. I never asked him what had gone between them and I believe that is why we were able to become friends. I simply sat with him until the pain had eased. It was he who introduced me to my Lewis and offered us the gold when he discovered that we had a dream of marrying and buying an inn.''

She looked closely at Aislynn then. ''He is a good man, a kind man and deserving of much love. You must have a care with his heart. For I have seen first-hand that, in spite of his seeming self-reliance, he can be hurt.''

Aislynn was somewhat overwhelmed with all she had just heard, but she could not allow the other woman to imagine something that was not, especially in the face of her care for Jarrod. ''I fear you have misunderstood. Sir Jarrod and I...we are not lovers. My brother, Christian, is missing and he is simply taking me to find him.''

The other woman's gaze seemed doubtful, but all she said was, ''Then I pray you find him, for I know Jarrod loves him as a brother.''

Aislynn nodded and said, ''I thank you,'' but her mind was reeling.

Sadona bowed, then turned and left the room, closing the door gently behind her. The silence that followed told of her presence outside. So stunned was Aislynn by the exchange that it was a moment before she realized Sadona was awaiting the closing of the lock.

Aislynn hurried to do so, leaning back against the door as she heard the woman's footsteps disappear down the landing.

So Jarrod had been in love, and he had been rejected. No wonder he was so very adamant about his freedom. He had been hurt badly enough that he had no desire to ever love again. His heart had been given to an Eastern woman who had called to the dark and mysterious part of himself—someone quite unlike Aislynn.

She had a vivid image of that blue ribbon and his reaction to her questions about it. How could any woman ever hope to win his love when he was so irrevocably bound to the ghost of one long dead?

Inside Aislynn was a strange hollow ache of regret. And even when she told herself that this was ridiculous, as she had her own life to live, her own marriage ahead of her, it refused to ease.

When Aislynn awakened to an incessant pounding at her door, she immediately knew who it was.

Jarrod Maxwell.

Ulrick would never allow himself to put on such a rude and autocratic display.

In spite of the fact that his manner was utterly maddening, Aislynn's mind was somewhat hazy as she sat up on her pallet. Never had she expected to fall asleep when she had lain down upon it after her awkward bath in the tiny wooden tub. Yet she had done so in spite of the thoughts spinning through her mind, thoughts of Jarrod and his love for a ghost.

Again came the pounding and, with it, Jarrod's angry voice. "Aislynn! Open this door at once!"

His autocratic tone chased any hint of grogginess from her mind. No matter how secretly sad or lonely he might be, the blackguard could not be allowed to dictate to her. Thus it was with deliberate unconcern that Aislynn rose and pulled the heavy woolen blanket about her for modesty. For she had dressed in a clean shift after washing her other shift and gown in the bathwater and hanging them from the windowsill to dry.

The moment she opened the door, Jarrod Maxwell strode through and slammed it behind him. He then

turned a black frown upon her and said in an accu-
satory tone, "Where is Sir Ulrick?"

She attempted unconcern. "If you must know, I
sent him on an errand."

"You sent him on an errand? Have you completely
lost your wits? He was to watch over you." His voice
was incredulous.

Calling on all her powers of self-assurance, Aislynn
moved away from him to settle upon the edge of the
pallet. "I have not lost my wits. And I will thank you
to keep a civil tongue in your head when speaking to
me, sir."

His hands went to his narrow hips as he moved to
glare down at her. "You will thank me? Good God,
Aislynn, but you can be quite insolent."

She shrugged, though her gaze narrowed on his.
"You accuse me of that when you come bursting in
here this way, treating me with a complete lack of
chivalry. But why am I reminding you of this when
we have had extensive discourse on this very subject
previously." She raised her brows. "Perhaps it is uncommon for a lady to be held in respect off in the
heathen lands where you have made your home over
the last years. It is not so here in England."

He fairly glowered at this.

She again reminded herself that it was not unrea-
sonable for Jarrod to treat her with some deference.
She had only sent Ulrick to find out about the man
who had looked upon Jarrod with such utter hatred.

She had been afraid for him. She still was, despite
his lack of appreciation.

But never would she have him know that now. He
was a knave and a fool.

Aislynn watched his set, angry face as she continued, "You might attempt to behave politely, Sir Jarrod. The results would likely surprise you."

The chagrin on his face told her that she had penetrated that outraged demeanor. Slowly he took a deep breath, then let it out. The too controlled tone of his voice told her just how difficult it was when he at last replied, "Very well then, Aislynn, I shall attempt to be polite, though the effort plagues me greatly. And you shall explain why you would send Ulrick on an errand when you knew that I had sent him to watch over you. And not only by my own wishes, but also your father's. You know full well that Ulrick and I have been charged with making sure you are safe until we have found Christian."

That made her waver in her angry defiance and she said with less antagonism, "How did you know that Ulrick was gone? He could have been in this very room keeping me company."

He grimaced. "It was Sadona who inadvertently gave you away by telling me that you had followed the knight's directions to the letter about keeping your door locked. She thought I would be pleased."

Aislynn found herself telling Jarrod the truth, though she did not expect him to be happy with her. "I sent him to make enquiries about the man at the market."

"The man at the market?"

"Aye, the one who attempted to challenge you to fight with him."

Jarrod took a calming breath. "I know of whom you speak. I simply do not understand why you would send Ulrick on such a pointless quest. That matter is over and done. It was the moment the madman left our sight.''

Aislynn shook her head. ''You must not disregard what I told you of him. He means you harm. I am certain of it.''

He ran an agitated hand through his thick black hair. ''I do not disregard what you say out of hand, Aislynn. I simply cannot fathom what reason he could have for bearing any personal animosity toward me. I do not know him. Aside from that I have other matters that demand my attention at the moment.''

''Other matters. What could be more important than guarding your life against possible harm?'' She threw up her hands in frustration.

He said slowly, carefully, ''I must find Christian. I will find Christian. None of us can rest until that is done.''

She looked at him. ''You will not be able to find Christian if that man does you ill. He...''

He held up a hand to forestall her. ''He will not do me ill.''

''I believe he will try, and if you are not attending, he could succeed. Why would you doubt me?''

He sighed. ''I do not doubt that you believe this, Aislynn. But I see no cause to become completely overset. You do not know those of his kind as I do. They go about challenging all who cross their path. It is a way of proving their manhood.''

She faced him earnestly. ''Even if that is true, it does not mean that he is not a danger to you.''

He sighed again, more heavily. ''I would not give him the benefit of reacting with trepidation. I have lived most of my life in a state of war, surrounded by those who felt I was their enemy. And yet I am alive.''

Aislynn bit her lower lip. She could not allow the matter to rest inside her. She knew, without knowing how she knew, that there had been something deeply hateful in that man's eyes as he looked at Jarrod. It was something that went far beyond any desire to prove his manhood.

And her concern for him overshadowed everything, including all that Sadona had told her. Jarrod must not take chances with his life.

She had done right to send Ulrick to find out whatever he could about the man. No matter that he claimed himself a man who preferred freedom to all things, Jarrod Maxwell seemed to make his presence felt wherever he passed. He left his mark on all, from the lowliest peasant child who might hold his mount, to Sadona and Lewis, to his long-dead love, as well as herself and her father.

In spite of his refusal to see to his own well-being, and the fact that he had treated her with such a lack of care, she could not see Jarrod harmed.

# *Chapter Eight*

Jarrod's frustration with Aislynn left him with a growing impulse to throttle her. At the same time he was aware of pleasure at her concern for him over the matter of this unknown knight. His pleasure made it difficult to maintain his anger toward her. But he could not simply allow her to act so rashly, even if she did accuse him of being unchivalrous by being angry with her. Jarrod was not in the least bit moved by her assertion that noblemen did not treat their ladies thusly. He knew a bit more than that about the ways of men and women. His own father had never raised his voice to his stepmother in Jarrod's hearing, true enough, but then they had never exchanged any but the most formal of words in his presence—ever.

He found himself watching Aislynn as she stared toward the open window. He allowed his gaze to glide over her delicate profile, that stubborn little nose. Clean and damp, the pale silken curtain of her hair fell down her back to her hips, soft strands of it clinging to the woolen cloth beneath it.

Jarrod's gaze widened as for the first time he realized that Aislynn was not fully clothed. Around her was a thin woolen blanket, which draped her small but womanly form most enticingly, embracing her every curve. From where she clutched it closed above her breast, he had an unrestricted view of her creamy neck and shoulders.

So lovely. Were he Aislynn's husband, their interactions could never be so stilted and formal as his father and stepmother's had been. They would...

Jarrod felt his eyes widen with horror.

He looked down at the scarred wood floor. He said roughly, "I will leave you and seek my own bed. We must make an early start."

"But you have not told me you would have a care." In her eyes he saw the raw fear as she moved close and placed a hand upon his arm.

He was infinitely aware of her hand on his arm and the soft white skin at the base of her throat. Jarrod felt his heart thud in his chest at her nearness. He swallowed. "Do not worry, Aislynn, I will be well."

Her voice was a husky whisper and now he heard the yearning beneath her fear, "I pray it be so. But I can not help it...I could not bear it if something were to..."

Without even knowing that he was going to do so, Jarrod held out his arms and she stepped into them. And then she was close against him, the blanket disguising little of the delicious line of her back and hips. He felt a rush of heat so intense it nearly made his knees buckle.

She strained up against him, her head thrown back, her breathing shallow. Looking down at her that way, her face flushed, her lips parted, Jarrod could no more

deny the invitation offered than stop the sands from
blowing across the deserts of his native land. He bent,
his mouth closing on those soft, beckoning lips.

Aislynn raised her arms to encircle his neck, feeling
her blanket slip away, leaving her standing there in
nothing but the gossamer-thin cover of her shift. But
she was not aware of any chill, for the heat engendered by Jarrod's lips, his hands, was enough to warm
her from the inside out.

Distantly she was aware of how immense this moment was. But she was too caught up in her own
feelings, the wonder of being in Jarrod's arms. His
strong hands slid down her back to pull her more
firmly up against him, his tongue flicking out to taste
her lips. Aislynn felt the world tilt and didn't care if
it never righted itself again.

Jarrod was on fire, his belly burning with wanting
for this woman. He deepened their kisses, urging her
to meet him, and she did. She returned his passion
equally and more, holding his head to her with desperate hands.

She slanted her head, giving back measure for measure as he kissed her with breathless abandon. Aislynn
was overcome with the fierce rush in her own blood
as she reveled in the heat, and hardness, and warm,
damp man-taste of him.

The increase in their passion brought with it a feeling of frustration. Jarrod wanted, needed, more of her.

Jarrod broke away from her, dipping his head to
nuzzle her neck. She tipped her head back, granting
him free access to that tender flesh.

Breathing heavily, his blood pulsing, Jarrod drew
back to look at her in the soft evening light from the

open window. He saw the heaviness of her lids, the wanting in those eyes that had now darkened to indigo, the mouth that was swollen from his kisses. His gaze dipped lower to where the peaks of her breasts showed dusky rose beneath the fabric of her garment.

He took a deep, shuddering breath. "So lovely."

His words sent a new ripple of pleasure through her and her voice was a hoarse whisper of longing. "Jarrod."

Overcome with a feeling of tenderness and desire so intense that it weakened him, Jarrod could only breathe her name into the silky curtain of her hair. "Aislynn."

Aislynn reached for him, wanting nothing more than to continue kissing him, to be held against him. She wanted...

When he dipped his head and flicked his tongue over the peak of her breast, Aislynn gasped aloud, as a shaft of delight so intense it made the muscles clench in her thighs shot through her. Involuntarily her fingers twined into the hair at the base of his neck, pulling him more closely against her. His groan of pleasure only served to increase the sensations inside her, creating a sweet ache in her lower belly, spreading down to pool at the joining of her thighs.

And when he seemed to sense her feelings, reaching down to cup his palm over her there, where no man had ever touched her, the ache deepened, intensified, making her thighs clench. Aislynn heard her own hoarse voice cry out with an emotion so naked it rocked her, "Jarrod, I...oh, help me. I burn."

Trembling with need at finding her so eager for him, Jarrod was powerless to halt the desire that drove him to answer her cry. Slowly he drew his hand away. With a gentleness born of sheer wonder at her responses to him, Jarrod picked her up. He marveled at her form, so light and delicate, yet womanly.

He kissed her as she raised her mouth to his, deeply, yearningly, even while he moved to the pallet on the floor. She held him to her as he lowered her down upon it, his head then dipping so that he could nuzzle the cloth of her shift from the tip of one turgid nipple. His mouth closed upon the naked, aching flesh and he groaned even as she reared up beneath him with a gasp of need.

His head reeling, his pulse pounding like a drum in his veins, Jarrod slowly realized he was hearing a sound, and that it was coming from outside himself.

For a moment, Jarrod could not reason what it could possibly be, his mind was so drugged with wanting for this woman. Then the pounding came again and, with it, a voice. "Lady Aislynn."

Sir Ulrick.

Jarrod pushed away from Aislynn, taking in her dazed and disheveled state. The nipple he had just plied so gently was still damp from his caress.

As she blinked in confusion, the knight's voice came again. "Lady Aislynn."

Jarrod rubbed a hand across his heated brow, trying to wipe out the sight of her as he reached down to take the blanket from the floor where it had fallen. He tossed it to Aislynn. In his desperation to keep from revealing their madness to her father's knight, to protect her from the censure such a revelation would bring, he whispered sharply, "Collect yourself."

She moved to sit up, her eyes, which had moments ago been dark and damp with desire, now filled with hurt and betrayal. Turning her back to him, she pulled the blanket close about her. Regret made his already churning stomach spasm, but he gave no sign of it as he moved to the door.

Jarrod jerked the door open, frustration coloring his voice as he said, "You should not have left her alone."

Sir Ulrick stiffened and Jarrod felt even more a fool for taking out his feelings on this man. He bowed, fully conscious of Aislynn, who moved to stand looking out the window. "Forgive me, I had no right to berate you I was only…"

The other man interrupted him, his expression grim now, "Pray have no care for that, Sir Jarrod. There is something you must hear. I have learned the identity of the knight who challenged you at the market."

Aislynn swung around from her contemplation of the darkening sky. "Yes."

Sir Ulrick addressed her directly. "The knight is one Sir Fredrick. He is in the employ of the Earl of Kelsey."

"The Earl of Kelsey." Jarrod took a step toward him, all other thoughts being driven from his mind by this name. He raised a hand to rake it through his thick hair. "God's blood, but I should have run him through. According to Christian and Simon, it was he who mortally wounded the soldier Jack."

He heard Aislynn's sharply indrawn breath as she stepped to the forefront. "I was right to think he meant you harm."

Jarrod took a deep breath, willing himself to think

carefully, not to react to this revelation though his heart pounded with rage at the very thought of the blackguard's temerity. But regret that he had missed this opportunity to do harm to Kelsey, who had destroyed the only home where Jarrod had felt he was more that an unwanted bastard, was so strong it burned in his gut. For no matter how many years had passed since Kelsey's betrayal of The Dragon, Jarrod had never forgiven that loss, nor would he. The Dragon had taught him not only the ways of knighthood, but of true manhood. His voice was a ragged whisper. "God rot his immortal soul."

Aislynn heard the rage in Jarrod's voice, saw it reflected in his dark face, which seemed even more exotic and mysterious because of it. She realized that anyone who earned this man's enmity was far from safe, but she knew too that the passion which drove that part of him also fueled his other passions—his desires.

And this only served to make her recall how close she had come to giving herself to him utterly and completely. The very thought made her face heat, for had not Ulrick come to the door...

Nay, she would not think on that. Jarrod would never have gone through with it. The very disgust on his face and in his voice when he'd thrown her the blanket told her that much. Why he had ever kissed her, touched her the way he had, she could not understand, nor did she see anything to be gained by understanding why when he so obviously regretted doing so.

She tried instead to concentrate on what she knew

of the Earl of Kelsey and his dastardly deeds. She knew that he had betrayed his own brother to gain an earldom and that not only Jarrod but Christian and Simon hated him for it. It was their very desire to gain vengeance against the man that had nearly cost Simon Warleigh his life. That Simon's forced marriage to Kelsey's daughter had ended in becoming a love-match and Isabelle's leaving her father's influence, was none of the earl's doing.

She noted that Jarrod rubbed the dragon brooch at his shoulder as he spoke through tight lips. "No wonder Sir Fredrick seemed uncommonly interested in this brooch. It marked me his enemy, for Simon had his own while at Dragonwick." She was somewhat surprised and unexpectedly admiring when he drew himself up, visibly besting those feelings of rage as he went on. "I would dear love to see the man dead, but I will put this behind me, for the moment. We go to Scotland in the morn."

In spite of all that had just passed between them, Aislynn faced him as if those passionate moments had never been. "Learning the knave's identity has revealed the seriousness of the situation. You must not go without reporting this to the sheriff. I saw the hatred in his face. He will stop at nothing to do you ill."

He frowned. "I require no man to see to justice on my behalf. When and if the time comes, pray God, I shall face Sir Fredrick head-on, and gladly."

Seeing that he would not be swayed, she clamped her lips tightly shut. Jarrod was so certain that he would prevail, yet she could not help knowing that the boundless hatred that still burned in the recesses of his eyes was equally matched in the other knight.

He turned to Ulrick. "We will leave at first light."

The knight looked at him. "Then you have learned some new information about the village we seek?"

Aislynn watched with surprise as Jarrod Maxwell actually blushed. "Aye, I have. If the directions given me are accurate, I believe we will be able to gain our destination before nightfall two days hence, if we make good speed."

Aislynn saw Ulrick's face light up with the relief she herself could feel. She did not even bother to question why Jarrod had not told her of this sooner. She knew why and her discomfiture compounded her inability to look at him directly. She said, "That is good news, indeed." The older man then swung around to face Aislynn. "You must seek your rest, my lady, if you are to undertake another such day."

Now that the rush of learning about Sir Fredrick had worn off, she was left with the pain and embarrassment of what had happened between her and Jarrod. It was impossible to look at him. Yet she must answer Sir Ulrick's concern. "I will be happy to be put to the test for such a cause. And make no mistake, I will seek my rest immediately, as must you."

She could feel the weight of Jarrod's attention upon her, and calling on her own inner strength, she faced him no matter that doing so made her throat constrict with pain. "Good night, Sir Jarrod."

He looked away. "Good night, my lady." Without another word, he moved to the door and left them.

Now she could feel Sir Ulrick watching her, and

she forced herself to also face him directly. "Good night." To this he bowed and made his own way out.

As he left, she asked herself why should she not face him? Nothing had really happened!

And it would not happen again, for clearly Jarrod loved the woman Sadona had spoken of so deeply that he had no room for another in his life. Not that Aislynn wanted to be in his life!

Aislynn did her best to sleep, knowing as she did that, rustic as her accommodations might be, they were warmer and drier than the tent would be on ensuing nights. Slumber was some time in coming, but when it finally did, it was a deep and dreamless state of utter exhaustion, both emotionally and physically.

It was Ulrick's voice at the chamber door that woke her. "My lady."

Slowly Aislynn sat up, her gritty gaze taking in the fact that the light filtering in through the edges of the narrow shutters was dim. She called out, "I am awake."

She rose as he moved away, and dressed in the gown she had laundered the previous afternoon. Covering herself in the enveloping amber velvet was, in a sense, like donning armor, for she'd felt too vulnerable in the shift that had proved little barrier to Jarrod's questing hands and mouth. It was with some sense of renewed energy and confidence that she moved to leave the room.

No matter what Jarrod might do or say, she would somehow manage to hold her own. She did not require his approval, nor his passion. Least of all did she require his passion, she told herself as she moved to the stair. Yet the words did not quite ring true in her mind.

When she reached the bottom, Aislynn halted, hearing the sound of Jarrod's voice as he finished off something he was saying with a rueful laugh.

Then came a voice that could only be Sadona's. "She is a good enough sort—your lady. She has been most respectful of me though I am far beneath her."

The harsh and quick reply stung more deeply than Aislynn would have thought possible, "She is not *my* lady."

The rejoinder was almost too quick. "I see."

Obviously all of Aislynn's assurances had been for naught.

The woman's tone was even enough, but Aislynn would have to be simple to miss the hint of knowing in it as she said, "As you say, Jarrod." She paused then. "You will have a care with her. She could be easily hurt."

It was much the same as Sadona had said of Jarrod.

A long pause ensued. Into it came Jarrod's voice, toneless, giving away nothing. "I owe you much, Sadona, of affection and respect, but you know nothing of which you speak. Aislynn Greatham and I mean nothing to each other."

The silence that followed was impossible to read, but Aislynn felt herself flush. Jarrod had said all there was to say. She meant nothing to him.

She drew back further into the shadows at the bottom of the stairs.

To her chagrin, Ulrick nearly collided with her as he came around the corner of the wall in preparation of going up the stairs. He halted. "My lady Aislynn. I was just coming to fetch you."

Aislynn had no choice then but to move forward into the light.

Jarrod stood in the main chamber with Sadona. His darkly handsome face was an unreadable mask as he turned to them, and Ulrick told him, "I have readied the horses."

Aislynn avoided looking into those black eyes as she preceded Ulrick. She looked instead to their hostess, though she was more than a little shamed at the way the two of them had spoken of her. She had no wish to appear anything but self-possessed. "Thank you for your kindness."

The woman dipped a curtsy. "I am honored to have had such a fine and gentle lady as my guest."

Only when Jarrod turned his back to say something to Ulrick, who had moved to stand beside him, did Aislynn look directly at him. She was amazed that, in spite of all, she still found him the most physically pleasing man she had ever looked upon. His raven hair was damp from a washing and had been combed straight back from his broad forehead. The dark cape he wore over his clothing only seemed to emphasize the width of those broad shoulders. Shoulders that she had clung to with such desperation and desire mere hours ago.

It was only by a sheer act of will that she forced herself not to turn away when Jarrod swung around to face her. The black eyes that had last night been so full of heat were now cold. "Are you ready, Aislynn?"

It was his coldness and the way he had spoken of

her to Sadona rather than the pain of what could not be that made her throat tight. This realization enabled her to hold her head high as she preceded him from the inn.

Throughout that day the land they traveled through became more difficult to traverse. The rolling hills steepened, the streams and rivers rushed through the vales more forcefully.

The difficulty of riding made conversation near impossible. She didn't believe Jarrod would have spoken to her even if it had not. That was fine with her, for she had wrapped a prideful silence about her that made it possible to go on, to hold her head high.

Yet as they rode on, Aislynn could not help wishing...wishing for things that she was afraid to even articulate in her mind.

Well after they had settled for the night, Aislynn lay looking up into the darkness. She wanted to believe it was the chill air on her cheeks that kept her awake.

She knew it was not.

Again she thought of what Jarrod had said to Sadona. Renewed resentment swept through her as it did each time she remembered his saying that she was nothing to him.

A groan of frustration escaped her. She could change nothing by repeatedly reliving the shame of it. Jarrod knew what he wanted. And that was not Aislynn.

Desperate to sleep, knowing that any sign of tiredness would be noted and disapproved come morning, Aislynn turned to face the wall of the tent. With determination she closed her eyes and pressed her cheek into the pillow.

She opened them again almost instantly, seeing the faint glow of the fire through the tent wall. And with it an image of Jarrod's darkly handsome face in her mind.

God's blood, what was wrong with her? The man was not that compelling.

But she knew that was a lie. He had made her feel things she had never even dreamed of, brought her slumbering body to life and, no matter how she hated him, her body, traitor that it was, only continued to yearn for him.

Aislynn shivered with frustration, and with that shiver came a sudden realization that she had not answered the call of nature before going to bed, having been too concerned with getting away from the man who plagued her so. As soon as the thought entered her mind, she knew that she would not be able to rest until it was answered.

Yet the notion of going out into the wood by herself now, with the heavy weight of night pressing down upon her, was less than appealing. She had promised Jarrod that she would not venture off on her own, but that seemed a long time ago—a lifetime.

Surely he could not fault her for not waking him. She need only go behind the tent.

So thinking, Aislynn tossed the covers aside and stood. Shivering in the chill, she quickly drew her cape over her shoulders and stepped out into the night.

She was somewhat relieved to find that the fire actually did more to light the area than she would hav imagined. Though it was dark all around them, the flames cast a gentle glow over the immediate area.

Aislynn listened to be certain the two men were asleep. She could hear no sounds from either of them. Feeling more confident with each passing moment, she moved around her tent, where the darkness was deeper, keeping the knowledge that the light was just a few steps away in the forefront of her mind.

Her task was completed quickly and quietly.

It was as she was rounding her tent in preparation of crawling back inside that she felt an odd prickling along her neck. Pausing, she cast a quick glance about the camp. A harsh gasp escaped her as her gaze came to rest on a face, a man's face, peering out from behind the tree nearest to where Jarrod lay.

The moment the sound left her, the face disappeared back into the shadows.

Almost instantly Jarrod Maxwell rose up on his bedroll, his gaze pinning her. "What is it?"

Aislynn pointed toward the tree. "I...it was a face. I saw a man's face there looking down at you."

Jarrod, sword in hand, was up and behind the tree before she could reach the fire. He moved around the tree, examining the ground as he went, then spun about to look into the depths of the forest, before disappearing into that thick darkness.

Aislynn held her breath. It was only minutes until he emerged from the forest and came toward her and Sir Ulrick, who had risen from his bed to stand beside her. The fact that her father's knight had drawn his own blade was not lost on Aislynn.

Sir Jarrod looked down at her. "I can find nothing. Tell me what you saw."

She took a deep breath. "I told you. I saw a face, the face of a man, looking out from behind that tree. He was looking at you, Jarrod."

"Did you recognize him?"

She shook her head slowly. "Nay, in the light of the fire, it was very strange, the angles exaggerated. I could not..." Aislynn grimaced. "But I do know it was evil. That much I know."

Jarrod rubbed a hand over the back of his neck as he looked toward the tree. "I can not see so much as a footprint." He looked at her again, his gaze searching, "I heard nothing."

"You were sleeping."

He shrugged. "Aye, but I am a very light sleeper." He frowned as he looked down at her now. "Pray what were you doing up and about alone."

Aislynn flushed. "I...I had to attend a personal matter."

Sir Ulrick spoke up. "My lady, you have given your word that you will not go off alone."

She scowled at him, surprised at this criticism from what she had considered a source of support. "I did not wish to wake either of you over such a small matter. I assure you that I never lost sight of the camp."

"Nonetheless, I trust you will not do so again," Jarrod interjected.

Aislynn swung around to face him, resentful of his commanding tone. "I trust you understand that I am able to complete some small tasks without your guidance." Who indeed was he to tell her what to do when he cared naught for her?

He glared down at her.

Aislynn returned the look, saying, "And now that we have gotten that taken care of, wouldn't it be wise to attempt to discover who I saw?"

Jarrod shook his head, replying slowly, "Aislynn, I searched the surrounding wood. I saw nothing."

She gasped. "Are you saying you doubt my word?"

It was Ulrick who answered. "Nay, my lady. I am most certain that Sir Jarrod is not saying such a thing. He is simply saying that you may be mistaken in what you thought you saw."

Jarrod nodded. "Aye. It is dark. You only glimpsed this face for a brief moment. Perhaps it was just a trick of the light in the shadows."

Aislynn drew herself up to her full height. "I know what I saw."

Jarrod shrugged, his tone not unkind as he said, "Who could it possibly have been, here in the midst of nowhere, in the dead of night? Surely thieves or anyone else who meant harm would have attacked."

Aislynn did not know who it had been, nor why they had run away when she saw them. Yet she did know that there had been someone there. She had not imagined it. She also knew that they could not have meant good.

She looked from him to Sir Ulrick. She could see the doubt in the older man's eyes. And his regret over it.

So be it. They did not believe her.

She held her head high. "The two of you may think what you will. I know what I saw. Do with the information as you see fit. And now I think I will return to my bed. Lest you have more to say to me.'' She frowned from one to the other.

Sir Ulrick bowed respectfully. Jarrod also bowed, but there were tight lines around his mouth. Without another word, Aislynn turned and stalked away from them.

It was some time before she fell asleep.

Jarrod went about the business of breaking camp with a heavy heart. He was completely conscious of Aislynn's continued anger with him. It was obvious in the stiff line of her back and the way she ate and prepared for the day ahead without looking at either him or Sir Ulrick directly.

He wished he could tell her that he believed her. But he had found nothing to indicate that anyone had been anywhere near their camp. It was true that the carpet of needles and leaves on the ground might hide footprints well, but there was not so much as a broken twig on any of the branches.

He simply could not encourage this fearful fantasy. Yet he felt a desire to soothe her hurt feelings. This desire was surely nothing but madness, for he did not mean for her to think...

What had happened between them could never happen again. She was a passionate young woman and had only answered his own caresses. That the very memory of her response heated his blood, he would control. He must do so.

As Ulrick led the horses away to drink before leaving, he found himself attempting to meet her gaze. To offer some form of apology, however silent.

Once again Aislynn avoided him as she stood feed-

ing her mare a handful of tender undergrowth that she
had specifically picked for her. He took in the dark
shadows beneath her eyes, which told of a sleepless
night. And as he did so he realized that, far from
detracting from her delicate beauty, this sign of vulnerability made her even more attractive to him. It
made him want to take her in his arms and…

He found himself approaching her. Surely there
was no danger of anything happening between them
here in the light of day. Nor any other time, he reminded himself quickly.

She looked up at him, her gaze cool, and Jarrod
felt a ripple of irritation pass through him. His incli-
nation was to leave her to herself, but something,
some sense of fairness would not let him.

Impatient with his own timidity before this tiny
woman, he spoke roughly. "Aislynn, I…" Her
haughtily raised brows made him halt. He began
again. "Lady Aislynn, I wish to tell you that I am
sorry for any disturbance I might have caused you by
questioning what you believe you saw last night. It
was not my intent to do so."

Those brows remained high as she looked him directly in the eyes. "Do not trouble yourself, sir. You
and I are nothing to each other."

With that, she swung around and stalked away,
leaving Jarrod feeling as if she had slapped him in
the face.

The words carried him back to a time he did not
wish to remember, a time that still had the power to
bring an ache to his chest. They made him remember
the woman to whom he had bared his yearning heart.
That day he had felt as if a part of him had died. As

he had stood in a tent, which had been erected on the fringes of an army camp, his shy but eager gaze had found her—a woman of dark and unusual beauty in spite of the differences in their ages and the ravages of her profession.

Jarrod being barely twenty, was a man, yet he still retained many of a boy's insecurities. He had come there with his heart in his hands. And she…she had faced him with a similar hauteur in her black eyes and said, "You, English boy, why do you come here and expect something from me? You are nothing to me."

Even now, nine years later, Jarrod felt the world tilt with the pain of that moment.

He drew in a ragged breath, forcing himself to gain control. He would not allow Aislynn Greatham, with a handful of words, to destroy his hard-won self-possession.

Yet he found himself watching her too intently as she allowed Ulrick to help her to mount with coolly civil thanks, still without so much as glancing in Jarrod's direction.

Unbidden, he realized that he now had some notion of what she'd felt when she'd accused him of ignoring her. Although that had been a completely different matter, he assured himself quickly. He had not chosen to withhold himself because of a fit of pique.

Again Jarrod reminded himself that what Aislynn thought of him did not matter. It was, in fact, the best thing for both of them that she held him in such disregard. Yet as he mounted and waited for them to fall in behind him with deliberate calm, he did not feel relieved.

All he felt was a sense of regret and an unfocused sadness that made the gray sky overheard seem bleak, the day before him long.

# Chapter Nine

Throughout the morning, Aislynn felt Jarrod watching her from his stallion. She would not have given him the satisfaction of knowing that she noticed if he were Saint George himself. At the same time she could not help feeling that he had been quite disturbed by their brief exchange before leaving camp. He had looked...well...shaken was the only way she could describe it.

This did give Aislynn some pause, especially as she had only repeated what he had said to Sadona the previous day. She thought her understanding of his feelings would please him greatly.

It was no bother to her when conditions worsened so that simply traveling forward became a task that demanded her undivided attention. The road grew narrower and more rutted as they went on. To the right of them, the sea crashed insistently against the rocky shoreline.

It was midmorning when Jarrod halted his stallion and leaned up in the stirrups. He studied the road up ahead of what appeared to be a sharp bend in the

narrow track. After a moment, he turned and came
back to meet them.

Frowning, Aislynn halted her mare and watched
Jarrod's face as he dismounted and came back to
stand at her horse's head. His expression troubled, he
pointed up ahead of them. "Come, I want you to see
something." If he had ever been upset with her, there
was no sign of it now.

So amazed and curious was she by this odd remark
and behavior that she forgot her own anger and took
his hand when he reached out to help her down. Yet
Aislynn was not unaware of the current that ran
through her in the brief and distracted contact.

Jarrod made no sign of noting this.

Holding back a sigh of irritation with herself, Aislynn followed as he led her to the spot where he had
turned back on the narrow road. She was aware of Sir
Ulrick coming behind them.

What she saw when she peered around the edge of
the bend in the rocks made her gasp.

The track no longer followed the brink of the water
from here. The cliffs ran right along the edge of the
sea here, and the path, which was too narrow for more
than one person at a time, rose almost straight up,
seeming to be cut from the rocks by some haphazard
hand.

As she watched, Aislynn could see that the spray
from the crashing waves had wet that ribbon-of-stone
path. This road would surely be slippery at the best
of times. She took a deep breath. "Dear heaven. It is
no wonder that few people dare to journey here."

Jarrod turned to her. "Precisely my own thought."

She looked at him. "You are certain we have followed the directions correctly?"

Aislynn did not require the nod Jarrod gave to know that they had done so. It was only a deep desire for it to be otherwise that made her ask such a pointless question.

Sir Ulrick spoke from behind her. "You can not think to go on here, my lady."

Aislynn turned to Jarrod and found him watching the knight with approval. Clearly he had only said what Jarrod had been thinking.

She drew herself up. "We must discover whether or not my brother is in this village. Or if he has been there."

Quickly Jarrod said, "I will go on alone and return to you with any news I learn."

Aislynn shook her head. She looked up at him, willing him to understand her position. "I can not agree to that. My father dreamed that I must be the one and I will honor his faith in me. I can not do otherwise."

He turned to stare out over the churning sea, the muscles in his lean jaw flexing. "Must you be so obstinate?"

She did not care for this characterization, for she did not imagine herself stubborn at all. She preferred the term *determined*. Yet Aislynn did not waste her energy in attempting to convince Jarrod Maxwell of this.

She simply met his eyes directly and said, "I will seek out my brother with or without your permission."

Sir Ulrick shook his head. "You father had no notion that you would be placing yourself in such peril when he charged you with this task, Lady Aislynn.''

''My father would have me heed his dream. After the way he lost my mother, he would feel that he had no choice. You must see that I have no choice.''

Sir Ulrick frowned, but said nothing. Aislynn was not blind to the fact that the stiffness of his posture indicated his continued objections.

Issuing a grunt of exasperation, Jarrod swung around to face Ulrick, ignoring Aislynn completely. ''I will see to her.'' The other knight nodded, albeit reluctantly and took a deep breath as Jarrod went on. ''You must remain with the horses, for we can not leave them and 'tis obvious taking them on would be impossible.''

The older knight nodded again. ''I will stay nearby with them.''

Jarrod sighed. ''A short distance back I did see a spot where you could erect the tent and await our return.''

The knight nodded again. ''I know the place.''

Aislynn knew she should be pleased at this easy capitulation to her wishes. But she did not feel pleased. She did not care for the way they had dismissed her from the rest of the conversation.

She told herself that she must ignore their opinion of her. She was only doing her duty in insisting on going on to the village. It was what her father had charged her to do.

It took far less time to hand the horses over to Ulrick than she would have expected. It was clear that once the decision had been made, neither man wished to linger over the matter.

Sir Ulrick's observation that night would fall soon explained their hurry. Aislynn knew that the path around the cliffs would only be made more dangerous once darkness had fallen.

She gathered the few belongings she would take and stood ready.

Whether Jarrod approved of her haste, she could not tell. He said not a word to her, only bidding Ulrick Godspeed as the older knight moved off with the horses.

Without a word to her, he turned and started up the trail, showing less care in traversing the rocks than she thought wise. But he could do as he would, could he not?

Gingerly Aislynn followed.

Pray God, Christian would be in Ashcroft at the end of this dreadful expedition.

It immediately became apparent that the trail was even more treacherous than it had appeared from below. The rocks were slimy beneath her slippered feet and the path was so narrow in places that her feet became stuck if she did not pay close heed. Aislynn was forced to attend to where she placed each careful step.

From the lead, Jarrod kept glancing back. Although Aislynn knew it was only because he had to look after her because of his promise to her father, she felt somewhat moved by this sign of care. It made her wonder what it might be like to be Jarrod Maxwell's woman, to have him there to care for her well-being.

But she knew that thinking on this served her naught but ill. Thus when Jarrod fell back to reach out a helping hand, she raised her head high and told him she required no assistance. Knowing her own susceptibility to him, she could not allow him to touch her.

The rigid set of his profile when he turned away would not sway her. Jarrod had made his intentions most clear and she could not allow her heart to soften toward him.

Her close attention grew increasingly more important as the path steepened toward the top of the cliffs. More than once, Aislynn stumbled and only managed to right herself in time to keep from tumbling back down the rocky cliff face. Only the knowledge that Christian might be at the end of this impossible trail kept her from stopping and telling Jarrod that he was right, that she did not wish to continue.

Finally she looked up to see Jarrod holding out his hand to help her the last long step to the top. Utterly exhausted, Aislynn did not meet his searching gaze as she took his hand.

When she stepped up onto level ground, he instantly let go of her hand and moved away from her. Aislynn did her best to ignore him, falling to her knees in the damp short grass as she sought to bring her breathing back to normal. She realized that her shortness of breath was caused more from the sustained anxiety of falling coupled with her own unhappy thoughts.

Jarrod waited there for a few moments, still not speaking, staring out at the wide view of steely-gray ocean and sky, which Aislynn had to admit would have been awe-inspiring under different circumstances. As it was, she could think of nothing save getting to Ashcroft and leaving it again—with Christian.

Thus it was she who turned to Jarrod as soon as she was able and said, "Let us go on."

He nodded, then hesitated. "I know you are angry, but I would we could make a truce for now, Aislynn. I would not be distracted from finding Christian."

Surprised but unwillingly admiring of his directness, she could not but acquiesce. She dipped a deep curtsy. "As you will."

He bowed with equal formality then turned and led the way.

The village, if one could call it that, was a cluster of no more than six or seven rather small but well-tended cottages, a blacksmith shop, and another building that appeared to be a business of some sort. At the center of the village was a well. There was no indication of life other than an elderly woman, who stood bent over the well as they approached. She looked up with obvious curiosity and even more obvious caution.

Aislynn was not surprised by this reaction at seeing strangers. She was certain that the method of getting here kept all but the most determined travelers away.

Suddenly Jarrod broke his silence, startling Aislynn somewhat though his tone was soft. "If you will permit, I will do the talking. The village folk may see so few strangers that they are leery of them."

Aislynn nodded, having come to the same conclusion.

Jarrod said no more, approaching the woman, who now stood watching them, with deliberate unconcern. Aislynn attempted to adopt a similar demeanor though her heart was pounding with anticipation at the thought that Christian might be close by.

Jarrod nodded to the woman and smiled. "Good day."

She bowed, her gaze taking in the fineness of his and Aislynn's garments. "Good day, my lord, my lady."

Aislynn nodded, deliberately feigning a casual stance to match Jarrod's.

Jarrod drew the woman's attention back to himself. "Wouldst you care if my lady and I availed ourselves of your well, good dame?"

She shrugged. "The well is there, my lord. You may partake of it as you like."

The words were not precisely welcoming, but Aislynn could tell that the elderly dame was pleased at his making the request when he could indeed take what he liked without doing so. Her assessment was enhanced by the fact the good dame herself reached out and took the metal ladle that hung from a hook at the side of the well and handed it to him.

Jarrod bowed. "You have my thanks." He then raised the bucket and dipped a ladleful.

To Aislynn's surprise, he handed it to her. Casting him a grateful look, she raised it to her dry lips. The water was sweet and cool and tasted better than anything before in her life. The exertions of the day had been draining.

Not until it was completely drained did she hand the ladle back to Jarrod. He dipped it again and followed her example.

The old woman raised her gray brows high. "Thirsty, aren't ye?"

Jarrod nodded. "It's quite a climb getting here."

She shrugged, her keen gaze assessing on his. "One needs have good reason to make the journey, then. Aye, my lord?"

He did not look away. "That is the truth of it."

She looked to Aislynn, who also met her gaze without wavering as she said, "Would you care to be tellin' me your reason then?"

"We are looking for my brother," Aislynn answered, totally disregarding their agreement that Jarrod should speak for them. She simply could not hold it in.

"This would be a strange place to look for the brother of a noblewoman. There is nothing hereabouts to interest such a one."

Jarrod cast her a frowning glance and Aislynn held her tongue. He said, "That is our own assessment, dear lady. Yet we have come here, even on the poorest of clues that he might indeed be here."

"You are that desperate to find this man?"

He took a deep breath, letting the truth of his concern shine in his black eyes. "Aye, we are. He disappeared from his home with little explanation and we have been searching for him for some time. The fact that he is known to have asked the whereabouts of your village is all we have been able to learn of him or where he might have gone."

As the woman opened her mouth to reply, a harsh male voice interrupted, "What are you about, Mother?"

Aislynn swung around to see a decidedly handsome young man, with thick dark brown hair and a pair of wary green eyes. He grimaced as he shook his head at the woman he had called mother.

The old woman looked down. "These folk are looking for someone. A man. The lady says he is her brother."

Aislynn moved closer, her gaze on the newcomer. "Aye, my brother has been missing for weeks and we have come in search of him. We have reason to believe that he may have come to Ashcroft. His name is Christian Greatham of Bransbury."

The young man shook his head, and his gaze slid from hers to his mother's. "I am sure you told them that we have seen no one who could be the brother of a noblewoman."

She looked down at her hands. "I was about to do that very thing, Sean."

Jarrod moved to stand beside Aislynn, who could not help wondering if the older woman was speaking true. Jarrod clearly felt the same, for he said, "Are you very sure of this?"

The man named Sean nodded, looking first Aislynn then Jarrod directly in the eyes. "Most sure, my lord. Ashcroft is a very small village and all would ken if there had been a stranger about."

Aislynn could barely contain her disappointment. Only now did she realize how desperately she had believed that Christian would be here in spite of their having so little indication that he was.

Sean interrupted her thoughts, saying, "Mother, 'twill be dark soon. I will help you carry the water back to the cottage." He reached out to take her bucket in hand.

Jarrod spoke up before they could leave. "Is there,

by chance, somewhere we might gain lodging for the night? I would be happy to pay.''

Aislynn was surprised at this request. Surely there was no reason to remain here. Jarrod's next comment explained his reasoning. ''The hour grows late and I wouldst not ask this lady to traverse those cliffs in the dark.''

The young man cast an assessing gaze over him. ''All the lodging you might find here about would be most humble.''

Jarrod shrugged, ignoring his lack of goodwill. ''That matters not. We would be happy to make our bed anywhere out of the damp.''

Sean shrugged. ''I know of nothing that would suit.''

The old woman frowned at him, ''There is no need for such a lack of hospitality, Sean. We can offer a dry bed.'' She then bowed to Aislynn, though her son glowered unpleasantly. ''If you truly have no care, my lady, you are welcome to sleep in the loft above the animals.''

Aislynn bowed in return. ''I thank you for your kindness, good lady. I am so tired that I might be able to lie down and sleep upon the hard ground. A bed of soft hay will seem as heaven.''

Her son scowled blackly but made no further demure.

The woman said, ''I am Hagar. Sean is my only child. If you will come this way with us, then I will see that you get a warm meal in your bellies before bed as well.''

Aislynn and Jarrod fell into step behind mother and son. Aislynn was not blind to the unhappy looks the

young man cast toward his mother in the growing
gloom as they made their way to a cottage some distance along the narrow road from the village.

The meal the kind woman set forth was simple, a
sort of stew with mutton and turnips. But as Aislynn
was tired, so was she hungry. No food had ever tasted
better to her, including the dark bread that the elderly
woman served with it on the well-scrubbed plank table in her small but scrupulously clean cottage.

She saw that Jarrod too seemed to be hungry, for
he ate with some enthusiasm. He appeared to have
much interest in their surroundings. He studied the
small cottage, taking in the sparse furnishings and dirt
floor, as well as the fact the sleeping quarters lay in
an open loft above the one chamber that served as
main chamber and kitchen. Jarrod also watched the
young man, who applied himself to his own food
while obviously feigning disinterest in them.

Although Sean had taken his own trencher close to
the fire, turning his back to them, the intent tilt of his
head showed that his attention was tuned to their
every word. Aislynn also noted the way he looked
toward them each time he turned his head to take a
bite from his bowl.

When the meal was finished, Jarrod stood. "We
thank you, good lady. And now if you will show us
to our sleeping quarters we will leave you and your
son to your peace."

As if she too was aware of her son's displeasure,
the older woman made no demure. She picked up a
tallow candle and led them into another structure,
which rested against the side of the cottage but could
not be entered from inside the main dwelling.

The interior was dim and smelled of fragrant hay and warm bodies. The soft bleat of a sheep told Aislynn the nature of the occupants before their hostess's circle of light fell upon them. She moved past the sheep to a ladder. They followed her up it, Aislynn in the lead.

When she reached the top, Aislynn scurried aside to allow Jarrod access to the low but sturdy loft. Hagar was already pulling the piled hay into some semblance of a bed.

Jarrod stopped her. "Pray, do not trouble yourself further, good woman. You have done more than enough."

She turned and looked at them, her gaze widening with seeming understanding. Quickly she looked away and nodded. "I will leave you a light." Hagar reached into a pocket of her gown and removed another of the tallow candles. She lit it and handed it over to Jarrod. With the same deftness, she moved to the ladder and down. It was no more than moments before she had left the shed, closing the door firmly behind her.

Aislynn took a deep breath, realizing that the woman thought...that she imagined they wished to be alone. She flushed, not daring to look directly at Jarrod.

Hurriedly she swung around and began to gather some of the sweet-smelling hay into a bed for herself. Jarrod was more than welcome to the one the other woman had started.

To cover her confusion, she said, "I suppose we will be leaving at first light."

Jarrod's reply halted her. "Perhaps not."

She frowned, trying to gain some hint of his thoughts from his face, which was unreadable in the flickering candlelight. "But why? Christian is not here. Has never been here." Again she felt a tug of sorrow, knowing that they now had no clue as to where they might find him.

Once more Jarrod surprised her. "Mayhap."

She sat down, making no effort to hide her confusion. "What are you saying?"

"I am saying I believe the son is hiding something."

She shook her head. "And why would he tell us a falsehood?"

Jarrod raked a hand through his black hair. "That I do not know. I only know that something is not right here, and I mean to get to the bottom of it on the chance that Christian is involved in some way."

She rubbed her brow, feeling her stomach churn. "If this is true, and Sean is hiding something about my brother, then I have very likely given us away too soon by telling the old woman why we are come."

Jarrod sighed. "Pray do not hold yourself to account for that. Your words did not hinder us. I do in fact believe the old woman was about to…"

He struck his palm with his fist in frustration. "Christ's blood, I do believe she did mean to tell us something. That is why Sean interrupted her."

He looked at Aislynn with approval. "And the reason Hagar wanted to speak was the truth you had told of your sadness and worry. Your honesty moved her to offer the truth. Whatever it might be."

Aislynn was surprised at Jarrod's approval. Even though they had agreed on a truce for the sake of

locating her brother, she had not thought it would
extend so far. In fact, she had expected him to be
angry with her for speaking when she had agreed not
to. She was warmed at the thought that they might
still find her brother here. Then she sighed. "What if
we are wrong? What if there is nothing to hide and
he is but a surly young man?"

"Then we shall be on our way with no more than
a few hours lost, for I do mean to get to the bottom
of this as quickly as possible."

Aislynn was overcome with feelings of gratitude
and yearning. Despite the fact that he did not want
her, Jarrod was a good man, a wonderful man. She
spoke from the depths of her heart. "Thank you, Jarrod. I...you'll never know how much this means to
me, how indebted I am to you for all you have done
and continue to do."

From where she sat, some feet from him, she felt
Jarrod stiffen, his voice as taut as the string of a bow.
"You may keep your indebtedness. As I have told
you many times, I do this because I care for your
brother."

The fact that he did not extend that care to her was
not lost on Aislynn, nor that their truce had only been
temporary. Could this cool and distant stranger be the
same man who had touched her, kissed her with such
passionate abandon? It did not seem possible.

She pushed the misery that rose up inside her to
the depth of her being, nodding sharply, forcing herself to meet that unemotional gaze. "Very well then."

There was no other reply she could make.

He looked away. "You'd best get some sleep. It

has been a trying day and tomorrow promises to be another.''

Quickly she removed her cloak and spread it over the bed of hay. Not waiting for Jarrod, she lay down and pulled the excess over her. In the heavy silence she listened as he attended to his own bed. She then gave a silent sigh as he extinguished the candle and allowed her the haven of darkness in which to nurse her battered emotions.

# *Chapter Ten*

When Aislynn woke the next morning Jarrod was already gone. But nearly as disturbing as his presence would have been was the fact that he had laid his own cape over her as she slept.

A pleasurable warmth spread through her body. Almost as if he had touched her.

Hurriedly she rose, and fighting an urge to toss the heavy garment aside, she folded it carefully and placed it on his bed of hay.

She wondered how she could possibly have slept through his leaving and why he should have let her do so. He did not know that she had lain awake long after his breathing had become even and deep, troubled by the physical intimacy of them sharing this small space, no matter how angry with him she was. He could not know of the images that had risen up to torment both her mind and body.

But he should have known that she would want to be with him while he sought out any sign that Christian had been in Ashcroft. Perhaps he had not been gone long.

Hurriedly Aislynn scrambled down from the loft and out of the shelter. The sheep were no longer in occupation and this told her that Jarrod was not the only one up and about. Not wanting to run into her hostess at the moment, Aislynn skirted the front of the cottage and made her way toward the tiny hamlet.

She walked quickly, barely noting the condition of the road, nor the steely-gray of the sky, which hovered low overhead, until she stepped into a puddle. Gasping, her shoes instantly soaked through, Aislynn realized that it had rained hard during the night.

Determinedly Aislynn set her mind to paying attention to where she trod as she made her way down the rutted laneway. It was riddled with murky puddles and she had no desire to get her leather-shod feet any wetter than they already were.

So occupied was she in this that Aislynn was nearly upon the two, who stood near the well where she and Jarrod had first met Hagar, before she noted them. It was a woman and a child. She cast a quick glance over the woman as she lowered her bucket into the well and the little one, who appeared to be a girl of no more than four.

Although Aislynn felt the woman watching her, she did so covertly as she went about her task. The child was much more direct, as children are, and stared at Aislynn with wide brown eyes.

Aislynn smiled at her and the child took a step toward her mother. Aislynn was not offended by this. She knew that little ones could be shy with strangers. She had a fondness for children and looked forward to the day when she would have her own.

When this thought brought a quite unwelcome image of the man who so plagued her, Aislynn drew herself up sharply.

Purposefully she spoke to the woman beside the well. "Good morrow."

The woman swung around to face her directly and Aislynn noted that she was heavy with advancing pregnancy. Her gaze took in Aislynn's long velvet cape. She bowed respectfully. "My lady."

She turned back to raise the bucket, which was now obviously much heavier filled with water.

Without thinking, Aislynn stepped forward. "Please, let me help you." She reached out to turn the hook on the opposite side of the well.

The woman grew still, looking at her in surprise. "There is no need…"

Aislynn smiled and said, "Nonetheless I will." She was quite used to doing this sort of activity at Bransbury.

The woman watched her for a moment, then nodded. They began to turn the winch in unison, neither speaking.

When the bucket reached the top, Aislynn lifted it from the hook before the other woman could do so. Aislynn then turned to watch the village woman as she lifted the hook that attached it to one end of the harness she would carry across her shoulders. At the other end was another full bucket. As she worked, the woman glanced over at the child, a frown creasing her brow.

Following her gaze, Aislynn saw that the little girl had positioned a rock so that she could lean up over the edge of the well as she dropped bits of something from her chubby fingers into the water below. The mother spoke firmly. "Watch now, Fi, that ye don't get too close."

The child jumped down and stepped back from the edge of the well, her cheeks pink with chagrin. Aislynn marveled at the mother's ability to pay such close attention to the child while she worked.

The young woman moved to attach the second bucket to her harness. She then stood and bowed. "Ye have my thanks, my lady."

Aislynn nodded. "I receive them most happily."

She was indeed happy to have something to do other than think of her own difficulties, if only for a moment. But now that the task was completed, she found herself wondering if the young mother might have some knowledge that could help her determine if her brother had been here.

Aislynn folded her hands over her midriff. "If you do not mind, good lady, there is something of import that I would ask you."

The young mother stood straight, watching her closely. "I know that ye have come to Ashcroft looking for your brother." She looked down at the ground. "Your assistance here changes nothing. I can tell ye naught of what ye seek, my lady."

Aislynn was not oblivious to the fact that the woman did not look at her as she spoke, and she felt herself frown with chagrin. "I did not..." She stopped herself. Although she had not offered to help for the express purpose of gaining information about her brother, she could not pretend that she was not interested in learning anything she could. She shrugged. "I sought no exchange of service. I thank you for being straightforward. To discover that you know nothing is to gain information.'' Aislynn bowed with civility.

The other woman smiled tentatively, ''I'll be about my work then.'' She reached down to raise the harness up to her shoulders. As she did, a soft squeal issued from behind them.

Aislynn and the other woman looked toward the sound, just in time to see a flash of color as the child disappeared down the well, another shrill screech issuing from her. That scream was loud with terror as was the one that erupted from her mother in the same instant.

Aislynn ran to look down the narrow chasm. She could see nothing, but the sound of hysterical sobbing and thrashing about in the water below was heart-rendingly audible.

Acting on pure instinct, Aislynn spun the rope from its rest, sending it back into the well. She called down. ''Take hold of the rope.''

The sounds of terror did not abate. Again Aislynn called down, this time more loudly, ''Take the rope.''

The screaming continued.

In desperation Aislynn turned to the young woman, who now sobbed violently at her side. ''The child will not heed me. You must make her hear.''

To Aislynn's utter frustration, the woman simply stared at her, her brown eyes glazed as if she could not understand.

Aislynn took hold of her arm, forcing her to meet her gaze, holding it as she said, ''She must take hold of the rope or she will drown.''

This seemed to penetrate her horror, for the woman caught herself in the next breath and leaned down into the well, calling out in a voice of authority. "Fiona, listen to me now! Ye mun take hold of the rope!"

The hysterical noises went on unabated.

The woman took a deep long breath and this time there was steel in her voice. "Fiona! Do as I bid ye! Now lass!"

At last the sounds of desperate thrashing quieted, although the sobs did not as the tiny voice called out, "It is cold, Ma. And dark."

Aislynn felt her own heart turn over in her breast. Yet she knew it could be nothing compared to the pain in the other woman's gaze, for simply looking into that bleak and bottomless agony was nearly too much to bear.

Aislynn knew that something must be done and now. Even if the little one was safely holding the rope for the moment, she would not be able to do so indefinitely. At any moment her panic could again overcome her.

Obviously the other woman had realized this in the same moment, for she tore at the string that held her woolen cloak, her eyes glazed with a madness born of desperation. Realizing what she was about, Aislynn moved to stop her. "Nay, do not try to go to her. It will do no good. You will never fit down the opening."

The young mother's tormented eyes fixed on Aislynn. "My bairn!"

Aislynn reached up to the clasp of her own cloak. "I am small enough to go." She took a long breath. "Once I am down there I will tie the rope around her and you will pull her up."

The other woman made no demure as she helped

Aislynn remove first the heavy cloak and then her gown, which would weigh too heavily once it was wet. Neither of them spoke further, for to do so would be to waste time that could not be afforded if they were to have any hope of rescuing the child.

All this was accomplished in a matter of seconds. And although she was focused on removing anything that might hinder her, Aislynn was not deaf to the choking sobs that continued to issue from the well.

Whilst Aislynn had disrobed down to her shift, the young mother moved with her to the edge of the well. Her eyes were deep dark pools of agony as she sobbed, "God go with ye, my lady."

With no more than a nod of assent, Aislynn took the rope in a tight grip and sitting on the side of the low stone well, hung her legs over the seemingly bottomless depths. With a deep breath she gathered her strength, as well as her courage, and slipped down into the narrow opening. She braced herself against the sides as best she could, putting as little of her weight as possible on the rope, for she did not wish to wrench it from the child's grasp.

Quickly she began to scramble down, bracing her feet against the cold stone wall.

It seemed to take forever with those horrific cries ringing all about her, but at last she reached the icy cold water. Aislynn wasted no more than a brief gasp of shock as it closed around her, for she also felt the form of the child brush up against her in the small confines.

Eagerly she reached out for the screaming child, filling her voice with all the confidence and reassurance she could muster. "I am here."

But this assurance did not have the desired effect. The little girl began to shriek even more loudly than before, and she flailed about in terror and desperation as she screamed, ''Mum.''

This made taking a firm hold of her impossible and Aislynn grasped nothing more than the edge of her sodden garments.

Horror swept through Aislynn when the child's voice became a gurgling sound as she slipped under the water. Quickly, with fingers more numb with anxiety than cold, she reached out again. This time she grasped a good amount of fabric and, with a cry of triumph, raised the child up in the water and at the same time drew her against her.

Aislynn's next breath was one of sobbing frustration as her own head submerged for a brief second due to the small one's continued frantic struggles.

Desperately Aislynn pulled her further up out of the water, speaking sharply in her fear, ''Be still, little one. You must let me help you or you will drown.''

To her utter relief the child stopped struggling and threw her arms about Aislynn's neck, clinging for dear life. Although she was hard-pressed to keep her own head above water with the little girl hanging about her neck, it was better than before and she was eventually able to brace herself so that she could catch her breath.

Only then did she hear the other woman's voice from above. ''What is happening?''

Aislynn called out as loudly as she could, the relief in her voice audible. ''I have her.''

Now it was the other woman who sobbed with relief. ''Thank God in his heaven.''

Bracing herself with her feet on one side of the stone well and her back against the other so that her hands would be free, Aislynn worked until she had the rope secured around the child's chest. She called up. "I have your babe tied to the rope. Pull it up now. But slowly."

The rope tautened even more and shuddered as the child began to be lifted above the level of the water. But once her weight was fully suspended above it, the movement stopped and she slid back until her weight was partially supported by the water.

The woman above called out, "One moment, I need only get a better grip."

Aislynn waited.

Again the rope tautened until Fiona was free of the water and again she fell back.

Again the process was repeated.

A groan of frustration and despair erupted from above. "I canna lift her."

Aislynn had realized this fact in the same instant. With a shiver, she felt the slime on the inside of the wall behind her. She felt the closeness, the dankness of the dark space and realized with despair that they had just begun this ordeal.

Steeling herself, she shunned that despair. She would do what must be done. With deliberate calm, Aislynn called out, "You will never be able to lift either of us. You will have to go for help."

"But how can I leave ye here?"

"You have no choice. We must have help to get out."

Jarrod eyed the blacksmith with frustration, but it did not show in his voice as he ran his gaze over that broad leather-encased chest. "I mean no harm to you or any other occupant of this village. I simply wish to find the man I spoke to you about. He is brother to the lady I am traveling with."

The smith's lips tightened as he continued to roll the piece of metal in the blazing heat of the forge. His voice was unconcerned, too unconcerned, as he spoke without looking up. "I wish ye well in finding the man ye seek, my lord. But as I told ye, I ken nothing of such as that."

Again, Jarrod was forced to swallow the bitter taste of his annoyance. He was many things, but foolish was not numbered amongst them. This man was, all of the villagers were, hiding something. Jarrod was certain of it, could feel it in his belly.

He was distracted from his unhappy realization as a female voice cried, "Help us, someone, ye mun help us."

Jarrod's gaze went to the smith as he tossed the metal he was heating into the fire. He too had heard the desperation in the cry.

The two of them hurried out into the lane, which ran directly in front of the smithy. A young woman shuffled down the rutted road, one hand supporting the weight of her advancing pregnancy as she hurried toward them.

The woman's voice had prepared Jarrod for the panic that glazed her gaze. It had not prepared him for the sheer misery he saw there.

She rushed to the smith, reaching to grasp his enormous forearm in a white knuckled hand. "Ye mun come quick, John. Fiona and the lady be down the well.''

A sharp flash of dread made Jarrod's stomach clench. He was not blind to the revelation of it in his own voice as he spoke sharply, ''Lady?''

For the first time the woman's gaze focused on Jarrod. ''Aye, the lady.''

Jarrod did not wish to imagine that it could be Aislynn. She had been sleeping when he'd left, safe and out of harm's way. But reason and his own sense of dread told him that it must be Aislynn.

He felt as if he were speaking from a long distance. ''Is it the lady Aislynn?''

''She didna tell me her name, my lord. All I ken is that she is the bravest of women. Went right down the well after me bairn when she fell.''

Without another word, Jarrod turned and ran toward the well where they had met Hagar the previous night. He did not imagine there could be two ladies in this small hamlet.

He did not stop until he reached the well. Still hoping and praying that he was wrong, he leaned over the side and called down, ''Aislynn.'' The raw panic in his voice could not be disguised.

The tentative cry of ''Is that you, Jarrod?'' in no way relieved him. Yet in spite of his distress, he was aware that she sounded more nervous than hurt or frightened.

This did nothing to alleviate his fear for her. It swept over him in wave after wave, leaving him weak.

Now was not the time to give in to such feelings. Jarrod knew he must focus on getting Aislynn out of there. He quickly realized that going down after her was not an option. The well was simply too small.

He called out, "Wrap the rope around yourself and I will pull you out."

She shouted back. "There is a little girl, Jarrod. She fell down the well. I have tied her to the end of the rope. You must get her out first. And hurry, for it is too dark down here for me to tell if she may be hurt."

Even as he began to haul the rope up, he was aware of the woman and the smithy arriving.

The woman ran to his side to peer down into the darkness. "My bairn. My Fiona." Her hysterical sobbing erupted anew.

He spoke to the smith without looking at either of them. "Please, keep her calm. The babe will fare better if she can not hear her mother crying."

The sounds of the mother's grief and fear became muffled, and for that Jarrod was grateful. He focused his attention on the task at hand.

Realizing that he might scrape the child against the rough sides of the well if he simply lifted it out by pulling the rope up by hand as he wished to, Jarrod forced himself to use the crank which kept the rope positioned in the center of the hole. And though frustration at the slow pace set his teeth on edge, he did what he had to do.

He was distantly aware of the fact that a small crowd was gathering around him. He paid them no heed as he continued to work at raising the rope as quickly as he could without jarring it. All the while he could think of nothing save getting Aislynn out of that black and forbidding hole.

When the still-crying child emerged, her mother pushed herself away from the smith's wide chest and reached out to take her daughter into her arms. Jarrod could see the pallor of the tiny face, saw the way she shivered violently in her mother's arms. His mind sent him a vision of Aislynn, so small and cold as she waited for the rope to be cast back down to her.

It was all Jarrod could do to force himself to go gently when he turned to separate mother and daughter enough to get the rope free. Despite the quaking of his hands, he forced himself to work patiently at the knot until it was undone.

The moment the woman had her child safe in her arms, once more she turned to Jarrod. "God bless your lady, my lord. She was here when Fiona fell. Fiona canna swim and she couldna tie the rope about herself. The lady said she mun go down after her." She glanced down at her daughter, her eyes filled with love and relief. "I couldna go down mysel, and I couldna bring myself to stop her. I couldna bear it if…"

Jarrod held up a hand. He needed no further explanation, for he understood that the mother would do anything to save her child, who had begun to shake as if with palsy.

The blacksmith took the child from her mother's arms and Jarrod said, "Take them home now. The child must be warmed. I will see to Aislynn."

The smith jerked his head. "Aye, my lord. You must indeed see to your lady."

Jarrod barely nodded to him before swinging back to the well.

Though he was glad the child was safe he felt no

relief. He was beset by the horror of the ordeal that, for Aislynn, had not ended.

Taking the free end of the rope, he tossed it over the side. "Aislynn, can you grasp the rope?"

Her voice echoed from the depths, "Y-yes. I am wrapping it around myself."

"Tell me when you are ready and I will pull you up."

"Aye," she called back.

Minutes seemed to pass as he waited, though Jarrod realized it must have been his own impatience that made it seem so. Nonetheless he found himself calling down, "Are you ready?"

She replied with obvious regret. "I—I am s-sorry. M-my h-hands are c-c-cold."

Guilt at being sharp with her stabbed at his chest. Before he could apologize around the lump in his throat, she called up again, "I—I am...ready."

Forcing himself to have a care when all he wanted was for her to be out of that dark hole, Jarrod began to draw her out. Again, it seemed to take far too long to pull up the rope. Yet just when he felt he might growl aloud with frustration, he saw the top of her head. And then, as he gave one last impatient tug, the rest of her emerged from the hole. The pale blond locks were dark and hung about her in a sodden curtain. Her face, as the child's had been, was far too pale.

His desperate gaze found hers. She gave him a half-hearted smile as she wiped her sodden hair back from her face. She closed her eyes and sighed, her voice coming in a hoarse whisper. "You have my thanks."

Although it was clear to him that Aislynn was trying to display a lack of concern for what had just occurred, the fear from the ordeal of being down in the well had left its mark. There was a haunted shadow in the blue eyes that had darkened them to azure.

Jarrod said not a word. He could not. The ache of protectiveness he felt was far too powerful, too poignant for any words. He reached out and pulled her into his arms, feeling the quivering in her icy form. He held her too tightly for a moment, replying in a husky tone, "It is all right, Aislynn. Don't try to talk. I will care for you."

She closed her eyes, seeming to be willing to allow him this without struggle. Their differences seemed not to exist for this moment.

Jarrod was once again swept by a wave of tender emotion. He was only able to set her away again because he had to. It was not until he actually reached down to remove the rope from around her chest, that Jarrod realized her state of undress. Every shadow was visible to his wayward gaze, which found the dark tips of her breasts.

Shocked by his own thoughts at such an inappropriate moment, Jarrod hurriedly slipped the rope from around her and pulled her back into the circle of his arms.

He could not bear to expose her to such attention as her near nakedness engendered. Even from himself.

He held her against him, still having a care to hold her so that as much of her was covered as possible. Only as he looked about them did he recall that the villagers had gathered to watch. Even in his distraction, he was aware that there were not as many left standing about as there had been. He could only imagine that the others had gone off to find out about the child.

This did not surprise him, for she was one of them. He spoke to no one in particular. "Please, the lady's cloak."

It was Hagar who appeared there to hand it to him. She must have been drawn by the commotion as the other villagers had been. He began to wrap the cloak around Aislynn's shoulders, and the older woman said, "Bring her ta my cottage. The fire will warm her."

She started away, carrying a bundle that must have been the rest of Aislynn's clothing. Jarrod lifted Aislynn up and followed her without hesitation. And as he strode after Hagar, he continued to hold the woman in his arms close against his heart.

Aislynn could not believe what was happening. Jarrod had not reacted as she had expected him to. She knew that he would feel she should not have risked her safety.

Yet he was not angry. He seemed...

Well, she could not allow herself to think that the tenderness she saw in his eyes was real. It was a construct of her own willful mind.

That Jarrod was not angry, had not berated her, was enough. It must not be misconstrued as anything more.

Aislynn was less relieved than one might think to be set down before the fire in Hagar's cozy cottage. Being held against Jarrod's strong chest was more comforting and stirring than she could have imagined, given the circumstances. Despite his heavy garments, she was aware of the firm beat of his heart, of the warmth and reassuring strength of his hard body. She wanted to tighten her arms about Jarrod's neck and keep him close, but she did not. She simply looked up at him, fearing that all her feelings were there in her eyes.

Jarrod's gaze held hers and her heart stood still, for in those dark depths there seemed to be something she'd never seen before, a gentleness that brought a warm flush from deep inside her. It was only as Hagar came forward to drag the damp cloak from her shoulders and drape a thick fur over her that Aislynn was able to turn away, murmuring "Thank you" in a voice that was husky and breathless.

As if Hagar's intrusion had broken some magical spell, which had prevented her from feeling the cold, Aislynn now began to shiver. The older woman turned to Jarrod. "I mun get her out of that wet shift."

To Aislynn's amazement two spots of color appeared over Jarrod's high cheekbones. Softly Aislynn said, "It is fine. You should go back and finish questioning the villagers."

He watched her. "Are you certain? I…"

She nodded. "I will be in good hands."

He nodded with uncharacteristic awkwardness. "I will leave you then."

Aislynn wanted to reach out, to call him back when he moved to the door of the cottage, but she knew that would be mad. Hagar distracted her from this thought, saying, "My Sean has gone fishing. He will not come in upon us."

Aislynn could only nod, as she heard the door close firmly behind Jarrod.

In what, to Aislynn, was an amazingly short time, the older woman had helped her to remove her sodden shift, put on a simple garment of soft white wool, and brought her a bowl of warmed broth. Gratefully, Aislynn sipped at the liquid, which helped to warm her.

Hagar seemed content to let her consume the broth in silence, sitting nearby. Yet as Aislynn did so, she soon began to note that there was an odd tension to the silence.

She looked into the other woman's plain but pleasant face. Odder still, Hagar seemed reluctant to meet her gaze.

Aislynn frowned. "Is something amiss?"

The other woman shook her head quickly—too quickly.

Aislynn grew even more certain that something was indeed wrong. She tried again. "Dear lady, it is clear that you are troubled. If there is something that I have…"

Hagar turned to her instantly, her gaze now round with horror. "Nay, my lady, dinna think it. Ye have done naught but good. And 'tis that which troubles me for I would repay your kindness in turn. Yet…" She bit her lip, her gaze going to a small chest beneath the one shuttered window.

Aislynn did not know what this could mean, but something, some sense of intuition told her to remain silent, as her heart began to pound with unmistakable anticipation. Hagar's uncertain gaze found her again and Aislynn, feeling as if she were being measured in some way, returned it with complete candor.

Hagar continued to watch Aislynn for what felt a very long time. And then finally, suddenly, she took a deep breath and said, "There is something ye mun know, my lady. We have not told ye the truth."

Aislynn held her breath, waiting, though somewhere inside her she knew before the words were said. "Your brother, Christian. He was here in Ashcroft."

She had suspected this, but the words hit her like a blow from a battering ram. For though she was glad, overjoyed to know that Christian had been here, that they might be able to determine where he had gone from here, the fact that they had been lied to brought up more questions than she could sort out.

Why had the villagers lied?

What had brought Christian to this place?

When had he left?

Where had he gone?

What if, in fact, the woman was wrong and it was not Christian she was speaking of at all?

Before Aislynn could say a word, the older woman stood and went to the chest. From it she removed a sheet of parchment. Seeing what was on it, Aislynn knew without doubt that her brother had been here. It was a drawing and done in a manner that was unmistakably her brother's.

Aislynn looked into the other's eyes, her voice no more than a whisper as a horrifying thought came to her. "He is alive?"

Hagar nodded quickly. "Aye, alive and well."

Relief swept through her in a dizzying wave as she reached for the drawing in a shaking hand. Quickly she took in the fact that it was of a woman's profile, a very lovely woman, with large almond-shaped eyes, a regal nose and full lips. She also was aware of the symbol that graced one corner, the same that had been in the sketch of the dead soldier, Jack. Yet she did not take the time to wonder at this now.

She looked up at the other woman who was blurry due to the tears that had sprung up in her eyes. "Thank you. Thank you. You have no idea how grateful I am that you have told me this. But why has he not come home to us, or perhaps he has even now when I am here looking for him?"

Hagar shook her head. "That I dinna ken."

Aislynn frowned. "I do not understand. Also I do not understand why, if you knew so very much, you lied to us when first we arrived. I told you that he was my brother."

Hagar looked into the fire. "I ken it might be best if I began at the beginning. Ye see when first he came to Ashcroft your brother was quite ill, near unto death itself." Aislynn gasped but Hagar instantly reassured her. "He is well now, as I have told you. I pledge my word on that, so worrying is useless."

When Aislynn said no more she went on. "He was found washed up on the beach beneath yon cliffs. He had no bags nor horse, nor any other means to mark his identity, but his fine clothes." She seemed to watch Aislynn closely. "'Twas the healing woman, Rowena, who nursed him back to the land of the living, though none of us thought she could, no matter how skilled she might be. My Sean, he was dead set against her keeping the stranger at her croft, it being some distance along the path into the wood from here.

But she would not be told what she might do, no matter how he railed.''

Aislynn looked down at the drawing. ''Your son loves this woman, does he not?''

Hagar sighed. ''Aye, for as long as there's been thought of any woman in his head. 'Twas why he took the drawing though he'd na right to it.'' Again Hagar paused to watch Aislynn before adding, ''Your brother was na alone when he left some days gone. He took Rowena with him.''

Aislynn stood, unconsciously allowing the drawing to slip to the floor. ''Why would he do that? And none of this explains what he was doing here.''

Hagar raised her gray brows high. '''Twas Rowena he came here for and 'twas he who charged that we were none of us to speak of his having been here. Nor would he say whence they were going.''

Aislynn understood none of this. She bent to pick up the sheet of parchment, her gaze coming to rest on the young woman. Aislynn was struck by the beauty and grace her brother had managed to convey in that simple drawing. He had also captured a feeling of uncommon strength and pride in that regal profile. And again she took in the dragon symbol, feeling troubled by it but not knowing why.

Aislynn looked to the other woman. ''What is going on? I do not understand. It seems the more I learn the less it all makes sense. Christian could not know this woman. He has only been back in England for a few short months. Most of that time has been spent with us, his family, at Bransbury and the rest with Simon and Jarrod, and I know Jarrod knows nothing of this woman.'' She shook her head, then felt her own brows raise in question as she looked to Hagar. "Lest your Rowena might have been in the Holy Land."

The other woman shook her head. "Nay. She had resided in no spot but this since her fourth year."

She moved to put her hand on the older woman's shoulders. "You must tell me everything you—"

At that moment the door opened. Aislynn looked to see none other than Sean standing there, his gaze on the drawing in her hand. "Mother! You didna..."

Hagar stood. "I did. This child saved young Fiona's life this day. I couldna..."

"You couldna tell what we are sworn to keep secret. That's what ye couldna do. Rowena's life may depend upon it." He came toward Aislynn, his hand outstretched. "Give it to me."

Aislynn could hear the misery in his voice, but she could not relinquish the drawing. "It is my brother's and you will not take it."

She turned and ran for the open door, desperate to keep him from taking this bit of Christian away from her. And as she ran, she could think of nothing save finding Jarrod. Only with him would she, and her brother's drawing, be safe.

# *Chapter Eleven*

Aislynn shivered as she noted that a light rain was falling. Quickly she shoved Christian's drawing into the long white sleeve of her garment, then raced toward the village. The water that had gathered in puddles soaked the bottom of the light wool, not to mention her bare feet, further robbing her body of heat.

And all the while her heart was pounding with alarm and relief at getting away from Sean before he could take the drawing. She also felt a growing glow of happiness. Despite her confusion about how Christian could know this Rowena, she now knew he had been in Ashcroft. He had been ill as her father feared, but was now recovered.

She must tell Jarrod so they could be on their way to finding Christian again.

The anticipation of telling Jarrod buoyed her as she ran on. It was not until she had passed the smith's shop, that she saw him walking toward her on the road.

His gaze found her at the same moment. His expression of surprise soon changed to concern as he saw her sodden state. "Aislynn, what the devil are you thinking? You should not have come out dressed like this, especially after your recent dunking."

She rushed to meet him, her eyes catching and holding his as she anticipated his reaction to her news. "Jarrod, I can not talk about that now. I had to come to you. Sean was threatening to take this from me." She removed the rolled-up sheet of parchment from her sleeve, seeing Jarrod's eyes grow wide with amazement as she did so.

"Christian."

She laughed, tucking it back into her sleeve. "Aye. He was here. As you suspected, they were lying to us. Hagar told me all. Then her son appeared and..."

He frowned. "You say he tried to take the drawing from you. I will—"

She stopped him with a hand on his chest. "Nay, put all thoughts of him aside. There is a girl involved, a Rowena, and it seems Sean is in love with her."

"A girl! Aislynn, what are you speaking of?"

"The drawing is of her, but we must get in out of the rain before I show it to you more closely. Her cottage is in the wood. We may find our answers there."

He reached out to take her shoulders in a tight hold. "How do you know this?"

"As I said, Hagar told me. Sean came in and stopped her." She met his gaze with certainty. "He will allow her to tell no more, for he has some fear that doing so will endanger this woman. But I think Hagar has told me all she knows."

"But if they might know more..."

She shook her head. "Any further information

would need be coerced from them and I would not wish to cause that dear lady any more troubles with her son. And he is only doing what he feels is right, Jarrod.''

He grimaced. ''Very well then. We will leave them be.''

She nodded, feeling unaccountably pleased that Jarrod would follow her wishes in this. At the same time she shivered as a cool breeze pressed the woolen gown against her back and a large drop of rain fell on her cheek.

Now Jarrod's brow creased in a frown that was as much from worry as anger as he said, ''What am I thinking? You should not be standing here in the cold.''

She began, ''I am not so very...''

Then before she knew what was happening, she had been scooped up into Jarrod Maxwell's arms for the second time in one day. So surprised was she that for a moment Aislynn could not utter a sound.

Without a word, Jarrod started back in the direction of Hagar's cottage.

Finally, trying not to think of the warmth and hardness of his chest against her, she said, ''Please, you need not do this. I can walk.''

He made no reply but to keep on walking.

She said, ''What if we are no longer welcome at Hagar's home?''

This time he replied, ''Then we will find another place to get you warm, but we must get our belongings.''

Aislynn felt a thrill of something she could not name, and all from realizing that with Jarrod to protect her, no one would ever take anything from her. If only…

But there was no "if only." It would be much easier to resign herself to things as they were if he were not carrying her against the hard warmth of his body. Unfortunately, try though she might, Aislynn could not help noting the strength of him, the damp male scent of his nape.

Earlier in the day she had been distracted by not only the painful memories of being down the well, but also her relief at being free. Now her wayward mind was left with little to keep it from wandering to things it should not.

She was beset by the memories of what those strong hands had felt like on her body, the most intimate parts of her. She knew the taste of those lips, which were now only inches from her own gaze. And though they were set with determination rather than soft with desire as her memory so raptly recalled, they were no less distracting when she thought of their touch on her heated flesh.

He took her not to the cottage, but to the animal shelter where they had slept. Aislynn did not question why.

He set her down at the foot of the ladder and she hurried up it, Jarrod coming close behind her. When he reached the top, she looked into his face for the first time since he had picked her up in his arms. His expression was dark, showing no sign of the tenderness she had seen before. He spoke abruptly. "We must get you dry."

Stung, Aislynn looked away while he retrieved his cloak from where she had folded in and placed it upon his bed of hay. *How long ago that now seemed.* And when he turned back to her, his face appeared stern and hard.

Aislynn wrapped her arms around herself, feeling the cold air on her legs, which she suddenly realized were bared nearly to the knee. Blushing, she awkwardly tugged at the woolen garment in an effort to cover them.

His voice was tight as a strung bow as he said, "You will need to remove it."

Aislynn, far more chilled by his sudden cold demeanor, was driven beyond reason to cry, "What have I done now that you would be so cool?"

His gaze narrowed, giving nothing away.

She went on. "You do not have to be so cruel. I have asked nothing of you, Jarrod."

He became very still and his voice was barely audible. "I am not being cruel. I..."

Aislynn waited in silence for him to continue, praying that he might help her to understand how he did feel. And finally when she could bear it no more, she blurted, "I know of the woman, the one in the Holy Land, the one whom you loved, still love. The woman whose ribbon you carry. Sadona told me all she knew."

Jarrod grabbed her by the shoulders. "How dare you discuss me behind my back?"

Aislynn could feel her eyes going wide as she took in the sudden and ragged depth of his anger. "I did not... She only thought to help me understand."

He laughed bitterly, interrupting her. "You understand nothing. My feelings for the woman you spoke of are not at all what you imagine." He looked away, the muscles working in his lean jaw as he turned back to her and said, "The woman Sadona told you of was my mother."

"Your mother? But Sadona thought…she said the woman was a…"

Again a bitter laugh escaped him. "And she was. Yet I would have cared naught for that if she had wanted me. Yet she did not. When I told her who I was, she sent me away, informed me that I was not to return. I should not have expected more from a woman who would give her own child away, believing she would never see him again."

Aislynn was not blind to the raw pain in him, a pain that made her heart soften in the face of his anger. "I…forgive me. Sadona did not know."

He held her gaze. "No one has ever known. Not even Christian or Simon. And I have no notion of why I would say so much to you, other than that you seem determined to worm your way into places where no one else has dared to tread."

"I will never speak of it again." She turned away, blinking back regret and sorrow.

Jarrod stood, tossing the cloak onto the hay beside her. "I will leave you alone to dress." He swung around to go.

Her mind reeling from not only his hostility toward her but all he had revealed, she reached down to grasp her sodden skirts in her hands, finding the task too much for her trembling arms. Determinedly she tugged again, groaning in frustration as her limbs refused to work the way they should.

Then, before she even knew what was happening,

Jarrod knelt before her, pushing her hands away. "Let me."

The brusqueness of his voice only served to further hurt her. Feeling her throat close up, her eyes stinging with tears, Aislynn whispered, "Please, please, I can not bear it. I meant you no ill and beg you to hurt me no more this day."

With a groan of anguish and relinquishment Jarrod pulled her into his arms. He held her close against him, whispering, "Forgive me, Aislynn. I am a knave, a blackguard. I do not mean to be cruel. It is my own wanting that makes me fight you so."

Those wet blue eyes turned up to his and time froze for one inexplicable moment as he read the need in them. And then his mouth found hers, with a certainty that this moment could not have been prevented no matter how hard he tried.

So delicate in his arms she was, so sweetly yielding. He reached out a seeking hand and came into contact with the curve of a hip.

His loins tightened as he realized that Aislynn had managed to remove her garment this far, baring her velvet skin to his touch. Though his manhood stirred, Jarrod held himself in check, knowing his desire was to go slowly, to enjoy every lovely inch of that form which had haunted his every moment since the night they'd nearly come together at the inn.

His lips left hers to brush against cheeks that were damp with tears. Silently he kissed them away, feeling the tightness of regret in his chest. Never would he hurt her. Far from it, for she awakened a tenderness in him that he had never even suspected he could feel, as well as passion. A passion he could no longer deny.

He felt her shiver against him and realized that she was still wearing wet clothes. More than happy to rid her of them, Jarrod gripped the end of the wool and pulled it upward, gently but firmly.

Aislynn made no demure, lifting her arms to aid him as he passed it over her head. Then quickly she pressed herself back against him, whether it be eagerness or shyness, Jarrod did not know, but he held her tightly, kissing those soft lips once more.

Jarrod moved his hands down to cup her small but womanly bottom in his palms. He felt that stirring again.

Aislynn gave a slight start as she felt the heat of his hands on her, feeling a pooling warmth in her lower belly. She knew not why he had changed so suddenly from anger to passion, but she was powerless to care, captured by her own inexplicable and inescapable desire for this man, who was mysterious and open at one and the same time. Mysterious when it came to himself and his past, open when it concerned kindness and generosity and faithfulness.

Jarrod continued to press his mouth gently to hers and, in a moment, felt a stab of satisfaction as her small hand came up to reach beneath his tunic and curl in the dark patch of hair on his chest. Feeling a thrill of pleasure at the touch, he continued to ply her mouth with his own, nipping and sucking at hers, drawing a response she seemed eager to give.

Jarrod groaned deep in his throat, unable to withhold the sound of his pleasure, hearing an answering moan from her. Even more ardently now, his mouth moved from hers to trail over her soft cheeks and then down the delicate line of her throat.

He leaned away from her to pull off his tunic.

When he moved back to her, Aislynn contacted smooth bare flesh over hard muscle. She sighed at the immediate quickening of her pulse. She tilted her head back as his lips left hers to press hot kisses to her face and neck.

Her heart thudded in her breast as the warm sensations that turned liquid found their way even lower in her belly. Aislynn had never felt so...so very... Her hips arched as if her body understood far more of what was happening than did she. Her hands, which moved with utter abandon over his hot, smooth chest, seemed to have developed a will all their own.

Jarrod felt himself harden even more at her touch, at her nearness. There was something about this woman, her soft warm woman scent, the velvet of her skin that caused his pulse to pound with a dizzying beat. With unexpectedly trembling arms, he laid her back into the softness of the hay. In the gentle light that trickled through the rough board walls, she was lovelier than anything he could have imagined. She was small and delicate yet so perfectly formed, all woman from the top of her white-blond curtain of hair to the tips of her tiny little toes. The curves in between were full and all female. He dipped his head to her breast and she reared up beneath him, holding him to her tightly.

Never before had being with a woman been such a banquet of taste, touch and feeling.

Aislynn's mind and body whirled with ripple after ripple of inexplicably delightful sensation. It was as if Jarrod had awakened some slumbering force inside her, a fiercely passionate creature that cared for nothing but her pleasure.

She held him to her, instinctively laying claim to the feel of his flesh, his touch, to him. Even the ragged sound of his hot breath against her ear was strangely thrilling.

Aislynn slipped one hand to his chest and over that tantalizing expanse of firm flesh, across a corded neck. She tangled her fingers in thick, coarse hair. A low sensuous moan was her reward. The sound made the fine hairs on her body stand to attention, leaving a delicious tingling along her flesh.

"Jarrod, Jarrod," she moaned with naked wanting.

He heard her need and felt an answering desire inside himself. Slowly he leaned up on his elbow, his hands unexpectedly unsteady as he gently slipped his other hand down her belly, for a moment enjoying the rousing quivering of that flat plane beneath his hand, before dipping lower. His fingers found her and he swallowed hard at finding her so damp, so eager for him. A fierce, driving need such as he had never experienced coursed through him. "Aislynn," he whispered.

His mouth came back to her and she leaned up, meeting him without restraint, her mouth hot and wet with longing. When he eased her back into the hay and placed his hand on her thigh, Aislynn opened to him without hesitation and his manhood throbbed in response.

Jarrod closed his eyes, breathing deeply as he tried to get hold of himself. But when she gasped his name once more, Jarrod knew he could wait no more.

Without breaking the contact of their mouths, he moved over her, sliding between her silken thighs, and found her. As he hesitated at the barrier of her maidenhood, she rose up beneath him and it was breached.

She gasped, as he did, his mouth leaving hers as he held himself immobile by gathering shreds of self-denial that he had not known he possessed. Hoarsely he whispered, ''Pray, forgive me, I did not mean to cause you pain.''

Aislynn could not deny that it did hurt, yet the ache that had been growing in her from the first time he'd kissed her was far more compelling a master than any mere physical pain could ever be.

She whimpered in frustration, her body tightening on him convulsively. ''Please go on.''

For a brief instant Jarrod Maxwell became very still, and then, ever so slowly, he began to move inside her and Aislynn sighed with relief. But that relief was short-lived, for as he moved, she seemed to draw the same instinctual rhythm from her own body and the ache began to grow more pronounced.

Her breathing quickened and she found her hands reaching out to hold his lean hips of their own accord. She knew nothing beyond the fact that the feelings inside her seemed to be building beyond what she could bear, what anyone could bear. But the feelings were oh so wonderful, so pleasurable, that neither could she bear for them to stop. She felt as if she was climbing toward something she had never known, some inescapable summit and that only Jarrod could guide her.

And when she did not believe there could be any

more ecstasy in all of creation, she arched as a burst of pleasure rolled over her. It was so intense the world disappeared and she cried out in inarticulate joy.

Jarrod was aware of her release and the sheer intensity of it, in spite of his own building need. He held her, reveling in her abandon, when she cried out and arched beneath him.

Only then did Jarrod give in to his own passion, which, now that he had given it free rein, quickly grew to a fierce white point of unutterable pleasure. "Aislynn!" Her name escaped him without conscious thought.

When he stiffened and arched against her, Aislynn felt her own body press against him. She knew that he had gone to that same peak of joy where she had just been, and that she had been the one to take him there. She choked back a sob of happiness. It was awing, that this strong, deeply private man had been moved beyond his accustomed control of himself because of her—Aislynn.

Slowly he rolled away from her to lie on his back in the sweet hay.

Aislynn took a long, deep breath. Only as the feelings ebbed did she begin to feel a sense of self-consciousness and uncertainty.

And when she turned to her side in the hay, it was clear that Jarrod felt the same. He wiped a trembling hand over his face. "Dear God, what have we done?"

Gingerly she shook her head as she pulled the cape up over her and sat up. "I do not know. I…"

He halted her with a raised hand. "There is no need to try to explain. We have allowed the fear and worry we have felt for Christian and emotion over my foolishly telling you about my mother to carry us away. And there is really no significance to the tale of my mother. I have put it behind me years ago.''

Aislynn did not know what to say. Clearly this was not true or he would not have kept the truth to himself for all these years. Not even telling Christian and Simon.

Oblivious to her thoughts, he went on. ''You are not to blame. It is I who should have done something to prevent this. I have taken that which was not mine to take.''

She turned to look at him. ''I am not a helpless child, Jarrod. I thought we had settled that. I am as responsible for this unfortunate episode as anyone.''

He grimaced. ''So be it then. What should we do about this *unfortunate episode?*''

Too many times Jarrod had made it clear that he had no desire to be tied. Now she understood that he had been so hurt by the events in his life, by his mother's rejection, that he had no desire to love. She shrugged. ''What is there to be done?''

He looked away, his lean jaw flexing. ''We could be married.''

Her eyes grew round with horror. Not at the notion of marrying him but of how strong a reaction of yearning there arose inside her. To cover her own unwanted feelings, she spoke quickly, sharply, ''Nay. I have given my promise to marry Gwyn. I would take on my place as lady to his keep. I would also fulfill my father's faith in me.'' Though he had never said so directly, she knew her marriage was important to the peace of Bransbury.

His face was a stiff mask. ''I see.'' He gestured to

the flattened spot between them. "And what of this? Would you simply attempt to hide it from him? If he has the least experience of women he will know."

She raised her chin. "Do you imagine that I would attempt such a dishonorable act?" Her voice quieted. "I will tell him, and it will be his choice." She faced him directly. "But have no concern. I would not trouble you even if he were to refute me because of it."

He bowed. "So be it. You shall have matters to your liking." He reached out for his garments and pulled them on without paying her the slightest heed.

Aislynn, keeping her gaze carefully averted, did not know what to say.

At last he stood, the sketch Christian had made in his hand, and she realized it must have fallen loose in the hay when he removed her garment. He quirked a black brow. "I trust you will understand if I do not sleep here with you. I will take the drawing with me so that I may study it."

She looked up at him. "But where…"

"Let that not concern you. I will pay Hagar for another night's lodging and fetch you at daybreak."

Seeing the tightness of his body, Aislynn knew there was no point arguing. And how could she do so after what had just happened? Even now, when she knew that what they had done was terribly wrong, the sensuous memory lingered inside her body and mind.

Jarrod found no more than a fitful rest.

He waited until long after he had gone into the cottage to fetch Aislynn's clothing, as well as to pay Hagar for the second night's lodging, to reenter the animal shelter and settle himself in the corner against the outside wall. Aislynn had been right in that Sean had not left Hagar alone with him. Jarrod, feeling some sympathy for the poor woman, had asked no questions, but he had felt compelled to give his thanks for what she had told Aislynn.

She had accepted graciously in spite of her son's glowering looks and told him that she could not but return Aislynn's goodness in kind. She also insisted on giving him a small bundle containing bread and cheese upon which they might break their fast. Gratefully, Jarrod accepted.

He'd used extreme care in being quiet as he entered the shed. When he heard no sounds from above, he felt relatively certain that Aislynn was asleep and climbed the ladder to leave her gown and cape in the hay at the top of the ladder.

He berated himself for the images that came into his mind, her gaze dark with passion, her body soft and yielding against his. God help him, if only he could put it from his mind, for he felt nothing but a fool.

He had done something with her that he had never done before—going far beyond the unbelievable fact that he had told her about his mother, which he could hardly credit as being real. He had asked her to become his wife. And despite the fact that she had given herself to him with an abandon that had shocked and amazed him, she had said no.

What he could have been thinking of, Jarrod had no idea. He did not love her, had only thought to do the right thing, to act with honor. And perhaps to have the right to bed that sweet and willing body again.

Even now, his body tightened at the memory of the

passion they had shared. For not only had her responses been remarkable, but his own as well. Never
had he felt so alive, so lost in his own feelings as he
had with Aislynn.

It was nothing short of self-destruction to continue
thinking this way. She had made herself quite clear.
She would marry her Gwyn, her good and decent
man. She would be the lady of a noble keep as she
had been reared.

Jarrod would do better to plan their journey from
here. Now that he knew that Christian was well, he
could return Aislynn to her father with all possible
haste. Though he took out the drawing and studied it
with as much care as his distracted mind would allow,
he could see nothing that helped him to know whence
his friend might have gone. Though the image of the
dragon did give him pause, he could not quite fathom
why, and eventually gave up trying.

A trickle of light that filtered through the rough-
hewn walls woke him from that restless slumber and
he went to the end of the ladder, calling up, "It is
sunrise. We must be on our way."

Her reply was curt. "I come."

Good, he told himself. There was no point in their
making pretense that neither felt. Aislynn was no
more communicative when she joined him outside.
And without another word exchanged between them,
they started down the mucky road.

The path along the cliff face was no less treacherous than before and demanded their full attention.
Even after they'd traversed the worst of it, the tense
and unbreakable silence remained.

When finally they reached the camp that Ulrick had

made for himself and the horses, Jarrod could only imagine how exhausted Aislynn must be. Yet he could tell from the set of her slight shoulders and the determined tilt of her head that she would never admit it—at least not to him.

It was his preoccupation with her that made Jarrod slow to recognize the anxiety that dampened the knight's welcome as he came forward to meet them.

It was Aislynn who said, "What is it, Sir Ulrick? What has happened?"

"I believe someone was here at this camp, last eve. Someone who did not mean good."

Jarrod looked at the older man. "Why would you think such a thing?"

Ulrick shrugged. "After you had gone on with the lady Aislynn, I came back this way and made camp as we had discussed." Jarrod nodded as he went on, "The first night went well. But last night, after dark fell, the horses became restless, unaccountably so. I called out, thinking it might be some other traveler drawn by the light of my fire. I will admit that I would not have been averse to a bit of company in this desolate place." Ulrick scowled. "There was no reply and I thought that it must have been some animal that had startled them. But when I was feeding them this morning I saw footprints in the sand."

"Footprints?"

"Aye, directly behind the horses, where someone had used their bodies to hide his presence."

"How do you know it was a man?"

The knight grimaced, raising his own large boot. "No woman I have ever known has had feet nearly the size of my own, Sir Jarrod."

Jarrod did not question this assessment further. There was likely no woman in England with feet of such a size.

"And it was not someone who simply stumbled upon me, then was too shy to come forward." He made a sweeping gesture to indicate the high cliffs on one side and the churning sea on the other. "There is no place close by for them to have come from."

This also was true.

He recalled Aislynn's certainty that she had seen someone lurking about their camp the night after they'd left Clumney. She could have seen someone and that someone might still be interested in their movements. And there was only one man he could think of. "Sir Fredrick."

Aislynn was nodding as Sir Ulrick said, "I was thinking along the same path."

Jarrod turned to Aislynn with open apology and regret. "You asked me to notify the law of his aggression and I would not heed you. I have very likely put you both in grave danger by not listening. If this madman has gone to such lengths to follow us, he is undoubtedly determined to do harm." He did not wish to worry Aislynn by telling her this, but neither could he refrain from doing so. Surely, he reasoned, she would have a more than usual care with her person if she knew there could be danger in not doing so.

Aislynn looked at him with surprise. And in spite of the fact that she wanted to go on resenting and hating Jarrod Maxwell until the day she died, she was unaccountably drawn to him by his willingness to admit his mistake so openly, so regretfully.

But she forced herself to concentrate on the business at hand. "I thank you for your apology, but there is no point in belaboring what can not be changed. We must determine what we will do now."

Jarrod bowed and nodded. "We must move on as soon as we can be ready to ride. This position would be difficult to defend. And we must now have a care as we ride, as well as setting up watch when camp is made for the night."

Ulrick nodded. "Aye. I will ready the horses immediately." He hurried to do so.

Jarrod then turned to Aislynn. "You can help us to protect you, Aislynn, by keeping your guard and informing me of anything that might seem the least unusual."

For reasons she could not, or would not, even begin to examine, this show of faith in her judgment warmed Aislynn to the core. Aislynn replied, "I will," and turned away, unwilling to let him look into her eyes, see the truth of how she was feeling.

He spoke gently. "I am very sorry if this has frightened you, Aislynn. I thought to arm you against harm by telling you."

She looked up at him quickly, grateful for the fact that he had misread her reaction. "I am not frightened. I am pleased that you trust me enough to believe that I might be of help."

He shook his head, a rueful smile touching his mobile lips despite the gravity of the situation and all the other unpleasantness that had passed between them. "I should have known that you would not be frightened. You have proved yourself more than brave and willing to face difficulty head-on in the past days. As well as having your observations confirmed.''

Their gazes locked—held for what seemed an eternity. What had passed between them in Ashcroft, the things they had said and done, the things she had felt, suddenly seemed more real than anything else in her life.

Into the silence came the sound of Ulrick's voice. "The horses are ready.''

Jarrod stepped back, the spell between them broken, replaced by cool civility. "We must be on our way. It would be best if we moved into less treacherous terrain by nightfall.''

Aislynn cast her gaze out over the sea, calling herself ten times a fool for letting herself react to Jarrod yet again. She held her head high. "Aye, I am ready.''

With that, she moved off to allow Ulrick, who now stood watching them, to help her into the saddle.

## *Chapter Twelve*

They set out immediately. Jarrod took the lead, keeping a constant eye peeled for any sign of their unwanted pursuer.

The anxiety he felt over this was preferable to the prodding knowledge that Aislynn could, with a soft look, destroy the wall of reserve inside him. When she looked at him the way she had when he'd told her he had faith in her abilities, he wanted...

Damn her to hell!

He wanted nothing from her. God praise the day he could deliver her to her family and be free once more.

But as he quickened their pace, he was beset by a certainty that he might never feel free again. With that unhappy thought tugging at his mind, Jarrod set a pace that would see them far from this place by night-fall.

They rode for hours, leaving the cliffs of Scotland behind, passing into England without stopping, and on. Only when they came to a spot where the road curved through a dense wood did Jarrod slow their pace.

He was aware of Aislynn, who rode behind him and in front of Sir Ulrick. She had offered not one word of complaint as they traveled. Nor of anything else.

Looking about them, Jarrod saw that the shadows of the trees had become long on the leaf-covered ground. Yet he did not like the feel of this place, the forest, which was a mix of both deciduous and evergreen trees. These trees would offer too much cover to those seeking harm.

He did not wish to contemplate the notion that his discomfort with this wood might be caused by the fact that he had sometimes ventured this far afield as a lad. That it had been a relief to be away from the home where he had felt none of the welcome of a son nor the anonymity of being a stranger.

As these thoughts passed through his mind, Jarrod heard a soft but distinctive whistling sound that was accompanied by a rush of wind as something sailed past his head by inches. A soft cry came from behind him at almost the same moment.

He swung around, watching with horror as Aislynn slumped forward on her mare's neck.

Crying out, "No!" Jarrod leaped from his stallion, but he could not arrive in time to catch her before she fell to the ground with a sickening thud.

His heart stopped, then started again with fearful intensity as he saw the blood that stained the right shoulder of the pale velvet of her gown.

Dear God, his mind whirled. Someone had shot Aislynn.

Desperately he lifted her head. Seeing the way it fell back, he realized she was unconscious. Torn between concern for her and the knowledge that their assailant could still be there, he searched for the source of the attack, seeing nothing but those damned trees.

Concern for her brought his attention back to Aislynn's face, which was deathly pale. He lifted her in his arms, pressing his cheek to her breast. She was breathing. Relief rushed through him in dizzying waves.

She was alive. Thank God. Alive.

But she was bleeding, and badly, for the stain was spreading quickly.

He must…

Ulrick's voice intruded on his chaotic thoughts. "What has happened to the lady Aislynn? I was watching to be certain that we were not followed and looked around only in time to see her fall."

Jarrod swung around to see his own dread mirrored in the older man's eyes. "She is hurt but alive. I believe it was an arrow, for it narrowly missed me."

Ulrick turned desperate eyes on the surrounding forest. "But how? Who?"

Jarrod shook his head, trying to think past the pain that held his chest in a tight grip. "I know not, but we can assume it was the same man who has shown so much interest in our camp. I want nothing more than to find the bastard and see him dead by my own hand, but we must get this bleeding stopped or…"

Jarrod could not finish. He could not allow himself to even contemplate what might occur if he did not stop the bleeding. He feared she had a head injury, as well, which his questing fingers soon confirmed by the bump on the back of her head. It was bad, but the bleeding wound must take precedence.

As he set to ripping her gown out of the way, the better to see the wound, a terrible thought intruded upon his mind. The arrow had barely missed him. He was suddenly and utterly certain that the arrow had not been meant for Aislynn but for him.

It had missed him by no more than the span of a hand.

Guilt crowded into a heart already overrun by tumultuous emotion. Desperately Jarrod told himself this would not help him now. He must clear his mind, set himself to getting the bleeding stopped.

To indulge his own feelings now would be to risk the life that was quickly seeping between his hands.

He spoke to the other man without looking at him as he continued to bare Aislynn's shoulder. "Ulrick, you must make certain there is no further danger. For all we know whoever did this might be lurking out there, waiting for a chance to get off another good shot."

The knight drew his sword and moved off without hesitation. "Pray that I find him, sir. He will die with the taste of my blade in his belly."

Jarrod kept his attention on Aislynn. Once her shoulder was uncovered, he felt his heart twist again. It was so very fragile, the arrow wound an ugly intrusion into the soft flesh, but it was difficult to see how badly hurt she was with the blood flowing so freely.

As best he could, Jarrod examined the area. In battle he had seen many men wounded by arrow shot. He noted that it did not appear to have damaged the bones, for her shoulder moved freely. It seemed only to have torn the muscle. Awful as this was, it was far better than broken bones. He was aware of occasions when wounds such as that never healed properly, the arm being useless forever after.

He realized that he was only fixing on these details because he could not bear to think of what would happen, how he would feel, if Aislynn was to…

Dear heaven, could anything hurt as much as the thought of losing her? Jarrod did not think so, could not allow himself to wonder why. He knew only that his heart felt as if it had been struck by that arrow. And if her heart ceased to beat, he knew his would halt at that same moment.

He lifted her head, looking down into her face, the lids heavy on her closed eyes. Gently he whispered, "Aislynn. Aislynn."

Her lids fluttered though they did not open, but Jarrod knew that somehow she had heard him. "Stay with me, Aislynn."

Again her lids fluttered.

Jarrod wiped the cold sweat that had gathered on his brow. He wanted more than anything to pull her close against him and protect her with his body, to give in to his own feelings of grief and anxiety.

Yet he could not do that. He had to think clearly, to make every moment count.

He raised her gown and tore a long wide strip from the bottom of her shift. This fabric he knew was soft and far cleaner than any of his own garments. It would make the best covering for the wound.

Deftly, forcing himself to remember that this was for her own good, he wrapped up the wound. The fact that it was somewhat painful to her was evidenced by the grim lines that came to her brow as he worked.

As he worked to bind it tightly, Jarrod could not help knowing that he needed somewhere to take her, somewhere that she could get better attention than he could afford her here in the open wood.

And suddenly he knew where it must be. In spite of the fact that he had no notion of how he might be welcomed there, or even if they would turn him away, Jarrod had to take her to Kewstoke. Kewstoke, the place where he had grown up, but never felt a part of as he had at Dragonwick. God rot Kelsey and his minion.

It was her only hope.

With the decision made, Jarrod wanted to mount his stallion and ride without delay. Yet he realized he must tell Sir Ulrick of his plans.

Trying to still the impatience that was born of his anxiety, Jarrod called out, "Ulrick."

There was no reply but what could only have been moments later, the knight rushed out of the cover of the trees toward them. "I saw him, Sir Jarrod, riding hard away from here."

Jarrod stared up at him. "You saw him?"

"Aye, and though he was riding fast, I believe it was Sir Fredrick as we suspected. The man has a distinctive gray cloak."

Jarrod felt a renewed rush of hatred. Here then was another reason for him to hate Kelsey with all his being. The man seemed determined to kill those he loved most.

As soon as the thought entered his mind, Jarrod knew it was true. He did love Aislynn. The realization came in wave after enveloping wave of tenderness and need so strong they left him weak. When it had occurred he had no idea, but his heart could not recall a time when she had not filled it.

Just what this might mean to him he did not know except to be aware of the fact that when he was in a position to actually think about it, it would very likely bring him great pain. But not now, not when Aislynn's life was slipping away with each passing moment.

Forcing himself to do what he must in spite of his revelation, Jarrod stood with Aislynn in his arms and held her out to the older man. "I am taking her to a place called Kewstoke not more than two hours' ride from here. You must go on to Bransbury and tell her father what has occurred."

Ulrick hesitated, his brow troubled as Jarrod mounted his stallion and brought him near. Jarrod held out his arms and the knight shook his head as he said, "I do not know if I should leave her."

Jarrod looked him directly in the eyes. "I would give up my life for her. And her father must be told. It is the least we must do for him in the event…"

The other man nodded and settled Aislynn into Jarrod's arms. "I will see to it. And to the mare."

Jarrod nodded, knowing that there was no time to linger. He turned his mount toward Kewstoke, making no reply as the knight called out, "Godspeed."

He was lost in his concern for Aislynn, his uncertainty as to what he would find when he arrived at

the place he had once called home. Welcome or rejection.

Jarrod pulled on the reins, drawing his mount to an
abrupt halt directly beneath the tower, which over-
looked the gate. He called out, "Open the gate!"

The guard inside peered down at him in the darkness. "And whom should I say bids entry?"

Jarrod grimaced. "You may tell your master that
it is Jarrod Maxwell."

The man leaned out further from the window, his
voice filled with obvious shock and disbelief. "Jarrod
Maxwell. Brother to the Baron?"

"The very same," Jarrod shouted back. "Now
hurry for I have grave need…someone has been
hurt."

As the man disappeared back inside, Jarrod pulled
Aislynn closer into the circle of his arms. The darkness did not completely disguise the fact that the stain
of blood on her gown had spread since beginning
their journey.

Dear God, he prayed, let them admit him and let
them hurry.

It seemed an eternity later, but was likely no more
than a handful of minutes, that another man looked
out from the window. Although the voice had deepened and changed Jarrod knew that this was his
brother as he said, "Jarrod?"

"Aye, Eustace, it is I, Jarrod."

Immediately Eustace called out sharply, "Open the
gate. It is indeed my brother."

Thinking of little save his relief that he would soon
have Aislynn where her wound could be properly

seen to, Jarrod was also aware of a feeling of surprise that he had been so readily granted entry. The last time he had seen Eustace, his brother's face had been filled with triumph and resentment.

That had been the day Jarrod had left Kewstoke. He had looked up to see Eustace standing on these very battlements staring down at him as he rode away to start his new life with his then unknown foster father at Dragonwick. Jarrod recalled the regret that had torn at his own breast, the feeling of leaving all that he knew behind, even as he hoped that what lay ahead would be better.

And it had been. His father had, if nothing else, chosen a man who was worthy of all the honor and love that Jarrod had longed to give.

Jarrod shook his head to clear it. He did not wish to think on any of this now. Aislynn was hurt and nothing else mattered in the face of that calamity.

Not even his own confused feelings at facing his brother after all this time. Not even when he had no notion of how he would be accepted here. The fact that he had been granted entry to the keep could be a sign, yet of what?

He rode through the gate and into the courtyard, aware of the castle folk who had gathered there in the light of several torches, along with his brother, who stood on wide low steps to the hall.

The young lord of Kewstoke looked at him from eye level as he came to a halt at the bottom of those steps. He spoke without inflection. "Jarrod, I—"

Jarrod interrupted him, albeit as politely as he could, even as he slipped to the ground with Aislynn in his arms. "Forgive me, Eustace. I would speak with you on any matter of your choosing if only you will first help me to see to the lady Aislynn. She has been injured.''

Instantly Eustace motioned to one of the men standing there. ''Take her.''

Jarrod pulled her close against him. ''Nay, I will carry her.'' Only then did his brother seem to fully take in the desperation in Jarrod's face and tone. Eustace beckoned Jarrod forward. ''Follow me.''

Jarrod did so, looking down at Aislynn's face, so pale and still in the light of the torches that it made his chest tighten painfully. He had ridden fast and hard, thinking of nothing save the fact that he must reach help as quickly as possible.

And now that he was here, he could only hope that all would be well.

Eustace led him directly through the hall, calling out, ''Aida, bring mendicants and bandages to the west chamber.'' They did not pause to see if the summons had been heard, but moved up the narrow stairs that led to the upper rooms.

They entered a chamber that held a wide bed with heavy velvet hangings. Eustace pulled them back before turning to Jarrod, ''Put her on the bed. Aida will be here in a moment.''

As Jarrod laid Aislynn down, she stirred, moaning softly, and Jarrod felt his heart twist. With a gentle hand he reached out to smooth the hair back from her brow, which felt too cool beneath his trembling fingers.

''What happened?''

Jarrod turned back to his brother. ''She was shot

with an arrow." He went on with unmasked regret. "It was meant for me."

Eustace watched Jarrod closely, but before he could make a reply a brusque female voice intruded, "What is amiss here, my lord?"

Eustace swung around to face the round squat figure of a woman Jarrod did not remember from his time here. He motioned to Jarrod. "Aida, this is my brother, Lord Jarrod. His lady has been shot and appears to be bleeding quite profusely. She needs your help."

The woman trotted forward, not even remarking on the fact that Eustace had just told her that Jarrod was his brother. She took one look at Aislynn's blood-soaked shoulder and said, "Out with the both of you. And send May up to me with some clean water." She placed her bundles on the table near the bed and moved to Aislynn's side, the two men seeming to have been forgotten.

Jarrod wavered as his brother went to the door without hesitation. Eustace turned back to him with an expression of sympathy that surprised him, and he said, "Come, Jarrod, I know you are worried, but there are no better hands for healing than Aida's."

The woman looked to Jarrod, her gaze also sympathetic but undaunted. "You'd best be going. I can better concentrate on the girl without you to distract me."

Realizing that there was nothing he could say to refute this, Jarrod reluctantly followed his brother from the chamber.

For Jarrod the next hours passed in a haze of anxiety as he waited in the Great Hall for word of Aislynn's condition. Eustace stayed with him for a time, saying nothing when Jarrod told him that he would be happy to explain all when he knew that Aislynn would be well, but that he could not make conversation until then. He accepted this, seeming content enough with the silence as he ordered warmed wine for both of them.

Although in a state of anxiety, Jarrod could not help noting that his brother seemed somewhat older than his years. His slight shoulders were stooped and there was a pale cast to his pleasingly intellectual features, the wheat-blond hair receding from his high brow. And when he rose, stating in a strained voice that he must seek his bed, he seemed to move with slow and deliberate care.

Jarrod made no comment on his observations, feeling it would be churlish to do so, even if he were not so very deeply concerned with Aislynn's well-being.

It was not until much later that Aida finally came to Jarrod. She came up short when he stood at her approach and said, "Is she...?"

She nodded. "Aye, she will be well, I think. She has a bump on her head but came around enough to know that she does not seem rattled in the mind. Methinks 'twas loss of blood that kept her unconscious for so long a time. The shoulder wound had to be sewn closed, but with a few days of rest she will come right."

He closed his eyes as relief washed over him in a weakening flood. "Thank God." He took her plump hand in his. "And thank you, dear lady."

She patted his hand over hers. "You are most welcome."

He released her and started toward the upper floor. She stopped him with a sharp "Wait." When he swung around to face her, she said, "Pray do not wake her. She has been through much and, though I have given her a potion to aid her sleep, she may awaken if you disturb her."

He raked a hand through his hair and moved toward the door once more. "I will have a care."

She spoke again. "You will do her and yourself a service by finding a bit of sleep." When he opened his mouth to refute this, she went on. "I have placed a chair near the fire. You will find it and close your eyes."

Jarrod paused at the door and nodded sharply. He would agree to anything if only he could see Aislynn with his own eyes. In the sick chamber, the fire now warmed the room with both its heat and light.

Carefully and silently Jarrod moved to the bed, his gaze seeking out Aislynn. She was so small and delicate against the pillows, and her cheeks were still pale but not as they had been, for there was now the lightest trace of pink just below those high cheekbones beneath the fringe of her lashes. Her glorious hair lay spread across the pillow behind her and there was no trace of blood on either the white night rail she wore or on the bedlinens.

Again he was flooded with feelings of relief and tenderness that were so intense he had to reach out and grasp the bedpost to keep from staggering. Then, ever conscious of the healer's warning, he moved to the chair beside the fire to sit. He would gladly have stood there looking at Aislynn, loving her, for the rest of his life, but he would settle for being nearby. Because that was all he might have.

Jarrod had not thought to sleep when he had seated himself in the chair beside the fire. He had intended to do no more than rest his eyes, but when he opened them, morning light filtered through the shutters to lay across the stone floor.

Instantly he was on his feet and at the side of the bed. Aislynn was still where he had left her, so motionless and quiet. Too quiet.

Cautiously he moved forward, watching her for some sign of breathing. As he bent close, then closer still, she opened her eyes.

Joy soared in him as he met her confused blue gaze. "How are you..." She shifted slightly, grimacing, and he said, "Are you in pain? I will call the healer."

Aislynn shook her head, reaching out to halt him with the hand on her uninjured side. "Nay, please do not trouble anyone further. I am only sore." Her brow creased then. "Pray what occurred? Aida could tell me no more than that I had been shot by an arrow and that you had brought me to your brother's keep." She studied him closely. "Do you mind very much, having to bring me here, I mean?"

He shrugged. "Do not even think on it. Eustace has been more civil than I could have expected."

She sighed. "So much must have happened for you to say such a thing. I wanted to stay awake to talk with you, but I think Aida must have given me something in the wine."

Jarrod nodded. "She told me as much."

Aislynn shook her head. "What did happen? I have no memory of it."

He took a deep breath and told her all, leaving out nothing from the point when he had heard the rush of the arrow just missing him, until this very moment. He was careful to include the fact that they believed it had been Sir Fredrick. He told her all except for his revelation of his love for her. That he would keep close for the rest of his days, for he knew that she was bound to another, a man who could give her all she'd ever wanted.

She sighed, calling his attention back to the matter at hand. "Sir Fredrick must hate you very much."

Jarrod's jaw flexed, and he could hear the ring of rage in his voice as he said, "I do not believe it can compare to the hatred I feel for him. He could have killed you."

"But he will continue to try to harm you," she whispered, her blue eyes uncertain. She was so lovely in her concern, and so very precious to him, although he knew her care was no more than she would give to any other. Jarrod felt a sense of regret that was devastating, tightening his chest until he could barely breathe. He forced himself to turn away before he said something that he—they—would be sorry for.

The sound of the door opening drew his attention. Aida stepped into the room and, directly behind her, Eustace. The healer approached the bed with energetic steps in spite of the fact that she too had been up half of the night. Eustace came more slowly.

Aida's voice and her observant green eyes were

marked by an innate good cheer as she said, "Ah, awake, I see."

Eustace came to a halt beside her, nodding to Aislynn. "I am Eustace Maxwell."

Aislynn bowed her head. "I am Aislynn Greatham and I must thank you for taking me in. I must thank all three of you, for it is only due to your care that I am alive."

Eustace shrugged. "Think nothing of it. I am happy to be of assistance."

Before Jarrod could begin to speak past the tightness in his throat, Aida broke in, "Good enough then, if you, my lord Eustace, and Lord Jarrod will leave us, I'll have another look at that shoulder."

Jarrod had no choice but to bow and leave with his brother.

Eustace led him to the clean and well-appointed hall, seeing that the first of the morning meal was just being served. When they reached the high table, Eustace indicated the chair to his own right. "Please Jarrod, sit."

Now that some of his anxiety for Aislynn had eased, Jarrod noted even more clearly how his brother had changed. His blond hair, the color of bright flax as a child, had darkened and thinned. And his body, though never as robust Jarrod's, now appeared quite slight. Only those gray eyes, so like their father's, were as steady and intelligent as they had ever been. Although now Jarrod did not see the same resentment that had marked their expression in the past.

Watching his brother closely, Jarrod took the spot he indicated. "Thank you."

The younger man bowed graciously as he began to

serve himself sparingly from the trays before them. "Your lovely young lady is doing very well."

Jarrod grimaced as he realized that he seemed to explain this to everyone they met. It appeared that others had noted his love for her even before he had known of it. Yet he must try again, for Aislynn did not love him. "Aislynn is not *my lady,* as your tone would seem to imply. She is the sister of my friend and I am merely escorting her back to her family." At this point in the journey, that much was true. He went on as his brother's pale brows rose high over skeptical gray eyes. "The lady is to be married."

The other man sat back. "I see." He said no more on it, but his gaze remained thoughtful.

Recalling his agreement to relate what had occurred when Aislynn was better, Jarrod took a deep breath and as simply as he could, explained about Christian's disappearance and their search for him. He ended with Aislynn's becoming wounded. When Eustace only nodded his head, Jarrod added, "I imagine that you wonder why I would bring her here of all places, and after all these years."

To Jarrod's surprise, he said, "The reason you brought her seems clear, as well as the fact that you will need to remain for some days, at least. She was grievously injured and your care for her overrode your reluctance to come to Kewstoke. Thus I assume you will leave at first opportunity. But while you are here, let us not speak of things that you have no wish to reveal. Let us be as men who are meeting one another for the first time. You will be my guest, nothing more, nothing less."

Jarrod did not understand why his brother was willing to make such a suggestion, but he felt only relief. He had no wish to rekindle pains that were better long dead. He nodded. ''You would have a most grateful guest.''

Again Eustace bowed.

Although Jarrod went back to the sick chamber as soon as the meal had ended, he was found himself at loose ends. Aida told him that Aislynn had been given a sleeping potion and that, for the sake of making a speedy recovery, she would be kept in this state as much as possible for some days.

As Jarrod wished for Aislynn to make a complete and steady improvement, he made no demure. Although he did yearn in the deepest parts of himself to see her, to hold her, Jarrod knew that the best thing he could do for himself and Aislynn was to stay away. His conversation with his brother had reminded him of just how deeply he felt about her, of how visible his feelings might be to others.

It had not changed her feelings for him. She was determined to marry her Welsh nobleman and live the life she had planned for herself. Furthermore, as far as she knew, he wanted nothing more from her than that which he had already had. Jarrod did not want that to change. He would not have Aislynn know he loved her.

Thus he found himself in the company of his brother.

And so it went over the course of the next days. They talked and, during their discourse, details about their lives were revealed. Yet it was as Eustace had said—they were two strangers coming to know one another.

And as the next three days passed, Jarrod began to realize something he had not expected. He found himself actually looking forward to their talks, the meals they shared in the hall where he had felt so much an outsider as a boy. Although he had not traveled anywhere outside these walls, Eustace had access to the very fine library of the monastery nearby and had read nearly every written work they possessed. He could speak at length on all subjects, be it geography or the influence of the church in the East.

Something else Jarrod began to notice, as the days passed, was the fact that Eustace did not ride nor even walk very far, and he often went to his chambers in order to study, where Aida was wont to join him for long periods of time. Yet Jarrod was reluctant to question him on this as he felt it would be a violation of the pact they had made to know each other as men. Thus he said nothing. He told himself that if there was one thing he was expert at, it was keeping to himself.

For if he could resist speaking of his love for Aislynn, which was stronger and more consuming than any thought or feeling he had ever known, he could remain silent on any matter.

# Chapter Thirteen

Aislynn woke to the sounds of commotion. Stretching her arms above her head without thinking, she quickly drew them down when she felt the stiffness in her right shoulder. But she was not completely disturbed by it, for the pain was not as great as it had been.

She wondered at the loud voices in the hall outside her chamber and the fact that they appeared to be getting closer by the moment. Unlike previous mornings, the healing woman had not yet arrived to give her another of her potions. Aislynn was not sorry, for she would not find it amiss to get up and see what had occurred in her time here.

Only a moment later the door of her chamber flew open wide and into the opening stepped her father. Aislynn could not have been more surprised were it King John himself. But her shock was soon forgotten as she threw back the covers with her uninjured arm and rose up beside the bed with a cry of happiness "Father!"

A wave of dizziness took her, and she swayed. But

she had no time to reach out for support as she was enveloped in her father's arms.

"Aislynn, my dear girl. My heart."

A tightness rose in her throat and she returned his embrace to the best of her ability, before pushing back. "Father, why have you come? You should not have left Bransbury."

He pressed her back to his chest. "I could think of nothing save making certain that you were well." He held her away from him, his gaze raking her from head to foot. "You are recovering?"

She laughed, though there was a sheen of tears in her eyes as she felt the wonder of realizing that her father had come to her. "I am quite well. They have coddled me like a babe and I have not left this room in all the days I have been here, having slept through most of them, though I am weary enough with that."

As he pulled her close again, Aislynn became aware of the fact that several others had appeared in the doorway.

Yet she knew that only one had the power to draw her attention from her father. Jarrod, whom she had hardly seen in all the time she had been here. Not that she had spent a great deal of time pining for him, but those few short moments when she had first wakened to find him beside her, his face gentle with concern, had left her yearning for him.

Now as their eyes met for the briefest moment, Aislynn realized that nothing, not potions, not separation, not even the fact that he did not want her, would ever dampen her awareness, her desire for him. It flared up instantaneously without fuel or encouragement of any kind.

Aislynn dragged her gaze away, not wanting Jarrod to see what she feared she could not hide. She was saved from having to try by the arrival of the healing woman.

Aida sailed through those who had gathered in the doorway like a ship under full mast. Even Jarrod stepped back with alacrity as she said, "You will all leave now. The lady must not become overtaxed."

Aislynn frowned at her, not letting go of her father, "But I would speak with my father. He has come a very long way to see me."

Aida shook her head. "This is your first time out of yon bed in days. It is time for your rising, but nothing must be done to excess lest you become overtaxed. You lost much blood."

Aislynn could not deny that she did feel a great weakness in her limbs even after this short time of standing. Her father looked down at her, seeing the truth in her eyes. Quickly he scooped her up in his arms. "The lady is right. You must rest. I will attend you later."

"But I want…"

Aida spoke gently, seeming to understand Aislynn's desire to be with her father. "After you have rested for a bit. The first time out of bed is the most difficult. Your strength will return apace, if you heed my advice."

Aislynn found herself deposited in bed once more. And though she was more than reluctant to see him go, her father shook his head firmly. "I will return."

Aislynn had no choice but to let him go. And as she did so, her wayward heart told her that Jarrod

Maxwell was also gone, for she could no longer feel the pull of his presence.

And then something even more painful than his absence came into her mind. Now that her father was here, Jarrod was free, free of his obligation to look after her, free of her.

Though Aislynn was forced to acquiesce to the healer's wishes, it was not so very much later that she insisted on having her father brought back to her. Now that she had had time to think, she was beset with questions about what he was doing here and how he could possibly have left his responsibilities at Bransbury.

Feeling much stronger than she had when he'd first burst in upon her, Aislynn was sitting in a comfortable chair before the fire when her father entered the chamber. He came to her, enveloping her in his arms as he had that morning. And this time, whether it was due to her quickly returning strength or because she was no longer stunned by her surprise at seeing him, Aislynn was aware of a strange anxious quality to his embrace.

Pulling away from him, she looked into her father's blue eyes. When he failed to meet her gaze, she was more certain. "Something is amiss."

He attempted to smile. "Nay, daughter, all is well."

She shook her head. "Do not try to prevaricate, Father. I know you too well. There is something."

He took a deep breath. "Aye, there is. But I had thought to wait until—"

"'Tis not Christian!"

He shook her head quickly. "Nay, not your brother. I have heard no word of him other than what Jarrod and Sir Ulrick have told me. It is…" He took another deep breath before going on. "It is Gwyn."

"Has something happened to Gwyn?"

His brows came together over his autocratic nose. "Nay, Aislynn, but I would as lief it had when I learned what he had done."

She threw up her hands. "You speak in riddles. I understand naught of what you are saying."

Her father sat heavily on the bench across from her. "Aislynn, Gwyn has married his cousin Leri. It seems he is the father of her unborn child."

Aislynn sat immobile for a very long moment. "Married! How can this…?" And then she remembered the things Gwyn had said to her that day—it seemed so very long ago, almost like another life— at Bransbury. He had been trying to tell her then. But she had had little thought for anything beyond Jarrod Maxwell, as she had had little thought for anything but him from the moment they'd met.

Then, as the numbness of surprise passed, she realized that far from being hurt or angry, she felt nothing but relief. Even if she had felt something besides friendship for Gwyn, she would not have been able to blame him for what he had done with Leri. She had always known he loved Leri. Clearly that love had gone deeper than she knew.

And love was not something that one could easily deny. Had she not given herself to Jarrod without thought to the consequences?

And as this went through her mind, Aislynn suddenly knew with a certainty which could not be denied that she loved Jarrod Maxwell. Loved him with all her heart and soul, had loved him from the first moment of laying eyes upon him. She also knew that she would love him all the days of her life.

That he did not love her seemed to have no bearing at all upon her own feelings. And this knowledge gave rise to a sense of helplessness that left her reeling.

Obviously seeing the shock and sorrow in her face, her father said, "Aislynn, I am so very sorry. He is a blackguard for hurting you."

She looked at him, calling upon all her will to hide her anguish as she said, "Do not feel pity for me, Father. I have never loved Gwyn that way. I simply am worried now that you will have no allies in Wales."

Her father's brow wrinkled in remembered amazement as he said, "Have no concern for that, for Gwyn has done one thing I thought impossible. He has managed to convince Llewellyn to treat with me."

This news pushed Aislynn's misery to the back of her mind for the moment. "But how?"

"I know not. I know only that he has. Perhaps it is guilt over knowing Gwyn has broken his promise to you in order to prevent his grandchild from being labeled bastard. Whatever it might be, he has called his folk to cease their attacks upon, not only us, but others in the area."

Aislynn sighed. "How wonderful, Father. And how greatly it will change our lives."

He closed his eyes. "Aye. Although I would have come here to see that you were well with my own eyes no matter what the cost, I have far less fear that there will be all-out war upon my return.''

She looked at him with concern. ''We may go immediately. I would not keep you away from your duties.''

Her father shook his head, patting her hand with his large, warm one. ''We will return, but not before you are well enough to travel.'' His lips thinned. ''Now that we know Christian is well we can return home and wait for him, though it is my intent to make known my unhappiness over all the worry he has caused us. I am sorry to have sent you off on such a journey with no need. My dream…I do not understand what it could have been about.''

Aislynn hurriedly told her father everything they had discovered about Christian's movements, including the fact that the woman who had healed him had been lovely indeed and that they did have a drawing of her.

In the end it was still very little. She would not have been able to answer any questions her father might have had even if Aida had not come in to insist that she must rest now.

Once back in bed, Aislynn was not unwilling to consume the sleeping posset the healing woman gave her. She only hoped that it might, for a time, ease the pain of knowing that she would likely be well enough to leave soon and that meant she would soon see Jarrod for the last time.

The next day, Aislynn was more restless, as with her returning strength came a deeper and deeper understanding of how much it would hurt when Jarrod was no longer in her life. Her sadness at this was brought sharply to life when Jarrod accompanied her father when he came to see her in the late afternoon.

On seeing him hesitate there in the doorway while her father came forward, Aislynn ran an unsteady hand over the skirt of the gown of rich blue samite Aida had brought to her. Though it was slightly large and had obviously been shortened especially for her, she was glad to be up and dressed.

As Jarrod then approached her where she sat in the chair before the fire, Aislynn realized that this was the first time she had been near him since realizing she loved him. And that realization had left her achingly vulnerable to the yearning inside her. Her pulse quickened, as did her breathing, and her heart beat so loudly she felt he would surely hear it. She could not prevent her eager gaze from focusing on each beloved feature with heightened intensity. Nor could she stop herself from watching each movement of those strong but supple hands that had touched her, awakened her, nor each movement of that lean, muscular body that had joined to her own with such passionate abandon.

The only thing she could be grateful for was that neither her father nor Jarrod himself seemed to note her reactions. Her father moved to run a gentle hand over her unbound hair as he bent to kiss her brow. His earnest gaze searched hers. "You seem stronger, dearling."

Still utterly aware of Jarrod, where he had come to halt at her other side, she swallowed hard. "I am, Father. I would be up and about the keep if 'twere not for the healing woman. She does insist that I must not overdo."

Jarrod said softly, "It is good to see you doing so well, Aislynn."

Her gaze skittered to his and away. "It is thanks to you that I am. You saved my life by bringing me to Kewstoke."

He seemed to tense. "It would not have been necessary had I not placed you in danger at the outset."

Her father patted her hand. "There is no need to berate yourself, Jarrod. We will not have it. Aislynn will be fine."

He exhaled sharply. "But it has all been for naught as we still have no idea of where Christian might be." He reached into his sleeve and drew out a roll of parchment. Instantly Aislynn knew what it was as he held it out to her. She carefully avoided touching him as she took it. "I wanted to return this to you."

Aislynn nodded. "Thank you." Then as her father leaned close to look at it, she spread the drawing wide. There again was the young woman from Ashcroft.

Her father frowned. "She is indeed lovely." He leaned closer. "There again is the dragon, just as in the rendering of the soldier from Dragonwick."

Aislynn, aware of Jarrod as she was, felt him stiffen. Looking into his face, she saw dawning comprehension as he said, "Why did I not see it before? Dragonwick is the key here, though I do not know what it might be. With Kelsey in power at Dragonwick, Christian would never go there. But he could get near by going to its closest neighbor. Christian has gone to Avington. He could not have arrived long after I left there."

As he said the words, Aislynn knew they were true.

For whatever incomprehensible reason, Christian had taken this woman to Avington. She whispered, "Then we too must go to Avington."

Her father rubbed a hand over his brow. "Aye, but not until you are well enough to travel."

She caught his hand. "I am much stronger."

Jarrod spoke sharply. "Your father is right in this, Aislynn. You have been very ill."

Frustration made her want to argue, but she knew they would not heed her. Thus she said, "Then we must be ready to depart as soon as I am, for I know 'twill not be long, perhaps even on the morrow. I grow stronger by the hour."

The skepticism on their faces was obvious. But Aislynn turned to her father, insisting, "You will make ready?"

With a soothing smile, he said, "Of a certainty, my love. We are as eager as you to see your brother and discover what he has been about, to return to Bransbury and our lives."

Abruptly Jarrod stood, bowing. "I will leave you to your own conversation. I will begin to make preparations for the journey as Aislynn wishes. I too am eager to see this matter settled." He raked a quick and distant glance over them both before turning toward the door.

Aislynn was stung by his sudden coolness. Feeling many times a fool for her preoccupation with him, she nonetheless watched him as he moved to the door with the fluid grace that was so much a part of him. That was why she noted the fact that when he reached it he paused, looking back toward them.

What she saw in his dark, depthless gaze made her

heart stop. For there was no mistaking the naked desire in those black eyes. And then he was gone.

Aislynn closed her eyes, no longer hearing her father's voice, no longer knowing anything but the fact that in spite of everything, Jarrod still desired her.

"Aislynn."

She looked into her father's worried gaze, as he said, "Is something wrong?"

She shook her head, noting that he was not looking at her but at the doorway where Jarrod had been standing. Blushing, Aislynn forced herself to meet him with a smile as he turned back to her. She said, "Nay, I was just thinking that Sir Jarrod has been so kind to us and that I am grateful. He certainly should not blame himself for what happened."

He nodded, seeming to accept this explanation easily enough, but as they continued to talk, Aislynn saw him glance toward the door with a thoughtful expression. Deliberately she ignored this, determined to avoid any conversation that included answering questions about herself and Jarrod.

There was no need for her father to know what had happened between them. He would certainly feel that Jarrod should do the right thing—marry her.

No matter how the thought of marriage to Jarrod, having a family, children with him made her heart swell, she had no such expectations. She knew how he felt about his freedom.

Yet she also now knew that he desired her, as she did him. And that fact was of great significance to her.

Very great indeed.

\* \* \*

The castle had long since grown quiet when Aislynn crept from her chamber. She moved, with unerring purpose, down the hall to the room the woman who had come to tend her fire had indicated was Jarrod's.

Aislynn knew what she was about. She loved Jarrod Maxwell and if she could not have him for life, she would take what little she could with her into the long, lonely years ahead.

After seeing his face in that one unguarded moment, Aislynn could allow herself to believe he would not send her away. When she reached his door, Aislynn did not hesitate to knock. She was too aware of how fragile was her courage. She turned the latch and the door swung open on silent hinges.

Her gaze went immediately to Jarrod where he sat on a stool beside the low burning hearth. He looked up, seeing her as he rose. ''Aislynn.''

She faced him directly, her gaze unwavering as she took in the fact that he wore naught but a pair of dark-colored hose that molded to his slender hips and emphasized the bronze expanse of his shoulders and smooth chest. ''Jarrod.'' Their eyes met and held and that now familiar awareness passed between them, making her stomach tighten.

He ran obviously unsteady hands over his thighs, drawing her gaze to their muscular length. ''Why have you come?''

She did not hesitate. ''Methinks you already know the answer to that question.''

He sucked in a quick breath of surprise at her directness. At the same time she noted that his lids flicked and became hooded above those exotic eyes as his gaze slid over her, obviously taking in the fact that she wore nothing beneath her fine white shift.

Jarrod did know the answer to that question. Had he not, the stirring in his own blood as he looked at her, clad only in that diaphanous white gown, her pale hair falling about her in a flowing curtain, would have told him.

Aislynn moved forward and carefully placed her candle on the table near him. He saw that her hand was steady, as was her gaze. He was very aware that her calm was at direct odds with his own demeanor. He could not deny the trembling in his body as she then came to stand in front of him.

Jarrod swallowed hard as his eyes moved over her lovely face. He now saw the heightened color along those high cheekbones, the flutter of her pulse at her throat as she raised her head to look up at him. Those two subtle signs told him she was not as unmoved as it had appeared.

Yet as his gaze met hers again he was altogether certain that her agitation was not brought on by nervousness, but by something deeper that was more stirring to his own blood.

Her voice was a hoarse whisper. "Would you have me stay?"

Would he have her stay? The very thought made his heart thrum, his breath quicken. She was so beautiful. The perfect contours of her form were not truly concealed by the gown, only tantalizingly veiled in hints of light and shadow. His body ached with the images her words conjured up. For he knew intimately how lovely she was, how soft the flesh that covered the curves and plains of her body.

Again Jarrod swallowed, knowing that he wanted what she offered more than he had ever wanted anything in his life. His realization that Christian would be at Avington had made him understand that it would soon be over. Aislynn would be out of his life forever, for he knew he could never go to Bransbury again and see her with her noble lord husband. He held out his arms, for there was naught else he could do.

Aislynn went into his arms, only realizing as he held them out to her how very afraid she had been that he might turn her away. Her relief that he did not do so left her limp and weak in his embrace.

But only for the space of a heartbeat. Closing her eyes, she lifted her face with a sigh of longing.

Jarrod's mouth found hers, his lips supple and warm, igniting a flame that raced through her and made her breath quicken. She raised her arms to hold his head down to her, standing up on tiptoe as she fitted her body to the hard length of his.

When his hands moved down her back to settle on her hips, she moaned, her body arching into his. She felt the hardness of him against her belly with a thrill of anticipation.

Unlike the first time they had made love, Aislynn knew exactly whence they were headed in this dance of desire. She stepped backward, looking into his eyes, taking his large hand in her own trembling one and backing toward the bed.

Jarrod stopped her, his breath hot on her ear as he whispered, ''Nay, my eager beauty, do not rush. Let me touch you.''

She shivered with delicious anticipation, closing

her eyes as a wave of heat raced through her. Then she opened them again as she felt herself being turned in his arms.

"Do not go from…" she cried, then subsided as she felt him press her back against the firmness of his body.

He drew her gown up the length of her body, slowly gathering it into his hands, baring her to the heat of the fire. And as he did so, Aislynn felt as if that warmth was an extension of his hands, his mouth, delicate but erotic on her skin. When he had raised it to the height of her breast, she sighed and lifted her arms, her breathing shallow and quick as he passed the garment over her head, then tossed it to the floor.

Completely naked now, her breath halted. She ran her tongue over her suddenly parched lips as he drew her back against him, his palms on the flat plane of her belly.

"I want to touch you," he told her, his mouth against her ear, the heat of his breath warming her.

Jarrod put his warm hands over her hips and slowly began to trace them up her sides. She sucked in a breath of pleasure and expectation, her stomach quivering. When his hands at last closed over her breasts, she moaned aloud, sagging back against the wall of his chest as his thumbs found her already erect nipples.

Gently he plied her breasts with his two large, warm hands, circling, squeezing gently, his thumbs applying just the right amount of pressure to those yearning tips. Thick sweet honey spread from those two sensitive points, seeping through her body to form a delicious pool of delight in her lower belly.

When his hand slid down again, tracing over her ribs, the flat surface of her stomach, then paused in the nest of golden curls at the joining of her thighs, she held her breath. But as his fingers slipped into the scorching damp of her, Aislynn gasped aloud, her knees buckling. She only managed to stay upright because she could not bear for the pleasure to stop.

Jarrod groaned, his half-open mouth finding the line of her jaw and lower along her throat. Her head fell backward on his chest, allowing him better access to that tender flesh. He was completely and utterly consumed by the heat in his own body, and the feel, taste and delicate rose scent of Aislynn.

Aislynn wanted, needed more of him. Without conscious thought she rubbed her bottom against his hardness and heard him utter a ragged gasp. A wave of sheer sensuality rose up inside her and she pressed back into him again.

Jarrod was aching, dying for her, and before he had even begun to enjoy her as he wished to. The unadulterated joy with which she took and gave pleasure drove him mad with need and an undeniable wonder.

Never in his years had he met such a woman, a woman who was unaffected in the joy in the sensuous delights of her body. His own pleasure was heightened by hers.

Aislynn's body ached, throbbed, with the thrill of his touch. But she was not ready to give in to the pounding of her blood. She turned in his arms, feeling a need to touch him, to bring him to the same level of desire that raced through her own veins.

As she looked at him, the dark and wondrous male beauty of him, Aislynn was overcome with a feeling of tenderness that made her heart ache. How dear and beloved he was to her. Would that she could take away all the hurts he had known in his life, heal the heart that knew not how to love.

But she could not do so, and all she had was this moment, a moment that must last her a lifetime. She raised trembling hands to slide them along his belly and he sucked in a gasping breath. She looked up at him, saw the fire that lit the depths of his black eyes and leaned forward to place her lips where her hands had been.

His fingers tangled in the heavy fall of her hair as she kissed his belly, her lips soft, sensuous, and shockingly confident on his flesh. When they closed over one of his hard nipples, he groaned and gently but firmly pulled her away, then bent to kiss her perfect rosy mouth.

He kissed her until his own head was spinning, his body aching with need.

Jarrod knew he could wait no more. He picked her up and moved toward the bed, his eyes on hers, seeing the raw need in those periwinkle eyes, eyes that had haunted him from the first moment he'd looked into them.

Aislynn continued to hold his gaze as he lay her back against the pillows.

When he ran a hand down her bare side, she shivered, her lids drooping, her mouth parting with the quickness of her breath. His voice was husky with passion as he said, "You are loveliness itself, Aislynn. You leave me with nothing but insignificant words to describe what is too beautiful for mere words."

She took his hand and raised it to her left breast. "My heart beats like a battle drum from the very sight of you."

He groaned and dipped his head to suckle at the very same breast. Now it was she who cried out with wanting. "Please, Jarrod, I want you so."

He went into her arms, his body sliding along the length of her. Her flesh was like silk against his, their contours seeming to meld as he slipped between her slender, velvet thighs.

When she lifted her hips, he slid into her. Her body was so wet, yet seemed to grasp him with an agonizingly sweet pressure. The sensation was indescribably pleasurable, making him close his eyes as he cried out, reveling in the sheer intensity of it as it rippled through his body.

Aislynn was afire with the sensations engendered by the joining of their heated flesh. To hear the hoarse sound of his voice and know that he was driven so far beyond himself because of her sent yet another wave of need coursing through her.

No matter what might come in the years ahead, she would have his reactions to remind her that once he had lost himself in her—Aislynn. She listened to the shallowness of his breathing as she moved beneath him, deliberately drawing him as deeply into herself as she could before withdrawing again.

And as she did so her own pleasure deepened, spiraling higher and higher toward the pinnacle that only Jarrod could take her to.

He stiffened above her, his face beautiful as the power of his passion took him, and she too ascended to the peak of unutterable ecstasy, dissolving in a shower of radiant light. Even before the delight had completely eased, she reached out to hold him to her.

He pushed back, rolling to the side, putting out his hand to brush the hair away from her face in a gesture so tender it made her heart ache. She looked into those black eyes. They were lit with a gentleness that was even more moving than his touch.

She allowed her gaze to move over his face, so exotic and yet so familiar at one and the same time. How was she ever to survive without him, to accept the reality of never seeing him again?

Her heart stopped then for one infinite moment at the renewed pain of her own thought. Jarrod was beloved indeed, more beloved than she had ever imagined any being could be.

Yet he did not love her. What she saw in those eyes was no more than the remnants of the passion they had shared.

She closed her eyes and a wave of exhaustion passed through her. As she felt it, she told herself that it did not help that she was still not quite fully recovered from her injuries. If only she could rest for just a moment, put aside the pain in her mind and heart. If only for…

# Chapter Fourteen

Jarrod lay there holding her for some time, before he became aware of a gentle tapping at his chamber door. He was protectively aware of Aislynn's presence beside him, her deep and rhythmic breathing. As soon as his passion had eased he had known that he should not allow her to remain here. She could not be found in his bed.

Silently but hurriedly he moved from the bed, realizing when the sound came again that it was not from the door that led to the hall, but the inner door, the one he believed connected to his brother's chamber. Hastily he drew on his discarded hose.

He opened the door, being careful to prevent anyone on the other side from seeing that Aislynn was asleep in his bed. It was Eustace. Hastily Jarrod stepped into the other room, not quite closing the door behind him in an effort to be quiet. As he did so, he wondered what his brother could want, for it was still full night.

One glance at his pale countenance told Jarrod that he would not ask. When a pale and listless Eustace

had retired in the midst of the evening meal, leaving
Jarrod and Aislynn's father to discuss their coming
journey, Jarrod had wondered if all was well. Yet in
spite of the mutual respect that had grown between
them, or possibly because of it, he had refrained from
remarking on it.

Eustace spoke rapidly. "I hope you will forgive
me. I could not sleep knowing you would soon be
leaving and there is something that I feel I must say
before…well, whilst the courage to do so is upon
me."

Jarrod replied evenly, "I am at your disposal,"
though he did wonder what could be so very urgent.

Then his eyes swept the candlelit chamber, and he
took a deep breath, momentarily forgetting about his
brother. The large table where his father had always
sat going over his ledgers, the large oak bed and other
heavy furnishings, were just as he remembered them.
This room, dark and filled with the ghosts of his
childhood, was the last place he had seen his father.
His father, whom he had loved no matter how impossible it had become for him to remain at Kewstoke.

In spite of everything that happened in his life, all
the years that had passed since that last meeting, Jarrod had never forgotten that day, had never wanted
to forget. Difficult as his life had been as a bastard
son, his father had, unlike his mother, cared at least
in part. If he had not he would surely have left him
far behind in the Holy Land when he returned home
to England.

It would have been the easiest thing to do. But his
father had never, to Jarrod's knowledge, taken the

easy road as far as his responsibilities were concerned. He had been one to drive himself to the limits of his endurance, even to the point of neglecting his wife and legitimate son, certainly leaving himself with little time for a bastard son.

But Jarrod did not wish to dwell on that now, or at any other time. He was a man, not the boy who had felt himself an onlooker in his own home. The Dragon had helped him to see beyond those hurts, treated him with the same respect that he had the other boys in his care, taught him that he was the center of his own being. This, Jarrod would not forget, even if being here did bring back into mind so much that he had thought long forgotten.

Squaring his shoulders, Jarrod went farther into the room where Eustace, garbed in an enveloping robe of burgundy velvet, had moved to stand before the fire, one hand upon the mantel. As he moved forward, watching his brother, Jarrod could not help wondering if it was for support. For the younger man was very pale and seemed more fragile than before.

Eustace began with preamble. "Aida tells me the lady Aislynn continues to improve."

Jarrod nodded stiffly, infinitely aware of her there on the other side of the stone wall. "Yes. She does well. Her father is eager to return home when she is able to travel." Jarrod did not care for the discomfort this thought brought. He hurried to continue, "And I...will try to find some clue to aid me in continuing my search for Christian."

Eustace nodded without meeting his gaze, his voice tight as he said, "I will be sorry to see you go."

Jarrod cast his brother a glance of surprise. Although he would be the first to affirm that they had come to know one another as he had never imagined they could, he was amazed at this reaction to his leaving.

He wondered what it might portend?

He was even more surprised when Eustace's next words confirmed what Jarrod had suspected all along. "Jarrod, I must tell you that I am unwell."

Jarrod was surprised by this change of topic but decided to allow it to go where it would. He watched that too lean face, the face that was a more sensitive, vulnerable version of his father's. "I thought as much."

His brother ran a weary hand over his wide brow. "I forget others can see what I can no longer hide from myself." Slowly he moved to sink down on the chair nearby, his gaunt face averted as he took a deep breath. Finally he said, "I would have you listen while I tell you..." He shrugged. "Well, while I unburden myself, if you will."

When Jarrod nodded, he went on. "I was very envious of you as a boy. I felt you were strong, brighter, and that if you were not here Father would have more time, more care for me. I soon realized that you had not been the problem. It was Father. He did not spend more time with me, love me, as I had envisioned he would when you were gone. He was as obsessed with his duties, his own interests, as he had ever been." He shrugged, looking directly at Jarrod then. "You knew him. It was not that he was unkind or cruel. He simply was not interested in anything but the estates—not even Mother, and I believe it was loneliness that killed her two years after you had gone."

Jarrod could only nod. "Aye, I did know his temperament, though I did not understand it for many years. But I loved him."

"As I did. I simply did not see that it was he who was to blame for the way he treated me. Not you."

Again Jarrod allowed his gaze to move over the room, the heavy walnut furnishings, the Eastern carpet and tapestries their father had brought back with him from the Holy Land, the large fireplace with the carved mantel and coat of arms above it.

He realized that his brother had not changed it in all these seven years that he had been lord here, not because he preferred it as it was, but because it was a way to continue to be close to their dead sire. All these years Jarrod had thought that his leaving had been for the best. He sighed heavily. Who knew, perhaps it had, for it had meant that Eustace had faced the fact that it was not Jarrod who had caused the problems in his life. And perhaps, in the end, it had been the making of Eustace.

For in spite of his obvious physical fragility, there burned in his brother's gray eyes a strength of character that had not been present when Jarrod had gone away. Here now, after all these years, he found a man who he would feel proud to call brother—aye, even friend.

If that was what Eustace wanted, at any rate. His speaking of these matters did not mean that he was willing to go so far.

Eustace spoke again. "I...you should know that Father did miss you, though he tried to hide it. I would sometimes see him late at night, walking the battlements and looking off toward the East. And I knew what he was thinking.''

The unexpectedness of this statement caught Jarrod completely unawares. He was shocked at the huskiness in his own voice as he said, ''It is good to know that I had that much from him. It is most unfortunate that he could not tell me in life, for that would mean that I had one parent who cared for...'' He halted, his jaw working.

Eustace held up a hand. ''What say you? Do you not know that your mother loved you so much that she begged Father to take you with him to England?''

His voice was filled with bitterness. ''Loved me? She loathed the very sight of me. I found her after much searching and she turned me away as if I was nothing.''

His brother shook his head. ''Nay, that can not be. Before he died, Father told me how she wept as she placed you in his arms. He said that it was near impossible to leave her standing there, that he loved her. I think, in fact, that Father would have been a very different man had she come to England with him as he bid her, that perhaps he had grieved for her all those years. But she refused. She told him that she would never be accepted by his people, just as she knew that you would not be by hers. Perhaps that was why she sent you away, Jarrod, for she did not wish for you to live with the stigma of her being...what she was.''

Jarrod sank down on the chair next to his brother. ''Could she really have wanted to protect me?''

''It could indeed be so.''

Jarrod's head was reeling. He moved toward the door, saying, "I must think. I…"

Eustace stopped him with an upraised hand. "There is one thing I would ask of you before you go. It is the very reason I had the temerity to waken you, for in the night, when mortality presses in upon your mind, it is what will come after you that seems to matter most."

Jarrod looked at him. "Aye, for what you have told me here this night, if it be in my power I will do whatever you ask."

Eustace took a deep breath. "I would ask that you come here to Kewstoke to live. That you would agree to stand as my heir."

Jarrod grew very still, his heart thumping as he realized he could not have heard properly. "What say you?"

Eustace made a sweeping gesture over his own slight form. "I will not long be in a fit state to see to the lands. I can barely do so now."

Jarrod moved toward him, realizing that his brother speaking thusly disturbed him more than he would have thought possible. "What of your sons?"

Eustace looked directly into his eyes. "I will never have a child, Jarrod. 'Tis no longer possible for me. For even if it was possible for me to find a woman who would take me as I am, I no longer have the strength to fulfill my duties as a husband."

"Have you seen a healer? Perhaps…"

He shrugged, his gaze holding Jarrod's. "I have seen many healers. Father insisted that I see many of them, though they all said the same thing—that I have a weakness of the blood, that there is no cure. When

Father died three years ago, Aida came to care for
him and I learned that she, of all those who had
tended me, knew how to treat the weakness, the
swelling of joints and the bruising caused by my ill-
ness. Yet she knows, as I do, that she can only care
for the symptoms. She can not heal.''

Jarrod stood silent, his chest tight with helplessness, knowing that there was nothing he could do to
change the fact that his brother was gravely ill. Eustace went on, ''Pray, say something.''

Jarrod shook his head. ''I know not what to say.
I...you have been given a great burden to bear. Yet
to ask me to stand as your heir...I would not have
believed it possible if I had not heard the words with
my own ears. I know not what to say. I have never
imagined myself as lord to these lands. The very
thought is so foreign to me.''

A rueful grimace twisted his brother's lips. ''I am
aware of the fact that you have chosen a freer and
less constricted lifestyle for yourself, Jarrod.'' He
shrugged. ''I have made inquiries about you amongst
the other nobles I am acquainted with and know that
you have amassed no small fortune in your travels. I
realize that if you wished, you could purchase lands,
a keep, and set up your own holding. And yet you
have chosen not to do that.''

Jarrod was shocked to know that Eustace had made
inquiries about him. He said, ''If you wished to know
of me, why did you not seek me out?''

His brother shook his head. ''I felt I had no right.''

Raking a hand through his hair, Jarrod stood. ''I
do not know what my answer can be. I must find
Christian before making any commitment. I tell you

though that I will give it most serious consideration before making a reply."

Eustace also stood, making a formal bow. "I thank you."

Jarrod moved toward the door, then stopped and turned back to his brother. "I ask a boon of you in return."

Eustace shrugged. "Of course."

"Do not speak of this in front of Lady Aislynn." As a knowing look came into his brother's eyes, Jarrod added, "Or anyone else for that matter."

Again Eustace bowed. "As you will."

As his brother's heir, Jarrod would no longer be the landless knight with nothing to offer a noble bride—a bride such as Aislynn Greatham, who longed for such things.

Yet he did not want Aislynn in that way. He thought of the way she had just given herself to him, having no illusions that, powerful as their lovemaking was, she meant for it to be anything more.

He had asked her to be his wife—he, Jarrod, not a landed nobleman—and she had denied him, had made clear her intent to marry her Gwyn. No matter how it hurt to be without her, would not having her for anything less than true love be even more painful?

For though he had learned that his mother might have cared for him, the pain of all those years could not be erased. Jarrod would know that he was loved, or continue his life as it had always been—alone. Being alone was at least familiar.

Yet it was with a heavy heart that he entered his own room and closed the door, which had remained slightly ajar after him. Approaching the bed with mixed feelings, he came up short as he realized that it was empty.

Aislynn had gone.

He looked toward the door. How much of the conversation with his brother she might have overheard he had no way of knowing. He had not meant her harm. He had only wished to save himself the pain of wondering if her change of attitude toward him might be based on his brother's offer. But, so be it. He did his best to ignore the ache of longing in his chest.

Aislynn looked up at the battlement of Avington Keep with a feeling of both relief and misery. The relief was that their journey was finally at an end. The misery had no particular source, but had been her constant companion from the moment she had overheard what Jarrod Maxwell had said to his brother the ill-fated night when she had given him, not only her body and heart, but her soul.

Waking to realize that Jarrod was not there beside her, she had gone to see if he might be on the other side of the partially open door, through which a sliver of light could be seen. What she had heard had finally and completely brought to an end any hope that she might have secretly harbored that he might care for her.

In very certain terms Jarrod had made it clear that he did not want her to know that his brother had asked him to be his heir. What had brought about this drastic change in their relationship, Aislynn did not know, nor at this point did it seem to matter. Jarrod would never accept his brother's love for him any more than anyone else's, including his mother's, or...

She would have no part in their lives either way.

She choked back a sob, her own. If only she need never see Jarrod Maxwell again, for how could she possibly face him after what he had said? Yet how was she to avoid him? This was his brother's keep, perhaps his own if he chose to accept the offer extended to him.

It was in that moment that she knew she could not stay at Kewstoke for even another day. She had gone to where her father was sleeping, waking him to say that they must leave before the others in the keep had arisen.

His shocked refusal was to be expected. But Aislynn had been prepared for it. She told him that Eustace had asked Jarrod to stand as his heir. She was afraid that Jarrod would refuse because of his promise to help them to find Christian. And there was no need for this to happen. They knew where Christian was and could go on alone before Jarrod knew what they were about.

He had told her that she was not strong enough to travel, and she desperately had admitted that she was not strong enough to stay. Her father had watched her closely, finally saying, "You are in love with him."

Unable to do aught but tell the truth in the face of his sympathy and love, she had nodded. "Aye, but he does not love me, which does not negate the importance of what I have just told you. We must give Jarrod this chance."

Thus the two of them and Sir Ulrick had set out ere dawn had broken. All that long way, it had been

Aislynn who insisted on riding till last light, and beginning again as the sun rose.

And gratefully there was no delay when they arrived. They were allowed entrance to the keep the moment her father called out, "'Tis I, Greatham."

A wave of complete exhaustion rolled over her when she rode into the courtyard, for she had been functioning on sheer will alone. But her tiredness was not so debilitating that she did not see the man who came running down the steps of the keep in front of the others.

Christian. Although she had been told that he was well, just seeing him made her heart sore with joy.

Then he was there beside her horse and Aislynn was looking into his dear face, that broad kind brow, the strong angular features, those blue eyes that were so like their father's. Her relief was so very great it left her light-headed.

When her brother reached out to her with a cry of welcome and happiness, Aislynn leaned toward him and felt the world spin madly, then go dark...

When she opened her eyes, she was in a bed, the rich, deep blue of the hangings creating a canopy over her head. Disoriented, because she did not recognize these appointments, Aislynn turned and saw that she was in a small stone chamber, and that she was not alone. Not only her father and brother, but two women and another man stood silently near the bed.

The man was of equal height and size to her brother, noble of bearing and feature, his hair very dark. She could only assume that this was Simon.

The two women were tall and slim, one with black

hair, one red. And like her father and brother, they watched her with concentrated distress.

The moment they noted that she was looking at them there was an instantaneous rush of concerned questions, though all were careful to keep their voices low. It was Christian who held up a quieting hand and moved to sit on the edge of the bed beside her. "Aislynn, Father has told us of your recent injury. You should not have traveled so soon—"

She interrupted him, albeit gently, "I am fine, only tired. The wound does not pain me over much at all." She did not add that any physical pain was far easier to bear than being near Jarrod Maxwell.

Gingerly Aislynn sat up, feeling the continued weight of their anxiety as her father moved to stand beside her brother. She rubbed her brow. "I would meet everyone."

Christian nodded. He turned to the others. "Aislynn, this is Simon Warleigh and his bride Isabelle." As they bowed politely, she noted that although her loose gown near disguised her condition, the slight mound of her belly betrayed the dark-haired woman's pregnancy. He then motioned toward the other woman, the one with bright auburn hair. "This is Rowena."

Aislynn bowed toward them all, saying, "I am pleased to meet you at last." Her gaze rested longest on the one named Rowena. The woman from Ashcroft, for she was easily recognizable from the drawing Christian had made.

Her father interrupted this tableau with a worried frown. "That is quite enough for now. You must rest."

She shook her head, casting him a reassuring glance as she sighed. "As I said, I am fine and feel quite silly about worrying you all. I was but tired." She looked to her brother. "I am most interested in hearing why you had us worry so."

He grimaced, looking toward the others, and Isabelle and Rowena stepped forward. He said, "I am very sorry, Aislynn, but I had been sworn to silence by a dying man. I could tell no one." He took a deep breath before going on. "I had been informed that The Dragon's daughter was alive and that I had to journey to Scotland to find her."

Aislynn could hear the shock and incredulity in her own voice. "Alive? But she was killed in Kelsey's attack on Dragonwick castle, along with her father."

"Mayhap not," Christian returned.

"Mayhap?" She looked to the young woman, who was even more beautiful than the rendering had indicated, with her lovely green eyes and fair skin. "Are you The Dragon's daughter?"

The young woman met Aislynn's gaze with complete candor. "I know not. Your brother believes I am."

# Chapter Fifteen

Jarrod leaped from his horse and strode up the steps and into the hall at Avington. Once inside he stopped short. There at the table they all sat—Isabelle, Simon, Christian, a woman who, in spite of the surprising brightness of her red hair, was unmistakable for her resemblance to the drawing Christian had made at Ashcroft, Lord Greatham, and Aislynn. That they had been enjoying their meal was evidenced by the pleasant drone of chatter that stopped the moment he appeared.

Anger rushed through him, an anger that had been brewing for days as he traveled toward Avington, being first delayed by his stallion losing a shoe, then by his having to find the beast after he had failed to tie him securely before rolling up for a few hours' sleep. Jarrod could only blame his preoccupation with just what he would say to Aislynn Greatham when he reached her. Without preamble he strode to stand before them, saying, "Well, well, is this not a pretty sight. All of you sitting about here without the least

thought to the fact that I have traveled the length and
breadth of England to find you.''

He fixed Christian with a glare, not even daring to
look at Aislynn, for he feared it might be the undoing
of whatever hold he had on his tumultuous emotions.
And Christian, God love him, had the grace to flush
as he said, ''Pray forgive me, Jarrod. I did not mean
to cause such a stir. It was only that I had sworn to
tell no one what I had been charged to do. And what
was I to tell even if I was inclined to break my oath?
I knew not what I would find when I reached Ashcroft. You see Jack had told me that The Dragon's
daughter lived and it was there I would find her.'' He
shrugged, his gaze going to the young woman. ''The
tale seemed so incredible. And does still. Yet here is
Rowena, whom I believe is indeed Rosalind.''

Jarrod was not unaware of the strange tension that
came into his friend's face as he looked toward the
red-haired maid. But this observation was lost in his
own shocked amazement at what Christian had just
said. Dazed, he sank down on the bench that someone
had placed beside him. ''Can this be true?''

The young woman shrugged. ''I know not. But as
Christian is so certain, I have come here to see if the
truth can be found.'' There was no mistaking the reluctance in those lovely green eyes.

It was indeed quite a fantastic tale. No wonder
Christian had been reluctant to share it.

But as his irritation with Christian faded, he was
achingly aware of Aislynn, though he still did not
look at her. He did not have to do so to know that
she would be so lovely that it would hurt his eyes to
look upon her. Again he allowed anger to cover his

confusion and pain as he turned to her father. "Pray sir, I do not mean to offer insult, but I can not understand why you would leave Kewstoke without telling me."

Lord Greatham bowed, his gaze flicking to his daughter and away. "Forgive me, Sir Jarrod, I thought only to prevent you from putting any more of your own life aside to look after mine. I knew that your brother had asked you to stand as his heir and…"

An immediate rush of exaltation and congratulations from both Simon and Christian drowned out anything else he might have been about to say. Both of them rose as one and hurried forth to embrace him with claps on the back.

So Aislynn had overheard his and Eustace's conversation. Now Jarrod looked to her with a frown. She met him with defiance and hauteur, being no less lovely for her ire. Those blue eyes were just as compelling as he recalled, and her hair, which she wore unbound, just as silken. As always his heart ached at the sight of her.

She had heard and had run away.

But he was prevented from thinking on what this might mean when Simon asked, "How did this come about? You have not even spoken to Eustace since long before we all went to the East."

Jarrod looked at him, his gaze direct. "As Lord Greatham has very likely told you, I took his daughter to Kewstoke when she became injured." He hoped the others did not note the fact that he could not bear to say her name, for doing so would only add to his difficulty in retaining a semblance of calm. He went on, "Eustace is much changed by time and...well, we have come to know one another differently."

Christian's concerned gaze flicked to Aislynn and back to Jarrod, before he smiled. "Then even as we mourn the reason for your going to Kewstoke, we must celebrate your good fortune, for there is none more deserving of peace within his family."

Simon met Jarrod's gaze and bowed. "Well said, Christian."

Jarrod was touched by their love and happiness for him and felt obliged to accept their joy for him as if it were a settled matter. He could not tell them that he had not, in fact, decided what he would do. For he did not know if, even for Eustace's sake, he could bear to remain in England, to risk the chance of seeing Aislynn with her husband.

Jarrod, not wanting to discuss the matter further, said, "It has certainly been a time of many unprecedented events." He looked to the woman named Rowena, noting that Christian was watching her as well. He told himself that this was none of his affair. He had acquitted himself poorly enough where Aislynn was concerned that he had no right to contemplate what when on between others.

He turned to Simon. "If Rowena does not know whether or not she might be The Dragon's daughter, how then are we to determine it?"

It was at this point that Isabelle interrupted to say, "Pray do not think me rude, Jarrod. We have talked on little else for days. I know you can not but be tired from your journey. I beg you leave this matter for just a little while. I, who have known so little of what family could be, would enjoy a few moments of your company. Who knows when all of us might come together once more, or what tomorrow might bring to us?'' Her sweeping glance included not only Aislynn and her father, but also Rowena, and there was a strange longing in it as she looked at the red-haired maid that Jarrod did not understand.

What he did understand was that she was wrong about one thing. To a certain extent he did in fact know what tomorrow would bring for him. And that would be pain and loneliness.

With as much chivalry as he could muster, Jarrod bowed. ''Your wish is my command.''

She smiled and the meal continued.

As he served himself from the savory-smelling dishes, Jarrod found himself unable to keep his eyes from Aislynn. To his relief she appeared completely engrossed in her meal, though she had eaten little if any of it. Very likely thinking on the fact that she could now return to Bransbury and continue her plans for her own approaching marriage, he told himself.

As if his attention had somehow beckoned her, she looked up at him in that moment. And the misery and anger he saw in her gaze before she quickly pulled it away made his heart thump with regret.

He knew she was angry at his telling Eustace that she was not to know of his offer to make him his heir. He knew that, after they had just made love in a way that had left him shaken, it must have sounded very condemning. On the other hand, in light of her coming marriage, what occurred in his life could have little import for her.

It was with very little enthusiasm that he ate his own food.

After the meal a listless Jarrod, along with Simon and Christian, retired to an antechamber to go over the details of all that had occurred in the past weeks and try to fathom whence they might go from here. Christian was determined to find a way to prove that Rowena was Rosalind of Dragonwick. And though Jarrod hoped for his friend's sake that it was true, there really seemed very little hope of confirming it. Though they would have welcomed Christian's father, he excused himself to go to his own chamber for a time. And Jarrod wondered if his leg might be paining him after all the riding he had done of late. This thought brought a reminder of how painful it had been to wake and find Aislynn gone from Kewstoke. He'd known immediately that he must follow, telling himself that he too wanted to make certain that Christian was there and that he was all right. Even as Jarrod had bid his brother goodbye, with the assurance that he would send him word of his intent as soon as possible, he had been consumed by irritation and frustration.

That Eustace's expression had been one of sympathy had not eased his unrest. He feared that his brother saw far more than Jarrod would wish him to, though he said nothing.

But he did not want to think about that now. Nor did he want to think of the maddening young woman who had set his unburdened life into such turmoil.

Christian seemed incredulous when he said, "I am somewhat amazed that Sir Fredrick seems to have undertaken a vendetta against you, Jarrod. 'Twas Simon who wounded him."

"Wounded?" Jarrod asked.

"Aye. A grievous wound to his shoulder."

Simon shrugged. "It also seems odd, given his behavior, that no one has seen any sign of the knight since his attack upon Aislynn."

Jarrod felt a renewed rush of rage at that reminder. "Would that we could ride to Dragonwick and call him out if he is there."

Christian shook his head. "None has more cause for anger against him than I, but we must recall what our efforts to gain retribution against Kelsey nearly cost Simon. The king is fully capable of taking not only his lands and titles does Simon give him the least cause, but our own as well."

Jarrod made no comment, though the words brought back his own uncertainty about his future. He tried to concentrate as Simon said, "We would be better served to concoct a plan that would prove Rowena's identity one way or another. Once that was done, and if she is Rosalind, we could approach our enemies' downfall from a new position. For as The Dragon's daughter, she may have some claim to the lands."

Seeing the longing that came into Christian's face, Jarrod saw that he did hope the tale of Rowena's being the heir to Dragonwick was true. And although Jarrod himself would be glad to know that Kelsey had not been able to accomplish all the evil he had attempted, there seemed to be something more in Christian's haunted gaze.

Yet mayhap it was because he was closer to the matter, after all that had happened in his quest to find the girl and bring her here. And mayhap Jarrod was seeing more between his friend and this Rowena because of his own preoccupation with Aislynn.

For in spite of all the shock and amazement and, yes hope, that this woman could indeed be his dead mentor's child, Jarrod could only give the matter half his mind.

It was not until he heard Christian speak of Aislynn that he found himself fully attending the conversation again. "My father understands that I must remain here for a time when he returns to Bransbury with Aislynn. Though he wishes for me to come home and take up my duties as his son and heir, he is willing to carry on as he has been whilst we try to discover if Rowena is Rosalind. He tells me that the peace Gwyn ap Cyrnain has been able to obtain through his marriage to his cousin Leri may not last. Her father, Llewellyn, has shown himself to be more unpredictable than not in the years he has held his lands."

Uncaring how he might give away his own shock and disbelief, Jarrod said, "Did you say that Gwyn has married his cousin?"

Christian frowned as he met his gaze. "Aye."

"But what of his engagement to Aislynn?"

He shrugged. "It is no more. And as she seems not the least distressed about the matter, it is of little import."

Jarrod ignored his unconcern, his lips tightening with animosity. "And, pray how long has your sister known of this?"

Christian shrugged again. "One would think it is since my father came from Bransbury. As he has had no contact with anyone there since, he must have known when he left."

Jarrod stood, his voice tight with anger as he said, "Where is your sister?"

Christian stood, as well. "I do not care for your—"

But Simon's hand on his arm halted him. "I think there is more here than either of us know, Christian. This is between Jarrod and Aislynn."

Though Christian continued to look unhappy, Simon replied to Jarrod's inquiry, "Methinks, Isabelle meant to take the other ladies into the garden for a walk."

Christian began, "But of what…?" and Jarrod strode from the room.

He did find the women in the garden with Isabelle, who was leading them through the grounds, one hand upon the gentle mound of her belly as she walked. But it was Aislynn who caught and held Jarrod's attention as he came to a halt before them. His narrowed eyes bored into hers. "I would have a moment of your time, Lady Aislynn."

She grimaced and raised her chin. "I would not leave my hostess so rudely."

To her dismay Isabelle cast them both an assessing glance. "Pray do not concern yourself, dear Aislynn. I do not mind in the least, for clearly Jarrod has something of grave import to discuss with you." She turned to the other woman. "You do not mind, do you, Rowena?"

Rowena looked confused and uncertain, but she said, "Nay, pray do as you will."

Aislynn's own eyes narrowed with rebellion, and she said, "I prefer not…"

But Jarrod gave her no further opportunity to deny him. He took her arm in a firm grip and led her away.

It became more than evident that Aislynn had only acquiesced in order to save the other two women from being privy to a scene when she jerked her arm from his.

She placed her hands upon her slender hips and glared up at him. "How dare you!"

"How dare I?" He gave back equal heat. "Why, in the name of all that's holy, did you not tell me that you were no longer engaged?"

Far from being quelled by his angry question, her own outrage seemed to be fueled by it. "Why, pray, would I? What could it possibly matter to you, Jarrod Maxwell? You have given no indication that the information would be of any interest to you. Nor can you say that you have shared everything about yourself with me."

Knowing that she was referring to what she had overheard he and Eustace discussing, Jarrod told himself that the two matters were completely different. Yet he could not deny a feeling of guilt.

Aislynn could not believe the temerity of this overbearing, insufferable—handsome, beloved man. In spite of the outrage burning inside her, there was another part of her, the part that loved him with all her heart and soul that basked in the sight of him.

He was obviously taken aback by her dig, having the grace to flush despite his angry scowl as he said, "You had no right to eavesdrop on my conversation."

She glared at him. "I was not eavesdropping. I was only looking for you when I woke and you were not…" Her face heating, she turned away, though she told herself there was no point in embarrassment. What did any of it matter? Jarrod did not care about her. And this fact only served to make his questions about her engagement all the more incomprehensible.

She looked up at him, seeing the consternation on his dark face. ''I ask again, what matter is it to you, Jarrod?''

He raked a hand through his dark hair. ''You knew when you came to me that night that you were no longer bound to Gwyn. Yet you kept it secret. Was it because you thought I might trouble you with another unwelcome offer of marriage?''

Aislynn let out a quick breath of amazement. ''Nay, Jarrod, such a thought would never have entered my mind, for I never took the first one seriously. I knew it was brought on by guilt and I had absolved you of that.''

''Guilt!''

''Of course.'' She threw up her hands in frustration and pain. ''You told me yourself that you want no ties, that freedom is your most sacred tenet.''

''You understand nothing of me. You who have been loved and wanted every day of your life.''

Driven beyond reason by his words, she moved forward to glare up at him. ''You know not of what you speak. I too have had loss in my life. I simply have not chosen to let it define me. When my mother died, when my father lost himself in grief afterward, when my brother went away without returning for thirteen long years, I believed that life could improve, that happiness was possible. It is your belief that all is lost when painful events occur that drives you and shapes your life.''

"How can you compare your life to mine? You know not what it is like to be born a bastard, to live in a household where you never quite belong. You can not fathom what it is like to have your own mother, when at long last you have found her, send you away as if you were no more than dirt beneath her shoes."

She shook her head. "You are correct in that I know not what it would feel like. But I do know that one can try to see if there is a possibility that the worst explanation might not be the correct one. Perhaps, as your brother said, your mother did send you away because she loved you so much that she could not bear for you to live the life she knew was in store for her."

"But I returned as a man, caring nothing of what others might think."

She clenched her teeth in exasperation. "Mayhap she could not bear for you to see her that way. How would you feel if you were she and your son had found you in such a state?"

His lean jaw worked as she took a deep, calming breath and sighed. "You have been so certain that you could live without love, that it made you strong. But you have never been without love. You have gained it wherever you have gone, from The Dragon, from Simon and Christian, from Sadona, in your brother, from…from those at Bransbury. It is in protecting yourself from having to love others in return that you have convinced yourself that you do not have, nor require love." She shook her finger at him in frustration as he continued to glare at her. "Ultimately it is each of us who must decide whether or not to give our hearts. And ultimately that is all we really have to give.''

Too angry to even try to convince him further, Aislynn turned, running down the path and into the keep.

''Aislynn!'' She heard him call out behind her, but she did not even hesitate. Realizing that she was far too angry and, yes, devastated by her own certainty that Jarrod would never allow himself to give his heart, she knew that she could not face any of the others just now. Thinking of nothing save getting away from them all, Aislynn went to the stable and fetched her mare.

The stable boy saddled her horse without question and Aislynn was able to gain her freedom from the keep in a very short time. Yet the feel of the cool wind on her face did little to soothe her battered heart and emotions.

What a fool she was to have fallen in love with a man like Jarrod Maxwell.

Her chest aching with regret and sorrow, Aislynn urged her mount across the flat grassland that surrounded the imposing form of Avington Keep, up a rise and into the cover of the forestland. Yet she had not gone more than a handful of strides when she saw, bearing down upon her, none other than Sir Fredrick. With a scream of frustration and rage, she tried to urge her mount in the opposite direction, but he was too quick for her.

He reached out and pulled her across his lap, then sped deeper into the wood. And as he did so, Aislynn's heart sank for she knew he could want nothing with her but ill.

* * *

Jarrod stood staring after her for what seemed an eternity. For during those moments, he felt as if his whole life, one scene at a time, was being reenacted before his mind's eye.

Was she right? Was it possible to see each thing that had occurred in a different way? Was he, as Aislynn had said, loved by so many yet not seeing it because he feared to love in return?

And if that was so, did it mean that the only way to change it was to openly give his heart without considering the consequences? Without considering the risk of rejection? And furthermore, if he was to do that, should he not begin with the person who mattered the very most?

Could he tell Aislynn that he loved her, knowing as he did that she could barely stand the sight of him?

Suddenly Jarrod knew that not only could he do it, but that he must. No matter what she might say to him, the hope of living without the loneliness that had been so much a part of his life was too strong.

And if what she said was true, that love was all there really was to give, then the depth of his love must count for something. He started up the path, not caring who might see him running to find her.

Yet Jarrod was hindered in his quest, for though he asked all he met whence she might be, none had seen her since the meal. Then at last he found a serf who had seen her walking toward the stables. Hurriedly Jarrod went there, only to be informed that the lady had gone riding.

Not bothering to tell the stable boy that he should not have allowed her to go out unattended, Jarrod asked for his own mount. He had no doubt that he would find her without difficulty. Aislynn would not go far. Even in her anger, she would not wish to worry her father.

Jarrod paused as he exited the gate, his gaze scanning the soft ground for hoofprints. Only one set failed to conform to the beaten path. He followed these.

He felt nothing, no hint of anything beyond his own determination to tell her that he loved her until he reached the top of the rise that led into the castle forest. There he found not only Aislynn's mare left unattended but also the recent prints of another horse. It was then that a sick feeling of premonition took him in its grip.

He began to follow the second set of hoofprints. It was some time before he was halted by what he saw up ahead of him. There, at the top of a knoll only sparsely populated with the trees that were bare and gray in the dying late autumn light, he saw them. Aislynn and Sir Fredrick. He saw that the other man was watching him across the distance, and Jarrod knew why he had picked that spot. Immediately he pulled Aislynn close against him and raised a hand to beckon Jarrod on.

His heart sinking but not knowing what else to do, Jarrod rode to them. As he drew to a halt and slid down from his stallion's back, he saw that Aislynn, though pale, seemed unharmed. For the moment. She looked at him with wide blue eyes, unable to speak around the hand he held over her mouth.

The knight smiled coldly. "Ah, at last, Maxwell. I have long awaited this day." Yet it was not his words but the gleaming silver blade that he held pressed against the tender flesh of her throat that made Jarrod's blood curdle as he cried, "Do not hurt her."

She strained forward. The knight jerked her back, pressing the blade deeper, and a thin trickle of crimson slid down that white skin. Jarrod roared, "I will kill you."

The other man issued a bitter laugh that confirmed his lunacy. "You may try. But not before you have watched her fall dead at my feet." He laughed again. "How accommodating you have both been this day. First the girl and then you."

Realizing that he did not know what to do, that he must stall for time as he tried to think, Jarrod said, "What do you mean? Accommodating?"

Sir Fredrick smiled coldly. "Why, she has been so by leaving the keep alone, and you by coming after her, and without your sword." He noted the scabbardless belt with approval. "I have been watching the keep for days and had almost given up hope of seeing my plans come to fruition."

Jarrod shook his head, trying to speak evenly and doing far better than he would have thought possible. "If you have been watching, why did you not try to take me when I came to Avington this very morn? Why strike out at this innocent girl?"

"Because I hate you all, all who wear the sign of The Dragon. You who have set out to destroy my master. I saw your face when this girl was hurt before." He smiled, his eyes cold. "I want you to suffer at the loss of her before I kill you. As I have suffered watching the slow and agonizing death of my master."

As the madman backed a few steps away, dragging

Aislynn with him, Jarrod again saw that he seemed to favor one side and recalled what Christian had said about his being grievously wounded. Could this weakness be employed to get Aislynn out of this situation alive?

Stalling, trying to buy them some time, he said, "What mean you the death of your master? He was alive and well the last I heard."

A wild light appeared in those piercing gray eyes. "Alive and well! His body lives but you have killed him, I tell you, taken away his will to live in taking that faithless, ungrateful Isabelle, God rot her soul. I pray that I am in position to do to her what I will do to this one, for I mean to kill you all, one by one and allow you the pain of watching those you love die before your very eyes." He pressed the knife close again, and a soft gasp of surprise and pain escaped Aislynn's lips.

Jarrod's heart thudded with helpless misery. Much as he wanted to set upon her attacker, he knew any rash move on his part would surely sign her death warrant. Calling on his self-control, Jarrod said, "I had no idea. One would think he would be well rid of her."

The other man seemed distracted by this thought. "Aye, yet it is not so. He grieves for her as if she had not betrayed him."

Jarrod knew that Isabelle's father had been angry at her leaving. Yet it was due to the loss of Avington, which he had hoped to gain through her child, rather than any love for Isabelle herself.

As these thoughts passed through his mind, Jarrod noted that Aislynn was trying to catch his eyes. Their eyes met and held for a quick moment in which she seemed to issue a warning before her gaze dropped to the ground beside him. Alerted by that warning, Jarrod cast only the briefest glance toward the ground at his feet and saw a large, heavy-looking branch.

To cover the exchange, which he did not even comprehend, he spoke to Sir Fredrick. ''None of us had any idea. Your master has seemed too levelheaded to allow himself to become so overset at such a thing.''

Luckily Sir Fredrick appeared to be too intent on his anger over the wrongs done to Kelsey to have noticed.

As the knight went on, warming to his subject, his rage and resentment coming fully to the fore, Jarrod again glanced at Aislynn. And she, infuriating damsel that she was, looked toward that branch before giving an imperceptible nod. Jarrod barely prevented himself from scowling, but Aislynn seemed to read his displeasure, for she scowled and nodded toward the ground again.

Jarrod did not know what she was about, but it was clear that she was determined for him to use the branch against Fredrick, but how could he hope to do so without endangering her life. He looked into her eyes again, distantly hearing himself replying to the other man's words when there was a pause in the diatribe, though he could not have told anyone what was said, as she silently made clear her determination.

Realizing that he had little choice but to try to follow her lead, Jarrod tried to communicate his acquiescence. She raised her brows to indicate her understanding. Bracing himself for whatever she might be about to do, Jarrod rested his hand low against his outer thigh. Yet it was he who was nearly taken off guard when, only a moment later, she pushed backward into the man who held her. The move came so unexpectedly that she actually managed to make him waver on his feet and drop his hand away from her throat to balance himself.

In the same instant, Jarrod grabbed up the branch and sent it sailing at Sir Fredrick's legs. Still reeling from Aislynn's shove backward, he could not absorb the shock and toppled to the ground, taking Aislynn with him.

But the arm on his weakened side was not strong enough to hold her and, before Jarrod could even reach them, she rolled away, screaming, "Jarrod!"

The knight lunged at Jarrod with the knife. Jarrod dodged in on his weak side, hitting him low in the belly, while reaching out for the hand with the knife. For a moment they grappled, but Jarrod, with two strong arms, was able to break the knight's hold on the knife with relative ease.

The older man fell back panting, stumbling to his knees. "Kill me then and have it done. I would have done the same to you."

But though he felt anticipation of doing just that, Jarrod looked to Aislynn. And it was not so much his own sense of compassion that stopped him, but the knowledge that he had decided to live his life with love. He had no need to murder a cripple, with no weapon to defend himself. If they met another day, perhaps things would be different. But not today.

He pointed toward the stallion that was tethered nearby. "Go. Get out of here and never return, for I shall only offer you mercy once in the face of the harm you have done those I love.''

The older man seemed confused for a moment, his gray eyes filled with disbelief. But when Jarrod simply stood there, he rose and moved to his horse. As he turned his mount to ride away, he looked back with an expression of suspicion, then prodded his horse away at a gallop.

Only when he was out of sight did Jarrod trust him well enough to relax his vigilance, and he turned to Aislynn. When he did she was watching with uncertainty. ''What mean you, Jarrod, when you said he had harmed those you loved? Did you speak of Isabelle and Simon?''

He shook his head. ''Nay. Though I am sure he has tried to harm them, I have no direct knowledge of any instances.''

Her expression gave nothing away, neither offering encouragement nor discouragement. ''Then...?''

He took a step closer to her, knowing that the time had come. No matter what might happen now, he was too tired of the past to prevent himself from attempting a better future. He spoke softly, but clearly. ''It was you I referred to, Aislynn. It is you I love.'' The moment the words were said he knew a rush of elation and release that made his head spin joyously before the world was righted again. No matter how she reacted, he had done the right thing.

She stood there without moving. ''But you said you wished to be free.''

He spread out his arms in supplication. ''I was an utter fool, afraid, as you had guessed, of being hurt. And when I asked you to marry me, you refused.''

"But I thought you were only..."

He grimaced. "Nay, I meant it from the deepest part of my soul. But when you told me you would not, that you would marry your Gwyn I could not allow you to see how badly I had been hurt."

She rubbed a hand over her forehead, looking down at the ground. "But I only said that because my marriage was important to the peace on my father's lands. And because I thought you had asked me because you felt guilty about what we had done."

He shrugged. "I felt guilty enough, that is true." He reached into his tunic and removed the blue ribbon he kept close to his heart. "You were right to think that this reminded me of a woman, for it is the exact color of her beautiful eyes, but very wrong about who she was. I purchased it for her from the peddler at Bransbury but then made every excuse not to give it to her. I loved her, then, as now, though I knew it not, and even if she continues to despise me I can not regret that I have told her."

She looked into his eyes then, her own gleaming with unshed tears of joy. "Despise you, Jarrod? I have loved you from the moment you walked into the keep at Bransbury."

He needed no more encouragement than this to move forward and take her into his arms. When his mouth met hers, she returned his kiss with a joy and abandon that could leave him in no doubt of her love.

At length he leaned back to look into her beautiful eyes, eyes bright with love for him. "You will marry me?"

"This very day."

He pulled back, though only slightly, as he

searched her face. "Would you very much mind living at Kewstoke? I know how much your home and family mean to you."

She smiled radiantly. "Where you are is my home."

Wonder made his heart throb with joy. "You do love me."

She raised her sweet mouth for his kiss. "For all time to come."

# CATHERINE ARCHER

has been a fan of romance novels for many years. Her dream was to write the kind of stories that moved her so much. Now, as a published author, she has the thrill of not only dreaming of romance, but of seeing the names of her characters in print.

Catherine lives with her husband, Stephen, and her three children, Katie, Stephen and Rosa, in Troutdale, Oregon. She loves meeting and hearing from readers. She may be reached by writing to P.O. Box 1216, Fairview, OR 97024-1216. If you would like a reply, please send a self-addressed stamped envelope.

**Pick up these Harlequin Historicals and partake in a thrilling and emotional love story set in the Wild, Wild West!**

**On sale May 2002**

**NAVAJO SUNRISE**
**by Elizabeth Lane**
*(New Mexico, 1868)*
Will forbidden love bloom between an
officer's daughter and a proud warrior?

**CHASE WHEELER'S WOMAN**
**by Charlene Sands**
*(Texas, 1881)*
An independent young lady becomes
smitten with her handsome
Native American chaperone!

**On sale June 2002**

**THE COURTSHIP**
**by Lynna Banning**
*(Oregon, post–Civil War)*
Can a lonely spinster pave a new life
with the dashing town banker?

**THE PERFECT WIFE**
**by Mary Burton**
*(Montana, 1876)*
A rugged rancher gets more than
he bargained for when he weds
an innocent Southern belle!

 Harlequin Historicals®

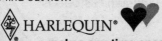

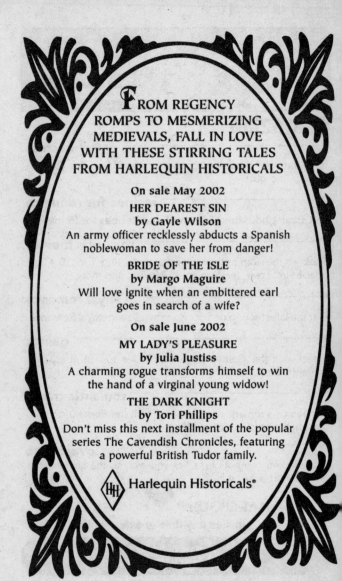